LK BILLIPS

The Coggery

An Annabelle Sweeting Mystery

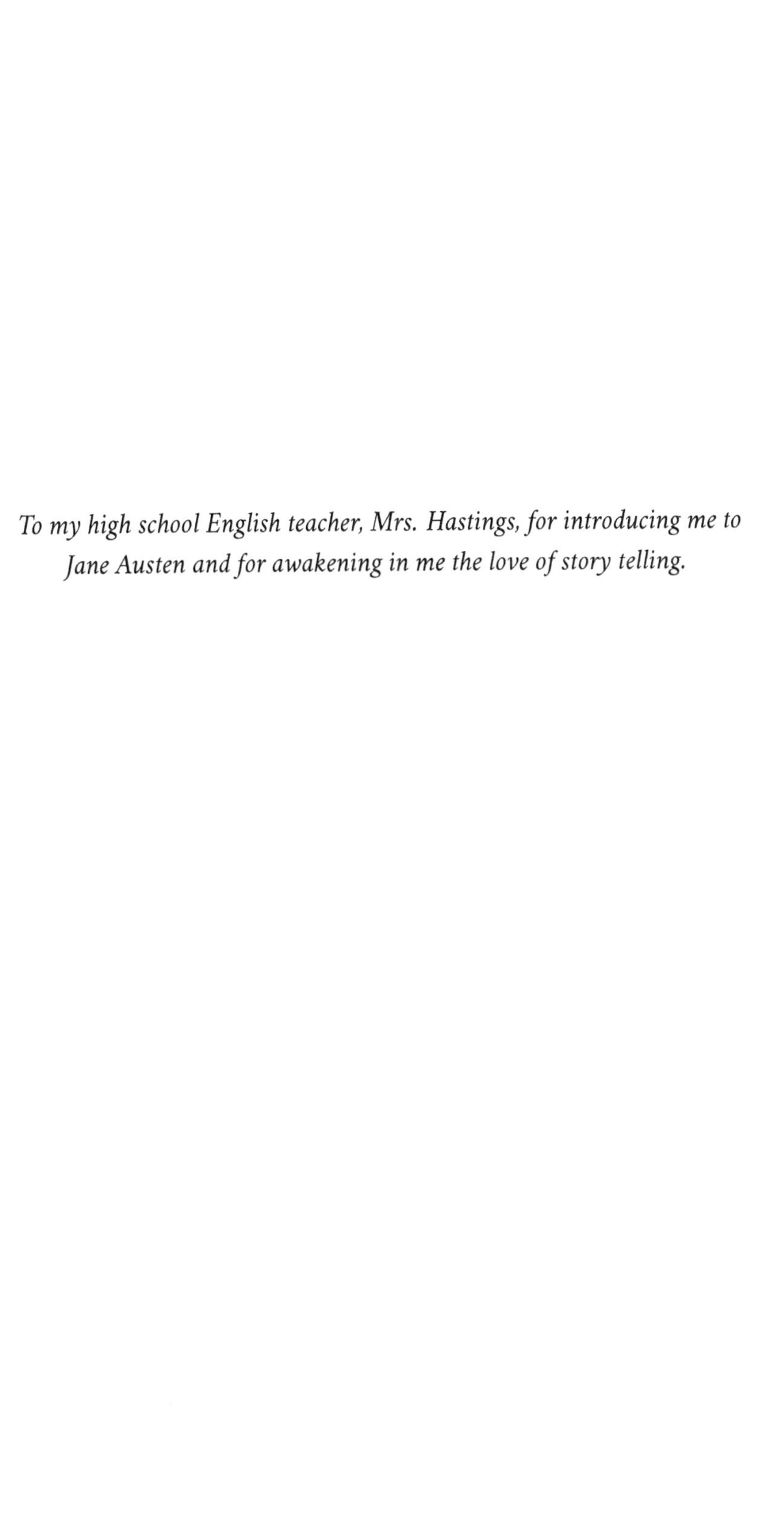

To my high school English teacher, Mrs. Hastings, for introducing me to Jane Austen and for awakening in me the love of story telling.

Contents

Preface

COGGERY

Meaning of 'coggery' (*Webster Dictionary*). 1 . Coggery [n.] - **Trick; deception**.

coggery · (obsolete) trick; deception ; 2. string · (dated, slang) A hoax; a fake story. ; 3. trickery · (uncountable) The art of dressing up; imposture ; 4. **cog**. (*OneLook Thesaurus*)

coggery1602–12. The practice of cogging; deception, trickery; also, concrete a ... A cheat; a **thief**; (in later use) spec. a sheep stealer. cheat1664 (*Oxford English Dictionary*)

Acknowledgement

I want to give a huge shout out to my husband, Paul. He has been a massive help getting this book up to snuff and supporting me through the fear and doubt that comes with releasing one's art into the world. I want to thank my daughter, Daniella, for her help and creativity when I needed a second opinion on my designs and for putting another set of eyes to my work. A thank you goes out to my mother-in-law, Fran. You are always the first to share, review, and cheer me on. I can't express how much that means to me. Thank you to Emily Thomas for her insight and unwavering determination to sift through the typos and make me look good.

I want to thank the readers who purchased my first story and now this one. Be it family, old friends or new ones, you give me the validation I need to continue this path, and I thank you wholeheartedly.

Chapter 1- Staying Busy

What is better than tinkering and time? Surely, I can't recall, but for fleeting moments of a dance at a masquerade ball.

It wasn't supposed to be this way. I, Annabelle Sweeting, ought to be out about town, thwarting crimes and cracking unsolvable mysteries. That is what my heart truly wanted. I had such success when I first arrived in London. An unprecedented string of murders led to an unexpected culprit, and I had helped unravel the mystery. It was a bit harrowing toward the end there, but really, when you took into account the tremendous odds we were facing, it was quite a victory. That all seemed to be behind me now. I couldn't help but feel glum as I stared down at the current project that occupied my attention.

Pulling my goggles over my eyes, I flashed a piece of metal into place. The lavender lenses blocked the majority of the brightness from my welding apparatus. Plus, they looked quite dashing. I had been working diligently for the past few months on a secret assignment for the Bergenhalts' upcoming costume ball. They were known to throw the most extravagant parties, themed with such detail. The height of society attends, and to be invited is an honor.

Lady Bergenhalt was a very inventive hostess, and this gathering should be nothing less than excellent. I had been sworn to secrecy, which was quite hard when my dear cousin, Mr. Jaime Nethersby, was always trying to peek within the confines of my tinker room. Fortunately, or unfortunately, depending on how I was feeling on any particular day, Jaime was asked to accompany his mentor, Lady Whipley, to France for business. She was at the forefront of the fashion world in London town, and Jaime was thrilled to be working by her side. Oh, how I missed him.

I had been asked to join Jaime at his home for the season, what felt like a lifetime ago, and decided to stay. My parents were none-too-thrilled to have a daughter who endeavored to take on the industrial world. They knew, however, that I was like this since I was a child, so there was very little shock if any at all. My cousin was more than exuberant to have me, and I felt we made a splendid pair of living companions.

Jaime had been gone several weeks now, and I was growing lonely without his upbeat and always intuitive company. I found myself working a lot more in my tinker room these days, but not really by choice. It was a rather sore subject, which meant it was constantly churning around in my mind. As an amateur sleuth, I felt riddled with doubt, and now this had happened. I remember the conversation vividly.

"Miss Annabelle Sweeting, you've gone too far this time. Do you know what kind of trouble you caused? Lord Daven is beyond angry and has been to The Yard personally to make his sentiments known. To accuse his friend and an honored man of the cloth, what were you thinking? The only thing we can do now is apologize and take you off the investigation," Chief Inspector Farthing bellowed.

"Chief Inspector, why are we backing down? Are you afraid of the nobility? This man has something to do with this, I know it! Constable Weston, don't you agree?"

That's when it happened. The chink in my armor was finally pierced. Constable Luke Weston was the first gentleman I met when I arrived. Something had sparked from that very first moment between us. A flame had been lit, flickering with an ever-growing intensity. We had agreed to work together, to take on this dark world side by side. Over the past few months, I didn't know what had changed. I never could have predicted what Luke said next, but it shattered me.

"Miss Sweeting, I think, perhaps, Chief Farthing is right. You have backed us into a corner on this one, but if you lay low for a while... we may still be able to salvage the investigation. I believe Father Gaverty wishes to help us with this inquiry, but we need to be cautious. I don't mean to be harsh, but I think you may have acted too rashly in jumping to conclusions," Luke said.

The memory made my cheeks heat with fury. We had solved several cases before that, and all without incident. The investigations were, I admit, less risky but no less important. When I needed him most, Luke abandoned me to bureaucracy, and I couldn't figure out why. I slammed my hammer on the workbench in frustration and let it fall out of my hand. It was almost as if the closer we got personally, the more he wanted to remove me from our investigative work together. The thought stung, and I lifted my goggles to wipe a few stray angry tears from my eyes.

I had been in town for almost a year now, and I thought I would be better versed in the way of things. It didn't feel like that at all. It felt like my found family was falling apart, and the more I struggled to hold it together, the more it came undone. I wished Jaime was home. He would know just the right thing to say.

The strain between Luke and I grew as the investigation, which I was no longer privy to, heated up. He stopped calling on me, as the demands on his time were required elsewhere. I think he also feared that I would try and pry out information when we met. Who could blame me, though? I couldn't let it go. It nettled me in my dreams, and I tried to reason with Chief Inspector Farthing, but he said they had a new suspect and it would be wrapped up quite nicely, to everyone's relief. He also told me a new investigation was underway and was surprised Constable Weston hadn't mentioned it to me. He gave me several small details and told me to ask Luke for more information. I sent a missive to Luke's apartment and waited for a reply for three days. When it finally came, I was shocked.

Dear Annabelle Sweeting,

I am most gratified that you wish to assist me in the search for justice, but I think your skills are better applied toward the realm of invention. I know you have lacked the time to focus on your passion with the barbarous cases that have come to light. I also see no need for us both to be in danger. I thank you for your help, but I think it best if we resolve your consultation assignment. Now you are free to open that boutique you had once dreamed of, and I will rest easier knowing you are not chasing monsters.

Your Constant Servant,

Mr. Luke Weston

Mr. Luke Weston, indeed. The audacity of the gentleman to try and choose my life for me. It would not be borne. Needless to say, I obtained the case files from The Yard the next morning. It appeared that he hadn't yet made it known that I wasn't consulting for him any longer, and I wasn't about to announce it. Luke tried to call the following day, and the Thursday after that, but I was always away from home, even if I wasn't.

Nathan Starling, one time pick-pocket turned travelling boy, and finally transforming into one of my dearest friends, joined me in this quest. He and I had been working on our own in secret. Starling and Sweeting could not be waylaid from the fray for long. After all, we were a formidable team.

The feeling of being watched brought me back to my tinker table. I turned to find Purgatorio, my mechanical manticore, powering up from his recharge. Purgatorio was also a constant companion, but a space still ached for the relationship I had thought I found with Luke. I smiled at the fierce metallic beast and thought about the other man who gifted Purgy to me.

Miro Nassar, now the Earl of Thetford, had been lost for a time after his family's fall from grace. The first case I helped crack brought his brother and sister-in-law to a most dire justice. I felt no guilt, however, for they were despicable humans.

Jaime thought the "ton" would be averse to any contact with the earl. The "ton" consisted of the very uppercrust of society who thought themselves superior and able to cast judgement on all of the fashionable world. If you were gossiped about, your standing in society could plummet based on the whim of the "ton".

Against my cousin's warnings I reached out and sent Miro weekly missives anyway. He was one of the first people I met when I came to the city and a good friend. I rarely mentioned Luke in my letters to Lord Thetford, due to our history together. Sometimes, I wondered if I had made the right choice. I am sure that was my hurt pride talking, but as I sat alone, it often penetrated my thoughts.

Perhaps after tonight's scheduled appointment with Nathan, I should reach out and invite Lord Thetford for tea. The more I thought about it, the more I found the idea appealing. I put my goggles back over my eyes and returned to my designs. Purgatorio gave a chuff as I struck out a pleasant melody of metal clashing. I smiled at the happy turn my thoughts had finally taken.

Chapter 2- Docks of Deception

1818- London Docks- Moonless sky with a chance of intrigue

I tried not to let the stench of the docks distract me from my mission as I crouched low behind a crate and peered around its edge. I knew I shouldn't be here, but the thrill of the hunt was too much to pass up. I watched as Nathan met with a tall, pock-skinned man by the bow of a schooner. I couldn't quite hear what they were talking about. Part of it was due to my distance, but most of it, if I was being honest, was due to the overpowering noise of blood pounding in my ears.

My heart was racing as I watched the exchange. I hoped it wouldn't grow heated. I could just hear Constable Weston now! His voice rang in my mind chiding me for such reckless behavior.

"Annabelle Sweeting, you take too much risk! What would your parents think, and to dress up like a lad to boot?"

I had to catch myself from giggling at that last part. I tucked my hair further into the hat I was wearing. I knew what we were doing was dangerous, but some things were worth the risk.

The smell of fish had me nearly gagging as I moved to get a better view between two crates. I envisioned myself as the sly fox on my parents' farm who was often spied on, trying to steal the chickens. Sleek and slender, I crouched down and watched the interaction play out.

Nathan was the first person I met when I arrived in town, and he had become as dear to me as a brother. His scuffed boots kicked at some gravel as he played the part of an impatient messenger. We both wore ragged clothing to blend in with the locals. We wore starchy brown pantaloons with matching vests, accompanied by off-white cotton shirts and brass-buttoned short boots. Nate had a heather grey porcupine hat, and I wore a dusty black bowler to engulf my long, auburn hair. I grinned at the memory of taking the ash from the fire grate in my room and making the streak that currently resided on Nate's right cheek. Raised voices brought me out of my thoughts.

"Whatcha mean, boy? I don't have the time to be messin'. You'll either take the package, or I'll find another hungry mouth to replace ya. There ain't a guttersnipe in town that would turn down this deal, I guarantee it."

"Settle it down, sir. I was just sayin' that for the speed of the delivery, it awt to be a bit more than the usual. Would I be any kind of gent worth my salt if I didn't at least ask, sir?"

"Aye, yawr a right, clever lad. Dangerous in this type of business. I respect the ambition, though. Alright then. Shall we shake on it? I'll give you half now, and if you deliver it before sunrise the second half will be waiting for you at the dock office. Ask for Pippin," the man said.

"Yes, ye got it, sir! I'll get it o'er there in no time at all," Nate replied with a dimpled grin.

I watched in awe as the boy I'd grown to love slipped seamlessly back into the guttersnipe I first met at the train station platform. He had a way about him, cunning and confident. It was strange to wonder where he gained that confidence, considering the dubious life he used to have. The man slipped a few coins into Nathan's outstretched hand and shoved the medium-sized parcel into his satchel.

"Make sure no one snatches it, you hear? And if you do get pinched, you don't know me, and you found the package just laying about. Understood?"

"Right-o!"

As they turned from each other to part, movement caught my eye from the end of the dock. Scuffling boots began to thunder down the pathway, and the sounds of shouting to "Stay put!" echoed through the empty fishery stalls. Nathan's eyes met mine and grew wide. He mouthed the word, "Run!", and took off through the labyrinth of stalls towards the east entrance. I took off towards the west. We had planned for this. We knew it might happen, but we were hoping not to be in the bobbies' crosshair. Our hopes were not relevant. We were to split up and meet behind the blacksmith's shop, where I collected discarded bits of metal for my creations. It was one of my favorite places to visit when I first came to London. But after last year's events and the poor death of that innocent maid, I still held a bit of fear entering its darkened walls.

I shook the memory from my mind as I raced through the man-made alleys of the dockyard. Stopping short at the edge of the gate, I looked for any sign of a constable having spotted me. I could make no shapes out. I was about to run through when a hand grasped my shoulder from behind, and I nearly leapt out of my boots. I don't know how I suppressed a scream, but only a high squeak left my lips.

"Sorry, Miss! It's me, Whitmore, your fellow night wanderer," he whispered. "Don't go just yet. There's something I needs ya to see. You've done me a right service, more than once, and I aim to helps you if I can," One-eyed Whitmore smiled a toothy grin.

He crooked his finger and beckoned me to follow him towards a path I hadn't seen when I first entered the docks. Hidden by a sheet of canvas, he led me deeper into a line of stalls that had seen better days.

"Where are you taking me?"

Beads of sweat started to accumulate on my forehead. I felt like I was entering a cavern that would never see daylight again. He turned back at me and smiled reassuringly.

"I won't let nothing happen to ya, Miss! I could never, nawt after the kindness you've shown. I must warn ya though, what I have to show you, is nawt good. It's downright evil, but you were the one that the guide is telling me to show, so I must do as it says."

"The guide, who's the guide?"

"Ah, I've said too much. Let's just say, I see things nawt a lot of people believe in, and these things, sometimes, they talk to me. I only listen to the good things though," he said with a wink in my direction.

I wondered if he thought that would alleviate some of the strangeness that his statement had just divulged.

"And these things, they want you to show me something… evil?"

"They said you were the right one, the good one, to help. You are the help that this problem needs. I don't know much more than that, sawry," he said.

He slowed his pace until we were near the end of the path. It was the second stall to the end, on the right. A weird breeze sailed through and fluttered the canvas flap revealing a glimpse of the stall. The flap swayed again, and tiny shoes were poking upward from the ground. It appeared as if someone was sleeping in the secluded spot.

One-eyed Whitmore stopped and pointed to the space.

"You must enter, I cannot follow, I can only lead the way."

He took on a faraway look, then shook his head and looked at me in confusion. He dug into his vest pocket and removed a charm secured to a leather strap. The token appeared copper and shined like a penny that had been polished many times. Perhaps, from a hand that sought it for comfort?

"Take this, it will keep you in the eyes of those who can help you, if help be needed. It's kept me safe, and they say you need it more than I now," he said solemnly.

He held the charm out so it dangled in the space between us. I took it from him and brought it up to my face, so I could see it clearer. It was an ankh- the symbol of life in Egypt. I marvelled at it for a moment. Looking up, I saw Whitmore running back the way we had entered. I wrapped the leather around my wrist and tightly held the charm in my palm.

Walking slowly, I moved the flap away from the stand and peered into the darkness. There on the floor was a young girl curled up. If not for the immense pool of blood circling her dirty blond locks like a halo, I would have thought she was fast asleep.

My heart retched at the same time as my stomach. I had to work hard not to release the contents of my dinner. It was shocking to see this innocent's shortened life bared before me. I looked up in search of some sliver of moon, some light to show me something other than the darkness I felt at this moment. If I was the help this poor girl needed, then the person responsible better be ready. A righteous fire burned in me, and I made a vow in the darkness. It looked like I was, again, going to be drawn into the depths of hell, but this time I was going to be prepared!

Chapter 3- Unfortunate Connections

Many things happen by chance, but coincidence is rarely one of them.

I do not know how long I looked up at the starless sky before I could compel myself to look down once more at the young girl sprawled at my feet. I knew the course of action needed, but the next steps I took were sure to get me into trouble. For one, I wasn't supposed to be at the docks in the first place. For two, I was dressed like a lad. And for three, Luke Weston, constable and lead detective assigned to the local murder investigations, was going to kill me.

I had met Luke, much like Nathan, by happenstance. Our meeting was in the train station as I entered London for the first time on my own. Luke had witnessed me snag Nate's collar as the little urchin tried to snatch my coin purse and offered his aid. I had struck a deal with young Nathan and saved him from a crueler fate. Luke, Nathan, and I ended up on a wild and often dangerous murder investigation. I narrowly escaped with my life, and the look Luke gave me as he almost lost me will forever be ingrained in my brain.

The truth is, I couldn't help getting caught up in the mystery of things, and if my conversation with One-eyed Whitmore held any revelation on the subject; these mysteries were clearly drawn to me. I squared my shoulders and looked down at the young body. If Whitmore or the guides, as the local mystic mage called them, were to be believed, then who was I to fight destiny? I turned around and opened the flap toward the narrow pathway out. I heard feet pounding towards me and made out a small figure racing my way.

Nathan launched himself into my arms and hugged me tightly.

"Ah, Miss, so glad you ain't been pinched. I saw that spooky Whitmore, and he told me you needed me. So I ran as fast as I could, I swear it," he exclaimed.

"Nate, calm yourself. Yes, I do need your help, but not for me. There is something quite shocking beyond that canvas, and I need to report it, which means we are probably in a heap of trouble. Do you still have the package?"

"Nah Miss, I thought it best to deliver it and be done with it without getting snatched up. Don't know what it was, but it ain't nothing good if they need the urchins of London involved. I have the address though, so we can stalk about there. What's in the stall?"

He looked around me, curiosity driving him.

"I daresay we have caught ourselves in another heinous mystery, young Starling. This one is even worse than the last," I replied.

His eyes grew big as he looked back at me. He turned toward the curtain and pulled it aside. Nate's face was away from me, so I couldn't see his expression. But as he hit his knees, I knew things were much worse than I thought. A gasp escaped from his lips as he leaned over the girl and moved a few strands from her face. I quickly stepped to his side.

"Nate, we can't touch her, we need to leave her undisturbed. You know that. What is happening?"

"I….I know her," he said barely above a whisper. "She…well, she was part of my home, my family, I mean. When I was at the hothouse, the sweatshops," he said.

He turned his face, and tears showed in the faint light. It was as if something had broken inside of him. This was a look I never wanted to see again.

"Oh, Nathan," I stretched my arms out wide, and he stood up engulfing himself in my embrace.

"We will find out what happened, okay? We will get Luke to help and Purgy too. You know we are an unstoppable team, and this will be no exception," I soothed confidently.

My insides twisted with the pain of seeing someone else in agony, someone I held dear. I couldn't wait another moment to wipe that hopeless expression from his face.

I put my fingers to my lips and let out a shrill whistle. I heard a replying screech from a far distance above. I held Nate to me while we waited for Purgatorio to find us. I felt Nate settle and then take a step away from me. He turned back to the girl on the ground.

"Her name was Gwennie, and she was really nice to me. I don't know what has happened, she wasn't just some novice on the street. She was right smart, miss. I don't know how that vagabond Whitmore found her, but he has some answers to give. I'm sure of it," he said, determined.

"You don't even have to ask…"

Before I could say another word Purgatorio swooped in towards us and landed on the ground, poised for any unseen adversary. His tail of spikes waived menacingly, catching the faint light streaming through the stalls of this dock. I stroked his smooth brass lion's mane, and he purred appreciatively.

"Purgy, we need Luke. I am guessing he might be part of the search on the docks. Can you lead him to us?"

"No need," Constable Weston said.

Nate, Purgy, and I all turned, startled to see Luke halfway down the narrow stall entry. As he got closer, his expression went from angry, to confused, then amused.

"Miss Annabelle Sweeting, what in God's name are you wearing, and does your cousin know where you are? I bet he would keel over dead to see you in that ensemble," he quipped.

"Constable Weston, I was just enjoying a nice walk along the Thames. I appeared to have taken too many back roads, but luckily dear Nate found me. As for my attire, well….. let's just stop playing this charade shall we?"

"Yes, let's. Now what was it that you needed that beastie to come find me for?"

Purgy chuffed at him, and Luke smiled back. Although he called him a beastie, it was with an affection that neither could deny. It could have had something to do with both of them being overbearingly protective of me, or some such nonsense.

I looked down at Nate.

"Are you ready for another battle, Starling?" I asked.

He nodded and squared his shoulders next to mine. I nodded back and grimaced. We turned in unison and stared at Luke. Purgatorio flew to my shoulder and perched there.

"Belle, I know that look, and it always means trouble," Luke sighed.

Chapter 4- Convincing Argument

Has looking for trouble ever been so easy? Probably shouldn't tempt fate.

"Constable Weston, I'd like to report a murder. I would also like to tell you that I have been requested to take part in the investigation, in a way, and I must insist you let me accompany you in it."

"Ahem...." Nathan elbowed me.

"Ah, yes, rather *us* in the investigation," I amended.

"Well, Miss Sweeting, by whose authority are you to be assisting me, do tell? I remember quite vividly the mishaps you encountered on our last investigation, and if I'm not mistaken, you were deliberately meddling in our current investigation involving some parcels of ill repute," he replied smugly.

"You know very well, Luke, that the vicar was a prime suspect in that case. Seriously, how many of the corpses had gone missing from his own parish?"

I didn't want to admit I was wrong on that one. We had received a case not too long after the vicious harpy of a jealous wife, Lady Talia Thetford, tried to kill me. Needless to say, Luke was weary of me getting involved in another case, and I was more than a little overzealous in trying to prove I was fine. This led to a clash of opinions, and me desperately trying to catch the culprit first.

The case that he so nicely was throwing in my face and what got me benched from the consultation role, I fondly liked to call, was the Grave Robber of Greenwich Village. Fairly fresh bodies were going missing from a graveyard in the village. We discovered that some of their organs and other bits were being used in botched experiments inside the living. Well, they were alive, but the decayed body parts had ended up killing them. It was quite grotesque. I found the link that all the recently deceased had held their last services at St. Alfege Church under Father Gaverty. I was so sure he had something to do with it that I was a little relentless.

Father Gaverty had some very powerful friends though, and Chief Inspector Farthing had to take me off the case. The culprit they ended up arresting was a parishioner of the church, but I suspected Gaverty had something still to do with it. I wasn't allowed to touch the case again. Chief Inspector Farthing had ruled it closed. I was put on the sidelines, and they were reviewing my helpfulness to the Yard. It was all quite a set down. Now I was trying to get back into Farthing's good graces, so Nathan and I devised a plan to get involved in the most recent case.

We decided to intercept one of the parcels that have been suspected by the bobbies to contain human organs. They were saying either a copycat or someone involved in the original Greenwich Village case was now moving the remains by way of town orphans. The unfortunate urchins of the city were now pawns in this sinister endeavor. We wanted to raise Nate's credibility with the contact so we could present what we found to Chief Inspector Farthing and somehow get back into action.

"Either way, human body parts are still being moved around the city for God knows what. We were just trying to use our talents to help. Maybe if you had tried harder not to have me completely shut out, we wouldn't have to go to such lengths," I huffed.

"Annabelle, you know very well I don't want you to be in more danger. To voluntarily put you there would be ludicrous. Besides, now you have more time for your inventions. Are you not preparing pieces for the next themed ball at the Bergenhalt's?"

"Do not change the subject. We have been summoned here by outside forces, and you must swear not to cut us out again."

"That's right, sir! We aim to find her killer, and you ain't gonna stop us," Nate chimed in.

Purgy let out a roar to add his own two pence.

"Let me see what you've found," Luke replied.

"Not until you promise," I responded.

"Who led you to this supposed crime scene?"

"Your favorite mystical mage, of course," I smirked.

"One-eye Whitmore? You have got to be jesting! I definitely don't want you involved now," Luke said.

"Constable Weston, I think you underestimate me, and I find it vexing," I replied.

"Fine, I promise you can assist me in the investigation in a regulated capacity. I don't want you going off on your own. That would be worse," he conceded.

"That is good enough for now, but I won't be treated as a child, you know. I have shown my worth, and if that horrid vicar hadn't high and mighty friends, this would never be an issue," I pouted.

"You are probably right, but danger is something you need not go looking for. It finds you quite nicely as is."

I nodded and led him to the stall where the young girl lay. Nate stood back a bit. He had a very solemn but determined face on and it worried me. As I pulled the flap open Luke took in the scene and sighed heavily.

"It never gets any easier, and so young," he mumbled.

He took out his notebook and jotted down descriptions as the poor creature lay before him. I took out mine as well and began to sketch the scene. A comfortable silence fell upon us as we worked.

Luke broke the quiet as he beckoned Nathan to fetch a couple of officers. He dashed into the darkness, and I looked at Luke in question.

"Belle, this is very bad. This girl is one of the informants we've been talking to about the parcels. You and Nathan have been meddling, and if this girl has been found out, I don't want to think of anything happening to Nate. You must tread lightly now," he warned.

"Luke, we didn't do anything too dangerous, I assure you. We believe the parcel Nathan intercepted was just a test. It seems that they are vetting the urchins first to find their worth. I am sorry we didn't include you in our plans, but we knew how you would react. Really, it was with the best intentions," I said.

"I know. You always act with the best intentions, Belle." He rubbed his hand over his face in frustration.

"I will take your advice and not stray from the path. Let us share what we know together, that always seems to work out best for us both," I replied.

"Yes, it does. I wonder when we stopped being partners, and started being adversaries?" Luke asked.

"I'm not quite sure, but I don't care for it. I like it much better when you include me rather than try to protect me. I understand your hesitation. Our first case was dangerous, I admit. I was there, and I was hurt. But if we went through life afraid of being hurt we would never really live, would we?"

"I hate it when you use logic on me. It's quite, how did you put it? Vexing," he replied.

I laughed and he smiled, as we stood looking at each other with a new appreciation.

"Well then, Miss Sweeting, let us get this case underway. Shall we call for Dr. Cannish?"

"Yes, Constable Weston, I believe we shall."

Chapter 5- The Darkest Alley

The shade of one's past is often etched with pain, but the light is what we always forget.

By the time we left the docks it was already morning. Nathan and I had travelled the side streets and snuck through the servant entrance to avoid detection from the rest of the household. We both retired to our rooms and fell asleep promptly. I woke up midafternoon to find the house bustling with daily chores and Nathan gone. A note informing me that he was dropping in on an old mate piqued my curiosity. I often wondered about Nathan's past, but I never knew the depths of the city in which he first dwelled.

He rarely talked about his time in the Brass Boroughs except when it involved some act of bravery on his part. Nate liked to talk about the train station though. He had such tales of his friends' ingenious trickery. He loved all the nooks and hidden spaces in the station and loved to watch people coming and going from distant places. When I asked him about the Boroughs he would flinch ever so slightly and then move to another subject.

I had never ventured past the street market myself. There was nothing on that side of town that had given necessity to such an excursion. I knew there was a whole other world on that side of London. Part of me was intrigued, but if it was anything like the docks, part of me was apprehensive as well.

I kept busy in my tinker room, straining to hear whenever the front door opened or closed. Hours went by and still no word from him or Luke. I was becoming a little stir crazy. I looked over my notes of the scene at the docks. It was clear to me that Gwennie was attacked. The huge gash on the back of her head wasn't caused by anything in the little stall we had found her in. Something or someone had struck her very hard.

Nate hadn't returned for dinner, and I started to worry for him. Luke had said that the dead girl was an informant. What if the villains discovered Nate was a party to helping the bobbies as well? It was all so unnerving. I couldn't wait any longer.

Stepping outside, I launched Purgatorio into the air. The sky around him was darkening. The sun faded to orange hues along the horizon. Purgy knew his prey, and I dashed to follow him on my newly-acquired motorbike. Nothing too bulky, just a nice modified bicycle that Miro and I had worked up. Ahh, Miro. The recently promoted Earl of Thetford was forced into hiding as the "ton" tore his family name through the gutters. I felt for him. He never foresaw his brother and sister-in-law for the lunatics that they were. He never could have predicted that his brother was a complete scoundrel, or that his sister-in-law would literally kill to keep her husband in line.

I kept my eyes darting between the road and sky as I weaved along the streets, keeping pace with Purgy as he made a path through the city. My mind wandered back to meeting Miro for the first time. Our first conversation was awkward to say the least, as I hailed his cab at the station. I smiled at the memory. I was glad we were still friends, and I wanted so much more for him. He was slowly building the trust back with investors that had bailed when news of his brother hit the papers. Some of the long-benched projects he had pitched to his brother were now seeing the light of day and getting recognition for their brilliance.

I lost track of time as we traveled farther into the Brass Boroughs than I had ever dared to venture. The smells got thicker, the people got thinner, and the buildings got more decrepit. Purgatorio slowed and started circling a tall white brick building on the left of Chancey Road. I neared the front and made out a faded wooden sign that read, "Second Chance Orphanage."

The steps were littered with children of all ages. They were dressed in clothes much like what Nathan and I wore to the docks, yet a little worse for wear. I scanned the steps looking for Nate among them. I looked up at Purgy still circling and signaled him to descend.

He swooped down, but instead of coming to me, he went to the side of the building. I edged my motorbike towards the wall and found an alleyway nestled between the neighboring building and the orphanage. I could see the glint off of Purgatorio's metallic hide as he descended, but then he disappeared into the darkness. Nothing but the faint stain of his red eyes indicated he was there. I parked my bike near the edge of the alley.

"You don't wanna be leavin' it there, miss. Don't ye know there be all types of miscreants about these parts," a small voice behind me said.

I turned to find a girl about Nate's age, wearing pantaloons, a newspaper hat, and a toothpick in her mouth staring at my bike.

"Well then, what do you suggest, young miss?"

"I will watch it for ye, for a fee that is. I'll take that nice bracelet ya got there, and make sure nobody messes with it," she replied.

"That's awfully nice of you, Miss...?"

"They call me Sadie, and no sweat."

"Well, Sadie, this bracer is not for you. It was given to me by One-eyed Whitmore, and he was very adamant that I should hold on to it. Now could you imagine giving away a gift from a friend?"

"Did you say...One-eyed? Oh well then, in that case, never you bother. Didn't know you was his friend. Nope, you just do whatcha need to do, miss. I will keep a good guard. You'll put in a good word with Whitmore for me, right?"

I was taken aback by her request. How bizarre it was to hear Whitmore talked about with such respect. For so long his name had been associated with the weird and uncouth. I had heard stories of his generosity among the Boroughs but had not met someone who held him in such high regard. Well, besides Nurse Gilda.

"You are well acquainted with him then?"

"Yes, miss. He comes by often enough, at least once a week," Sadie replied.

"Sadie, you may call me Annabelle. Do you know Nathan Starling? He is my friend and partner. I believe he is down that alleyway, as my manticore has led me here."

"You're Miss Annabelle Sweeting?" Her face grew bright, and her eyes were wide with awe.

"That I am, indeed."

"Nate, yeah I saw Nate nawt too long ago. If he's in Darkest Alley I'd say he was up to no good, Miss Sweeting, no good at all. That is where deals are struck and always with too high a price," she warned.

"Please watch my motor, Sadie. I must go in and see what Nathan is up to. I would not want him involved in anything too drastic," I replied.

She nodded, and I turned at a sprint towards the mouth of the alley. Her words gave me speed and caused the hairs on the back of my neck to rise. I hoped Nathan was not getting wrapped up in something he couldn't walk away from. I knew the dead girl meant something to him, but I hoped he wouldn't do anything foolish without me. I heard whispering and hastened my pace towards it. I could make out Purgatorio's eyes on a fire escape on the side of the orphanage peering down at what I assumed were Nate and his mysterious confidant.

"Shhh, I hear someone coming," Nate whispered.

"Why you little snitch, you set me up didn't you?" An unfamiliar voice accused.

"I would never, besides, would I warn ya to be quiet if I had? You're a right foul piece of work," Nate replied.

"Who's there, then? Show yourself, you eavesdroppin' buggar!" The unknown boy yelled in my direction.

They both came into focus as I closed the gap between us.

"Miss Anna! Whatcha doing in these parts of town, it's unsafe, it is!" Nate rushed to my side and grabbed my elbow.

"I could ask you the same thing, and who is this young chap? Why are you meeting in this wretched alley, and why didn't you tell me you were coming here?"

"You did bring someone here then, you scrap of rubbish. I thought you was fishy, been gone so long, all with the fancy Glimmers!" The disheveled boy declared.

"Brass before glitz, it's the code, Byron. I would never betray the code," Nate said.

"Well, then what do you call *her*?"

"Byron, is it? I am Annabelle Sweeting, and I take issue with anyone that questions the integrity of Nathan Starling. He is a man of his word," I replied.

Nate puffed up his chest at this praise and looked assessingly at the other boy. Byron appeared to be about two to three years older than Nate, and from what I could tell, he lorded it over him any chance he got. Byron turned a slitted pair of eyes towards me and took my measure. Not quite sure what he saw, I continued.

"As my partner, young Starling, I would have hoped that you'd have kept me abreast of any new leads. Why is this Byron fellow so interesting?"

"Byron is Gwennie's brother, miss," Nate replied.

I gasped and turned toward the older boy. "Oh young sir, I am very sorry for your loss," I said.

He had a look of genuine surprise on his face at my sincerity. I could tell he wasn't used to someone taking an interest in his feelings. Byron looked up at me, and I could just make out a puffiness in his eyes I hadn't noticed before.

"Yes, well, I told her to be careful, but she was always chasing the next best thing, you know," Byron replied. He seemed lost in his thoughts. I heard a kind of bewilderment in his tone.

"I should have done more to protect her, but she had a fire about her that could rarely be contained."

"Aye, I know about them types of lasses, I do," agreed Nathan.

I gave him a quizzical look, and he smiled softly at me.

"Yes, my dear boys. Sometimes a woman must act twice as rashly to earn her salt. That is just the way of the world. Unfortunately, Gwennie's gamble took a higher toll. Do you know how deep she was in, Byron? We need to find someone that saw her recently, or who might know the handler that was providing her parcels," I inquired.

"Now, ain't that the stick. The Mrs. is who she was working for. She had Gwennie taking parcels all over town. We—" he hesitated, lost in thought for a few seconds, "None of us thought nothin' bout it. Just thought it was 'orphanage business', as Mrs. Squires likes to call it. Nawt til Nate came did I even know there was other nonsense floating about," he paused.

He took his hat off and scratched the dirty blond hair beneath before replacing the dusty headpiece.

"Now that I think of it, there are a couple other girls the Mrs. has been sending out more often. There's um, Jane and Sadie. Yeah, those are the two. The boys are getting real sore about it, favoritism and all that," Byron said.

"Did you say Sadie? I just met her, she is watching my motorbike at the alley mouth," I replied.

"Ah, miss, you didn't? She is as cunning as they come. She'll steal the buckle off your belt while you're wearing it, she will," Nate groaned.

"She did seem quite a swindler, but once we talked about Whitmore, she seemed more than amiable. Do you think I was mistaken in that respect?"

Byron whipped his head around at the mention of our mutual acquaintance.

"You know One-eye?" he asked, relaxing visibly. "Oh that girl is right down obsessed with that crazy old fool. If you know him then I think you are safe," Byron said.

"Either way, I think we should be going, Nate," I said, feeling more ill at ease the longer we stood in the darkness of the confining alley.

Nathan nodded and turned to shake Byron's hand.

"Nate, give Byron direction to Bread Street," I said, "while I go handle Miss Sadie. Have him come around tomorrow eve, I think we might have a spot of work for him if he is game?"

I arched my eyebrow toward Byron in question.

A broad smile spread across his face revealing a missing front tooth. Somehow, it suited him.

"Most appreciative, miss. I am always looking for a way to fill me purse," he said.

I nodded and headed back down the alley. Purgatorio took flight behind me and startled the two lads. Apparently Purgatorio's stealth had improved enough that not even two seasoned guttersnipes had detected him. I couldn't help but smile.

Chapter 6- Catching Up

Nothing outweighs the importance of friendship except a truly heinous ensemble.

I reached the mouth of the alley and found Sadie giving the evil eye to a couple of younger boys taking a closer look at my motorbike. One had blond curly hair with a dimple in his chin. If he wasn't so dirty he would look just like a cherub. The other boy had dark red hair and freckles along his nose and cheeks.

"Oh come on, Sades, we only want a look-see. Why are you all up in arms anyways, she give you a coin?" The blond boy asked.

"Yeah Sadie, what she give ya, you're real rotten not to be sharing," the freckled redhead chimed in.

"It's not like that, Jeffie, she knows the sage. I need her to give him a good word for me. He knows things, and I don't want what happened to G to happen to me, you got it? So back off," Sadie warned.

"Ooooh, she knows One-eyed Whitmore, Lance." Jeffie, the cherub blond, looked to his friend.

Lance, the freckled faced boy raised his brow in surprise.

"Well, what makes you think he's gonna helps ya out? You ain't any better than Gwennie. She was a lot nicer too!" Lance taunted.

"Scram you little scrapes, or I'll give you a pounding!"

I emerged from the alley behind Sadie with Purgatorio perched on my shoulder. His eyes glowed red as we broke from the darkness. The two boys widened their eyes in fear and took off running for the safety of the stoop.

"That's right, run you beggars! Next time I'll box your ears for sure," Sadie called after them.

"You are quite fierce, indeed, Miss Sadie," I said from behind her.

She jumped and squeaked in surprise. Turning around, she started to point at my shoulder and back away.

"You've got a demon on your arm, miss. You…you, it's right there," she said.

"It's no demon, my dear. This is Purgatorio, my mechanical manticore I told you about. He might look the part, but he was a saving grace when I needed one."

Purgy's gears moved, producing a metallic purring sound beside my ear. I giggled as it tickled and gave my neck goosebumps.

"Wow, miss, it sure is something!" Sadie clammored as she stood gaping at Purgy.

"Sadie, can I ask you a question?" I said in the gentlest voice possible.

"Sure, I guess," she said suspiciously.

"I understand you knew Gwennie, yes?"

She nodded.

"I also understand that you and Gwennie have been taking parcels about town for the Mrs.?"

She nodded again. I could see the wheels turning behind the girl's unfocused eyes. My line of questioning wasn't making her comfortable, and I needed to get to the heart of the interview before I lost the chance.

"Do you know what happened to Gwennie?"

"Yeah, I heard. She was pretty quick too, one of the slickest sneaks around, Missus' favorite," she said with a sneer.

"So, do you know what is in the packages?"

Sadie shook her head now, but behind her eyes, I saw something that told me that wasn't exactly true. She started fidgeting with the button on her vest and darting her eyes between me and the orphanage front door.

"Sadie, I am in no way trying to get you into trouble. I want to help. If you ever have anything that you can tell me or need to tell me, you can find me on Bread Street, or find Nathan, or mention my name to Mr. Whitmore, and I will make sure to come," I said.

She looked at me with confusion and suspicion. I needed to say something to convince her I was on her side.

"When I see Mr. Whitmore I will be sure to put in a good word for you as well. Does that please you?"

A sneaky grin flashed across her face and then was gone. She nodded her head and started to walk away.

"Wait, here, this is for watching my motorbike." I handed her a few farthings and a brass button I had painted with a four-leaf clover. She looked down at her hand and fingered the button curiously.

"For luck, I always have a few tokens in my pocket, since you never know when you might need a bit of luck. I can tell you, it's served me on several occasions quite heartily," I said.

"Wow, no one's ever given me a present before. Thanks, miss," she said. She kept looking down at the button as she walked up the stoop to the orphanage. Her statement caused my stomach to ache weirdly. A sense of sadness and uncertainty took hold for a moment. Was this what it was like for Nate? Did he have no gifts, no one to care? It all felt so melancholy and made me want to help these children. Perhaps my dear cousin, Jaime Nethersby, might have an idea.

I was forced from my thoughts by Nate's sudden appearance from the alley.

"You ready, miss? We don't wants to be caught out of doors past dark in these parts, trust me," he said.

"Yes, well, let us be off. Did you walk here?"

"Naw, I took a ride on a truck delivering old parts from the track. Let's head toward the loco, we can bring your motorbike with us," Nate suggested.

"I don't think I've ridden the locomotive through town yet. Is it like the train I took from home?"

"It's faster, and a little more rickety. Most of the Brass use it, you see? It takes them to the mines and back, or to the factories uptown to work at the cotton mills. Just stick close to me, Miss Anna. The borough folk have a weary way about them, especially when the dark starts to take over," he warned.

His words created a sense of unease in me. Not so much for my safety, it was more the realization that I was still so naive to the ways of town. Perhaps it was also that this boy, a young man now, was so much more aged in that respect than I. It was unsettling to think of all the things he had seen, and now I was more curious than ever.

"Nathan, when we arrive home, after we ride this locomotive, can we sit down for a chat? I feel it's a long overdue one," I said.

"I thought this might be comin'. I know what you wants to say, and I think I'm ready for it. You've done me a kindness that I likely won't ever be able to repay, the best I can do is be honest as an oak tree," he replied.

I gave his ear a pinch as we walked toward the platform for the train out of the Boroughs. It was busy with people shoving for optimal position. Nate and I stood back from the crowd and watched as the steam clouded down the track indicating the loco had arrived. The doors opened with a dust cloud, worn people rushed out of its hull. As they made their way past us, no one looked up. They all walked solemnly with their eyes on their shoes, and their thoughts on their beds.

Nate tugged my elbow, and we rushed toward the doors to squeeze in with my motorbike before they closed. People stared menacingly at us for taking up more space, but Nathan just returned their cold stares. He had grown to have such steel in his spine, and it made me proud. We got off at the edge of town and traveled back to Bread Street.

I stored my vehicle in the motor park and headed inside my cousin's house. I dashed upstairs to change out of my dusty clothes and went to meet Nathan in the kitchen. I had made it just past the library when I heard my name.

"Cousin Belle! There you are, dearest! Come here at once, I must see you with my own eyes. It's been such a trial without your company, I assure you!"

"Jaime! You're back, finally. How was your voyage? Did you have a most splendid time? I can't wait to see all the wonderful silks you couldn't bear to leave in Paris," I enthused.

Jaime met me just inside the doorway and picked me up, causing a squeal to escape.

"Put me down, cousin!"

He laughed and swung me around so my feet couldn't touch the ground. Then he planted me down firmly and kissed my forehead. I had missed him immensely, and it felt good having us all under the same roof again.

Jaime had gone with his mentor to France for a 'fashion holiday', as they called it. Lady Whipley was all aghast about France being seen as the forefront of fashion in the eye of the "ton" and wanted to make sure her designs incorporated some of the latest trends. She would not be outdone by the French.

Jaime had told Annabelle all of this before he left, but she suspected he was as much of a fan of French fashions as anyone. He was nearly vibrating when he left two months ago. To say I had been lonely would be an understatement. I hadn't made the acquaintances I longed for yet, and after Father Gaverty had gotten me kicked off of the investigation,

I wasn't able to see Luke very much either. It was like a valley had opened between us. He was relieved I wasn't a part of any danger, and I was resentful for not being trusted or believed in. I had written to Jaime regarding it, and he offered a short-lived balm to the burn of it all.

Now that he was home, and I had better news on that front, I felt that things were finally falling back into place. I just hoped that Whitmore was right about me. I hoped that I would be able to help and that my instincts hadn't deserted me. I think that was what worried me. The realization that maybe, just maybe, I wasn't the right fit. The right fit for investigating, the right fit for Luke, or the right fit for London. The thought broke my heart a little. I squashed those ideas and just held on to this joy I felt at having my family home.

"You will not believe the delish numbers I have brought from Paris. Lace and silks, buttons and hairpins. This season is going to be overwhelmingly extraordinary," he raved.

"Much like you, my dear cousin. What, no feathers?"

"Oh Belle, you know me better than that," he teased. "It seems even the French are obsessed with them. I have so many wonderful new additions to my stock, it has me quite enraptured!"

"I am overjoyed for you, Jaime. I want to hear every splendid detail, but I must ask to postpone it. I am on my way to have a chat with young Starling. A new case has arisen, and it involves one of the children that grew up in his orphanage," I said.

"Oh, no! Poor Nathan! You are on the case? I thought that ancient inspector waylaid you for that tiff with the vicar? I was rather happy about it, I do admit. I know I was being quite selfish, not wanting you involved in more murder cases. I can see, though, that it was only a matter of time. You are of a relentless stock, and I dare say it makes you shine the brighter. Perhaps, too brightly. Do be careful, dear cousin. I shall join you in the kitchen, I would like to see Nathan as well, and give him my condolences."

Jaime and I walked together down the hall.

"Cousin, I know that you worry for me. I also know that you doubt me. I can't help thinking maybe I am failing in some capacity, that I am looking for things that are not there. Mayhap I should sit this one out? But then I see the girl's small body in my mind's eye, Nathan's dear little friend. Then adding the words Mr. Whitmore said to me about being the right person to help, makes me want to try. I know I must do something." I confided.

"Oh Belle, I do not doubt you. It's rather the opposite. I see the dragons you go off to fight, and I see how your bravery pushes you forward into the flame. I only worry that the flames will burn too hot one day. You are clever and intuitive, always have been. But there is a darkness that would seek out that light and try to snuff it, and that I just could not bear," he replied.

"I see."

"No, I think you still think I doubt you. Annabelle, you were born to do this, to discover truths. What I am trying to say is, don't let the search for truth consume you, and don't let others make you second guess your abilities, because that is when you stumble," Jaime said.

"This is why you are so dear to me, cousin. You are there to catch me, so I do not fall," I said.

I smiled warmly at him, and he returned my grin. We stopped for a moment and took a breath together. Jaime grabbed my hand and gave it a light squeeze.

"Without exception," he replied.

Chapter 7- Nathan's Tale

A person's life is almost always dictated by the environment from which they have grown. To use those lessons for good or bad depends on that person's will.

We found Nathan in the kitchen, below stairs. The cook, Trish, had long since served dinner, but we had all been away from home for it. The leftovers were dragged from their storage and placed on the big wood block in the center of the room by the fireplace. We moved a few chairs over, and we all sat down with a hearty plate near the fire. Jaime, Nate, and I had become so familiar with each other over the last year that we worked wordlessly as we gathered the items and made a picnic spot. I waited until we had all indulged in some supper before I broached the subject weighing heavily on our minds.

"Nate, I know I've not asked, and I know you didn't want to say before this, but I fear it is time you tell us of your place in the world prior to our friendship. I knew you were in a tight spot when I met you, but I did not know what you had left behind or who. Can you please share with us, and perhaps it could help find out what happened to Gwennie?"

Nathan let out a big sigh and stared into the fire. I didn't want to push too hard. I knew finding a friend slain must be terribly traumatizing, and to have to relive a part of your life that was equally so was a large request. Nate looked at Jaime, and he nodded encouragingly.

"As you may have guessed, I wasn't from a good home. I don't remember too much about my mother, she died when I was very young, but my father was a very hard man that worked in the mines. He thought a man's worth was measured by his strength, and he was always trying to show his off. One day he showed off a little too much and ended up in a brawl at a bad pub in the Boroughs. The man he fought was a local snake, a real cobra he was. Strike ya as soon as yer back was turned. I heard it from a lass there that he was done knocked about proper by my pa. When pa turned his back to dismiss him, the snake pulled a knife and struck him down," Nate said.

"I'm so sorry, Nathan," I replied.

"Well, they got the bugger. Hung him up good and high in the center of town for it. But that didn't stop them from sending me off to the children's home. No next of kin would claim me, and no one would watch out for me. And so I went."

"Were you part of the Second Chance Orphanage?" I asked.

"Naw, not at first. I was at a different place. The Foundling Hospital, but it was not to be. Rooms were filling up too quickly there, and I only was able to stay a few months before one of our guardians sold several of us to a local sweatshop. That's where I met Gwennie and Byron. They were lucky to have each other, and I was lucky to have found them. There were a few others that I became mates with too. Cabbage, Markus, and Mary were also sold off from the hospital. I guess not all children were worth saving," he said.

I wanted to gather him in my arms and squeeze him, but I knew I wouldn't want to hear the rest if I did. I watched as his face scrunched up in thought. Perhaps a memory of what happened next.

"The shop was very bad. The foreman, Scabs, we all called him, as he had horrid sores all over his face, would hit us with a branch from an oak tree outside if we didn't meet the quota for the week. He wasn't a good man.

I thought we were saved the day Mrs. Squires came to the shop. She admonished Scabs and paid him for about half of his workers. She told us we didn't have to work in those shops anymore and that all we had to do to earn our stay at the orphanage was run some errands for her. For a time, it was good, and that's what we did. We were the youngest kids there. The older kids sneered at us with some secret we weren't privy to.

Then one day a new bunch of scavengers came in. That's what they called all new children that the Mrs. brought in, scavengers. Mrs. Squires said we were old enough now to start really pulling our weight. She separated the boys and the girls. The girls met with Milda, and the boys with Samson. They were the eldest at the orphanage and taught us how to pickpocket, move like shadows, and open doors that were locked. I would be lying if I said I didn't think it was fun. There was something about getting a Glimmer's coin that made you feel victorious. Why were some people so blessed with their situation, but us Brass were stuck starving in the dirty streets of the Borough? It felt like we was Robin Hoods," he admitted.

"I have often thought the same, dear Nate." Jamie said. "However, I was on the lucky side of the coin. Well not quite so lucky, as I lived through a different kind of hell growing up, but I always wondered why God had shown such kindness to some so undeserving but challenged those with goodness. I still struggle with this at times, so I try to do my part with what I do have now, and recognize those I can help."

Nathan looked at him in surprise. I don't believe they had ever had such a personal or truthful conversation as this. It was like their experiences were creating a bond of survivors. Those, I had come to find, were the most enduring.

"So Mrs. Squires recruited children from work houses and then taught them how to steal for her?" I asked. "I'm not quite sure if she's a saint or a devil. It seems all the children are the ones that are really losing out in this. And now, poor Gwennie."

"Yes, miss. I'm not sure abouts what is twas in the packages, but I aims to find out," Nate declared.

"Nathan, we must be careful. Something Luke said to me earlier has me wary. He told me that since we got involved by the docks we may have put ourselves in more danger than we thought. I think we must observe a few things first before we rush in. I have learned my lesson about announcing my thoughts too soon. I will not let you fall to the same fate. We will bide our time and make sure we have a few more pieces to this growing puzzle before we leap into the fray. Do you agree?"

Jaime interrupted. "I think that is a very wise and mature statement, cousin, and I am happy you take that stance. Also, we are calling the constable Luke again, are we?"

He arched an eyebrow in my direction. I ignored him completely except for the uncontrollable blush that tinted my cheeks.

"Nate?"

"I know what you is saying miss, but I am not going to lie, it will be hard for me not to do what I've been taught to do. After all, sneaking around is what I do best. I trust your feelings though, and if the mage is on your side, I can't turn my back on the signs. I'll follow your lead, for now," he agreed.

"That's all I ask. We are partners, are we not? It is our job to watch each other's backs. I will not let your friend's murder go unanswered, but I also will not let you go into the fray unprepared," I said.

Chapter 8- Laying Low

To sit on the edge of history and not participate is both living and dying at the same time.

I stood studiously behind Constable Weston at the morgue the following morning. Doctor Cannish examined Gwennie with his usual candor, but I didn't comment. I let Luke take the lead and ask all the questions. I wanted to exercise my most valuable weapon, observation. It seemed to have escaped me of late. I watched the matted blood being removed from her hair. The harsh wound was made clearer with each spray of water.

Her right arm and wrist were covered with bruises. I glimpsed a sliver of white hair along her head as he washed the blood away. I took out my notebook and began to write down all that I saw. I kept Cannish's commentary within hearing range but didn't let his observations dissuade my own.

A time or two, I felt Luke's gaze on me, but I ignored it and kept a vigilant study as the exam proceeded. I wasn't trying to be distant or cold, rather, I was letting people lead me – dimming my light so that theirs could shine. It was a weird experiment, but I felt it was fruitful in the end. Doctor Cannish was finishing up when he turned to me.

"Well, Miss Sweeting, I must say you are out of sorts today. Dare I say that Father Gaverty has your knickers in a twist so you're on your best behavior? If that's the case, I don't care for it a jot. Enough of this nonsense, I need that quick wit and your outlandish theories. They tend to lean towards being correct," he said.

I was taken aback by his proclamation. Was I so transparent? It appeared so, at least to the studied eye of the doctor.

"Well, I didn't want to interrupt your observations," I explained.

"Malarkey, that's never stopped you before. Is it this cranky constable that's got you off pace?"

Doctor Cannish pointed at Luke, giving him a harsh expression.

"Me?" Luke sputtered. "I brought her in here, didn't I? If anything, I am breaking the rules to have her participate, I assure you."

"Oh, really?" I couldn't believe his gall. "You are breaking the rules for me? I wasn't fired from giving council on any other case besides the grave robbing one? How is it that you haven't included me in any since?"

"Aha, now we are getting somewhere," Doctor Cannish chimed in.

He sat back in the chair by his desk and watched as we continued our standoff.

"Miss Sweeting, I assure you, if your talents had been needed in any other case I would have called upon you. I am a very capable investigator on my own, as well you know. I have earned my place in the Yard, and I don't need to run every case past you," he retorted.

"I never said you weren't capable, Constable Weston. It seems, however, that you think that I am. You questioned my judgment, and made me out to be reckless. I can assure you I am well up to any task. And furthermore, you would have never discovered this body if not for Nathan and I," I said.

"And you would never have discovered it," Luke hurled back, "if not for One-eyed Whitmore. Perhaps I should invite him into the investigation, as he always seems to have his finger in a pie of some kind."

"Tell me once and for all, why don't you want to work with me any longer?" I demanded. "I know it cannot be due to protecting my feelings. You have clearly thought nothing of my feelings in regards to this conversation," I said bitterly.

"This is hardly the time, nor the company to be having this conversation, Miss Sweeting," Luke replied.

"I don't mind a bit, please continue," Doctor Cannish smirked.

I nodded towards Luke to continue.

"Fine then, have it your way. Miss Annabelle, you almost died. Who in their right mind would want someone they regard more highly than everyone else to be put into that kind of danger constantly? Is it so wrong for me to want you to find a different path for your skills? A safer path?"

He looked at me earnestly. His eyes were fierce with emotion that I haven't seen from him in months. Luke's words were so different from his actions of late. How could I believe he held me in such tender regard if he constantly excluded me. It was like he had put a wall up between us for fear of some unknown force tearing me away.

"Constable Weston, I understand your concerns, but could I not say the same for anyone in your line of work? Is it right for me to ask you to put yourself in such danger alone, when I have a contribution to be made. Life has always been uncertain, and yes danger exists in your world, but doesn't it exist everywhere? Is it not better to be in danger together, than to be separated by the fear of it?"

He shook his head a few times, but I would not let him derail my current train of thought.

"I have promised to not act rashly, can you promise the same? I think I know what has happened now, and I am none too happy. You took the allegation against me, that I was incorrect against the vicar, and used it to push me out. Perhaps I shall need a new liaison to the Yard then, if you do not trust me enough? "

He blinked at me a few times in disbelief. It was clear that he never thought of having me investigate with any other constable before.

"Annabelle, please."

"No, I think I've heard enough today. Doctor Cannish, thank you for letting me sit in on your exam. I will be at Claymore's later for dinner. Perhps you can stop by, and I can ask you a few questions on the case? I will buy you a meat pie?"

"Miss Sweeting, you know me well. Yes, I shall be there. Good day, young miss."

I turned and walked out of the room without saying another word to Luke. A tear began to well up in my eye. As the distance grew between us, I heard one last thing.

"Son, you can't snuff out a fire that burns that brightly. She belongs here and you know it. If you're not careful, you'll push her right out of your life," Cannish said.

"I feel like either way I am going to lose her," I heard Luke confess.

I walked the rest of the corridor alone and thought, *maybe you already have Luke, maybe you already have.*

Chapter 9- Pickpocketing 101

Thievery is a skill much like art. You have to hone and practice it, but the consequences of failure are much more dire.

I sat across from Doctor Cannish later that night, and we went over all that was discovered today. I noted a few marks on the young girl that he had missed, and the unexplained white streak of hair that was visible after the blood was washed away. I made it a point to ask Nate about it before my meeting with the doctor, and he confirmed it wasn't natural. Doctor Cannish noted that there were a few chemicals that could be used to turn hair this color, but he would have to look into it further to be sure.

"You know I'm not a replacement for him, right?" the doctor murmured.

"What do you mean, Dr. Cannish? Of whom are you speaking?"

I knew very well of whom he spoke, but I didn't dare own it. It was best to see how observant he was instead of filling in the blanks for him.

"For Constable Weston. I know you two are having a tiff, but I am not an investigator, nor do I wish to be," he replied. "I talk to the dead, or severely sick, because let's be honest, they rarely talk back. Trust yourself, there is not a single person I know that is more attuned to this job than you, neither man nor woman. Don't let the fears of your failure cloud your methods. I am not a man who goes out of his way to help people, so don't take this lightly. Understood?"

I breathed out a huff and looked into his sincere brown eyes. His observations were dead on, and I could scarcely believe his compliments.

"Doctor Cannish, I thank you. I must be honest, I *was* doubting myself. And the fact that Constable Weston did nothing to waylay those fears injured me deeply. So your words mean very much indeed," I replied.

"Yes, well, enough of that. I can't have any doe eyed females chasing me about now can I? I will have a talk with Chief Inspector Farthing. If you really want to get assigned to a new officer, I suggest you do so. Perhaps that will kick Weston right in the breeches," he said.

He stood up and bowed. I watched as the door shut behind him and looked around the room. I wasn't looking for anything in particular, but a set of green eyes staring back at me caught me off-guard. They weren't as brilliant as Miro's, more like a light meadow green. They led down to a sharp nose and the stern set mouth of an older woman I did not know. I smiled awkwardly and turned away my gaze.

I stowed away my notebook and coin purse. I signaled the server to clear the dishes and collected my other items on the table. I noticed Doctor Cannish had left a note on the table for far more than our meals were worth, and I smiled. He might be a dodgy old curmudgeon, but he was really quite kind.

I settled up with the servant and headed towards the cooling afternoon air. I had just crossed the threshold to the outside when I felt someone moving fast behind me. The stranger bumped into me on my left side as they passed, and I looked to see the green-eyed woman swiftly moving away. Before she could distance herself too far, I hooked her elbow. I patted my pockets while still holding her elbow, and although my coin purse was still intact, my notebook was no longer in its designated space.

"Don't you know pickpocketing is a young scamp's game? Now, do be so kind as to hand that notebook of mine back. I am not above getting the bobbies involved, so don't try to deny it," I said.

She stared at me with a mix of surprise and venom. I couldn't fathom why I would receive such an angry glower, so I inquired.

"Do I know you? Perhaps the correct question is, do you know me?"

The woman revealed my notebook from her right skirt pocket and handed it back to me.

"You've been snooping around my place enough, young miss, to make anyone suspicious of your intentions. Those children have it bad enough without some priest accuser sniffing around them. I'm only watching out for what's mine," she retorted.

"You're Mrs. Squires, aren't you?"

"Aye, and you're the right nosey, Miss Annabelle Sweeting. I've heard all about you, and twas nothing good. So just keep your distance, hear?"

"Mrs. Squires, I have done nothing but give my condolences to a young man that lost his sister. I would never harm someone who has been so generous to our unfortunate youth. I would dearly like to know who has been spreading such false rumors to make you think otherwise," I cooed.

As her face softened I knew I was on the right path. If I wanted information from her, a verbal altercation would get me nowhere. I proceeded to flatter her in the hopes that she would become an asset.

"A woman in your position is very important indeed, I could not even fathom the struggles you must endure, and all for the sake of the children. What did you think I possessed that would afflict your mission, praytell?"

"Oh, well. I didn't realize. Yes, yes it is difficult. I heard that you were making trouble for some of my young wards. I apologize for the misunderstanding. You clearly are not out to hurt the poor dears, then?" Her eyes searched mine seeking some kind of tell.

"Of course not. I was concerned about what happened to Gwennie, but who wouldn't be?"

"Ah, yes," Mrs. Squires said. "She was one of my dearest girls, and will be quite missed. Unfortunate, indeed. Are you helping with her case then? I saw you meeting with the death doctor," Mrs. Squires said.

"The death doctor? Oh, Doctor Cannish! I am sure he would be thrilled to hear that nickname. Yes, I am consulting on the investigation. Is there anything you would like to add? You know, about Gwennie that could help us find her killer?"

"Um, well, no, I mean… She was a right fine miss, and one of my best…students. I mean, she did her letters quite well, you see? Anyway, I don't know anything that could help, I'm sure," she stammered.

"That's too bad. Well, if you do think of something please send word. I am easy to find, apparently. Oh, and one other thing, never crook your finger when you pinch a wallet, it's pickpocketing 101," I said.

Echoing the words Nathan had used when he tried to teach me a few things had made the impression I desired. Mrs. Squire's face turned pale. I wondered at the boldness of such a woman to not only track me down at dinner but to be as brazen as to try to steal from me. Something Luke had said about not accusing a suspect from the start seeped into my mind. Although I loathed to admit it, perhaps a little less flippant intensity and a little more tea and scones were in order; to get the information I needed. The foul use of the children in her care was only a part of what this guardian was keeping, and I aimed to find out what else was behind those serpent eyes.

I turned and reached for my motorbike before she could respond. I touched the brim of my hat in salutation as I took off down the road toward Bread Street. There was much I needed to think about now, very much indeed.

Chapter 10- Decisions, Decisions

A gear that is not moving will rust and crumble. A passion that is not pursued will do the same.

The next morning I woke early and dressed in semi-professional attire. I wanted Chief Inspector Farthing to see me as an asset and not some chit off the street. It was high time I stopped hiding behind the coattails of Constable Luke Weston. For my part, I wanted to be an equal, to have my opinion valued like it once was. Somewhere along the way, it felt like I was being taken care of rather than being taken seriously. Today I would forge the path that captivated me.

"My dear Belle, you are looking quite determined this morning," Jaime quipped.

I walked into the dining parlor and collected my plate of the morning's offerings at the breakfast bar. I took my seat and began eating with gusto.

"You are worrying me, Belle. I haven't seen that look in your eye since we decided to get back at that disgrace for a boy, Jared. I remember you soldered his bike chain to its frame right outside the market down the lane from your parent's farm. He tried to ride away and fell straight on his face. Served him right for trying to cut one of your little sister Casey's pigtails off at church, but I had never seen you so focused," Jaime sighed.

"Yes, well I am going to Scotland Yard this morning," I replied, spreading butter on my toast.

"Indeed, and what business are you conducting there, may I inquire?"

"I am going to meet with Chief Inspector Farthing about pairing up with a different constable in the area. He has often given me credit for adding value with my observations to a case and I think I have a chance of still contributing if I am direct with him. I want to pursue being of assistance, and I don't think Constable Weston wants the same," I replied.

Jaime drew back, "Oooh, drawing a line in the sand are we? How delicious! I was wondering how long it would take you. Playing second fiddle was never your strong suit, cousin. Shall we dine together this evening and you can tell me all the torrid details of what I missed while I was away?" he asked.

"Jaime, do you find pleasure in my misfortunes? You are unbearable sometimes. I daresay if I didn't love you so, I'd hide all your feathers from you and make you wear grey!"

"You wouldn't!" Jaime brought his hands to his mouth in mock horror. "You well know I adore you and Mr. Weston together. I am always on your side though, and if that fool of a man cannot see what he is doing then I guess it's up to you to shed some light on it. I think I know what this is all about, but it is too good to let this play out," he said.

"That is very unkind of you, cousin. How can you just leave me so utterly naive when you clearly know what is happening, and I do not?"

"If I told you, you would not believe me, and I've found it best in these circumstances to keep myself apart from warring parties." he explained. "You'll find your way, my dear, and be better for it. Plus, I could be completely wrong, and then we would both have egg on our faces. No, you go to your meeting and strike fear into the hearts of all who doubt you. I look forward to dining with you tonight," he finished.

"I've been meaning to ask you something," I said tentatively. "I thought that since it has been quite a few months, and the "ton" has moved on to rather more exciting gossip, we could take tea with Lord Thetford some time in the future?"

Jaime raised his eyebrow at me.

"You are quite the feather ruffler. I think that is a most intriguing idea. Yes, let's invite him here, two days hence. Just enough time for news to spread," he added.

"News to spread? What are you speaking of?"

I pursed my lips at his cryptic words.

"Oh, nothing, cousin. You better be off to your appointment, I can't wait to hear all about your new partner," he said. Jaime stood abruptly and left the room before I could inquire any further.

I finished breaking my fast and put on my new hat and matching gloves. It was a miniature magenta top hat with a black and silver dragonfly pin. The dragonfly tail held a secret compartment for bobby pins. One could never have too many bobby pins. Stewart, a good friend and our house butler, helped me put on my long coat, and I headed for the motor park. I placed my riding goggles over my eyes and climbed aboard my motorbike. I was risking my tightly pinned hair to the wind, but I felt confident it would hold its shape and integrity.

I pushed the button and kicked the pedal on the right side of the bike. It buzzed to life, and steam puffed from the small exhaust pipe. Purgatorio flew from the second story window and circled from above. He would follow me to The Yard. As I released the brake, I felt freedom take over me. I was sure that after today that freedom would be all-encompassing. I would not allow it to be any other way.

I arrived in time to find Chief Inspector Farthing finishing a cup of apparently very good tea through his open door. He up-ended the cup, looking for more content, while sitting behind his desk. I knocked gently on the door frame and waited to be acknowledged.

"Ah, Sweeting, good morning to you." He motioned me to enter and waved towards a chair in front of his desk." What is it that I can help you with?"

"Good morning, Chief Inspector," I said, taking the proffered seat. "I wanted to inquire about getting assigned a new liaison. "There has been a breach of trust in the partnership between Constable Weston and I, and as such we've found that we should no longer be working together. However, I wish to continue assisting Scotland Yard, and was hoping I could do so in the same capacity, with a different officer. Perhaps a pair of fresh eyes could assist whoever is trying to crack this new case?"

He looked at me sternly for several minutes. I knew this look well. This was his weighing and measuring routine that sent most constables running for the hills. They found it was better to pretend that their request was never made than to take the heat from that stare. I was made of sterner stuff, I had just forgotten that recently. I wasn't forgetting at this moment though, as I looked back into his hard grey eyes. Then a smile came to his lips, making his ridiculously long mustache quiver.

"Yes, yes, that is just the ticket. We shall have you partner up with Quincy. He's new off the training force, but I dare say he has a quickness about him that you will find helpful."

He drummed his fingers on the desk and continued to smile.

"I can't, however, take Constable Weston off the young girl's case, you see? He's already invested a lot of time as I am sure you have as well. I will need you two to finish this one out, and then we can make the transition. Fair enough?"

My hopes of a quick clean break were dashed. I felt my shoulders slump, and a little of the wind flew out of my determined sails. One more case together. I wasn't sure if I was happy or about to burst into tears, but I kept my composure.

"Don't look so put out, Miss Sweeting," Chief Farthing said. "I dare say you will get this case solved in no time, and be on to bigger and better mysteries before long. Besides, Constable Weston has come a long way, wouldn't you agree? I daresay I can't understand why you wish to break up such a successful and productive team. I admit the Greenville Grave case went a little sideways, but that was all politics. Happens to all of us. If you aren't ruffling someone's feathers from time to time you aren't doing a good enough job," he said.

"Really? I thought you were quite upset with me, sir," I replied.

"Well, at the time I had to give a good scolding, of course. You'll learn that in the business of murder you need to have a tough skin. Not only from what you see, but what you hear. Don't let a few harsh words deter you from solving the puzzle, Miss Sweeting. I know this is probably something I shouldn't tell you, as you are quite the unrelenting bloodhound, but it's my duty not to see a sharp mind like yours go to waste. Now will there be anything else?"

"No, sir. Thank you, sir!" I said, standing up.

"Good, good, now go help solve this case. I hate it when the crimes involve children."

I nodded and turned to leave. It was amazing how much the people around me were supporting my endeavors. I was finally starting to believe that, yes, this is what I was meant to do. Why, then, was there still a voice nagging me? Could it be the one person I wanted approval from was denying me, and the doubt left was overwhelming?

I respected Constable Weston's opinion more than anyone else's. I had realized that his complete dismissal of my desire to continue the investigation was unpardonable. I would make my mark on the world without him. Well, at least after this case. It looked like the time had come to meet with my soon-to-be ex-partner. I didn't know if it would lead to severing our other relationship as well. It seemed inevitable at the moment. Who would want to be romantic with someone who neither trusted nor supported you?

I walked out into the street and adjusted my hat, smiling up at the sun. One thing was for sure, I was not going to doubt myself again. It did nothing but make me depressed. Purgatorio screeched from the sky, and I waved my hand out. He dove down and landed on my forearm.

"Purgy, it's time to get to work. Let's pay a visit to Constable Weston. It's high time we got a few things in order."

Chapter 11- A Duel of Wits

A heart cannot truly love unless a bond of trust and respect is forged. Oh, how I long for that!

I followed the laughter to the back of the pub that Luke often frequented for luncheon. A boisterous group of officers was hurriedly eating and telling jokes as they went. I found Luke in the back with Constable Harold Williams and Constable James Tallon. They had been friends for several years and helped us out on occasion over the past year. Purgatorio was perched on my shoulder as I made my way to their table. Constable Tallon noticed me first and elbowed Luke.

"Annabelle?" Luke said, in obvious surprise to see me. "I mean, Miss Sweeting. What are you doing here? I mean rather, did you receive my letter? I tried to call several times this week, but you were away from home. Is everything alright?"

Williams and Tallon snickered as Luke fumbled.

"Constable Weston, it appears we are not in agreement on the point of my career path. In turn, I have taken the opportunity to meet with Chief Inspector Farthing to relieve you of the obligation. I have been directed to see the Gwennie murder through with you, but then I will be assigned to assist Constable Quincy beyond that. I wanted to come by and thank you for your help over the past year, and wished to see when you would be available tomorrow to go over the current case," I said.

The shock on Luke's face was palpable. I hadn't realized his face could turn such a multitude of colors. Williams and Tallon stood up abruptly to leave the table.

"We'll see you down by Prescott Street, Weston," Tallon said.

They didn't wait for an answer, as it didn't look like Luke could physically give one at the moment.

"Luke, are you alright?" I asked, turning my attention back toward him. "Do you need some water?"

I wasn't sure what to do, he had been sitting there silently for at least two minutes. I finally sat down and shook his stacked hands. His eyes met mine, and there was a strange lost look to them.

"No, no I am well. I mean I don't understand. Why would you ask for another partner?"

"I thought it was obvious. You don't want me investigating with you. If I can't investigate with you, I must find a new liaison, no?"

"Belle, I don't want you investigating at all. Don't you see the danger? I want to…"

"You want to pursue me romantically," I interrupted him, "but without the headache of having me investigate murders, yes?"

"Yes. What I mean is, I admire your ambition, and you are good at many things, I just need you to be safe. Is that so wrong?"

He looked at me with such hurt and confusion. If he couldn't understand I didn't know how we could continue in any capacity.

"Luke, I don't need to be taken care of, I need to be seen as an equal. I need to have my opinion trusted, and my ambition supported. That is the kind of partnership, and dare I say it, *relationship* I am looking for. Is that so wrong?" I retorted, throwing his own question right back at him.

We sat there looking at each other. Neither of us wanted to give in, and neither of us wanted to give up. I longed for him to just say he could understand. That my presence and input on the case meant more to him than some made up fear he had of my peril. Couldn't he understand that we were cut from the same cloth? Puzzles and mysteries and justice that needed to be sought out are what we craved. How could I prove to him that I was just as capable, and why did I feel I needed to?

"I need to think," he finally broke the silence.

"Shall we meet on the morrow to discuss the case?" I asked. I didn't want to waste more time on a subject we couldn't compromise on. Best to stick to the facts and move on.

"Yes, that will be fine. Actually, I need to follow up on a lead first before that. Can we meet the day after?"

"This lead, do you not need assistance? I can accompany you."

"No, no. I must go on my own. It was asked of me to come alone. I understand it's a sensitive matter," he replied.

The sting of being excluded had me feeling petty. I said something next that I had not planned on revealing.

"I will be having tea with Jaime and Lord Thetford the day after tomorrow, but the evening is free," I replied.

I looked up through my lashes at him, waiting to see his reaction. His eyes seemed to darken as he took in my words.

"Lord Thetford? I hadn't realized you renewed your acquaintance with the gentleman. Am I to be replaced in all aspects of your life then, Belle?"

Me, replace him? I could scarcely stay composed at the accusation. It was he who was cutting me out.

"Mr. Weston, I am surprised at you. That is quite ungenerous of you. I was under the impression that you were distancing yourself from me. I can see now we both have a lot to ponder on. Let us hope we can find common ground enough to find justice for Gwennie, yes?"

"That's never been in question. I have no doubt that we will find the culprit; it's the cost of finding the truth that wrecks me," he replied.

I arched a brow in question.

"Never mind that for now, I must be going. I will see you the day after next, Miss Sweeting. I look forward to hearing what you've discovered."

Luke stood up, bowed to me, and moved swiftly to the door. He looked back before he exited the pub, and a determined glint sparkled from his eye. It made me nervous, and for some reason, hopeful.

***

"And that's all he said?" Jaime said when I had returned home and told him of my confrontation with Constable Weston. "Cousin, what cryptic words from an otherwise rational man. You do find yourself in such interesting predicaments. At this rate I won't have to go to the theater this season," he joked.

"Jaime, do not make light of my situation. I fear I am once again out of my element. Today started out so promising. I felt like I was finally setting my own course. But he has power over me, and I know not what to do," I admitted.

"You forget, you have power too." Jaime said. "That is what love does. And when two people are so strong willed it can be hard to fight their need to lead and compromise. They either succeed and come out stronger, or…"

"Or what, Jaime?" I asked, flashing him a stern look.

"Or they realize they cannot find enough common ground to keep their love alive, " he finished. "A painful realization, but let's not dwell on that now. Let us think of happier things. I have to tell you all about my journey. It was quite something, indeed," Jaime exclaimed with delight.

I tried to join in with his enthusiasm, but the words that he said sat like a rock in my stomach. The thought of completely severing ties with Luke was crushing. We had shared so much together, good and bad. I thought that is what strong relationships were built upon. I couldn't see myself giving in to only being a supportive wife and not pursuing my own goals and dreams. If that was not where we were heading, then what were we really doing?

I suddenly realized I hadn't heard a word Jaime had said in the last few minutes and tried to catch up to where he was in the conversation.

"And then there was this rude servant that was treating Lady Whipley quite like a pariah, but I donned him with a most fetching hat with bright green feathers to match his waist coat, and he simply beamed. You should have seen the transformation, Belle. So now I am convinced as ever that feathers can make any ensemble better, and the people wearing them happier! Lady Whipley was quite miffed by the whole ordeal but couldn't help but giggle when I stuck a peacock feather in her towering bun," Jaime laughed.

"You didn't, cousin! You are beyond bold! I daresay it was a wonderful affair," I said.

"I most certainly did, it was quite diverting. I only wish you were there to share in my triumph. Alas, I have brought some wonderful items home with me for you. I do hope you put them to good use, and if you are grateful, I would dearly love a clue to the Bergenhalt's theme this year," he pouted.

"I knew it, you scoundrel! Trying to trick me into telling," I scolded.

"Not telling, just a hint. Please?" he begged.

"Oh, alright, but you mustn't say a word to anyone else, understand?"

He squealed with delight and nodded his head fervently.

"Only a small clue," I told him. "How about a little riddle to make it interesting?"

"You do love the dramatic, cousin. Yes, I am most amenable to that idea," Jaime said.

I tapped my chin for several minutes piecing a puzzle together. It had to be general enough to have several options, but precise enough to result in the correct answer. I beamed with anticipation as I recited the clues.

"A river longer than the Thames leads to my enchanting halls. Three shadows cast a fearsome shade when the sun is on the horizon. My glory is in my history," I said.

"Oooh, how fun. I will need to think about this a little bit. The River Severn is bigger, but it isn't known for shadows that I can think of. What a grand puzzle indeed!" Jaime exclaimed.

"I'm glad you like it, now maybe we can get on with some better conversation while you wheedle it out," I quipped.

"Yes, cousin, as you wish. Are you all set for tea tomorrow with the new Lord Thetford? I got a missive today saying that he will be bringing a new invention with him to show us. If his letter is any indication, it should be quite illuminating."

"Really? That sounds most intriguing," I said, my mind racing as to what kind of invention it might be. "I am looking forward to conversing with him again in person. It seems a hard position to be in, don't you think?"

"Yes, I can well believe it is. I've been in some tough scrapes myself, but to have not just one relation but two be caught in such deplorable actions must be very trying indeed. I do hope you aren't overextending yourself, though," Jaime said.

"How so?"

"I merely mean to suggest that you be cautious. I know you are angry with Mr. Weston, and if you were to be too amiable to Lord Thetford, it would be seen as a statement."

"To what are you referring, what kind of statement?"

"I can see that I will need to spell it out for you, so let me speak plainly. If you start entertaining Lord Thetford, it will be looked upon as though you have given up your attachment to Luke. Is that really something you are ready for?"

I thought for a moment about how I would actually feel if Luke really wasn't in my life anymore, and I knew instantly it wasn't the outcome I wanted.

"Honestly, no. But surely one tea will not set the "ton's" tongues wagging?"

"Perhaps not, but do be tactful, my dear. I fear you are in for a hardship or two, and I would hate to see you enter such treacherous waters unprepared," he said.

"Very wise council. I thank you and will be on my best behavior, I assure you," I replied.

"Yes, let's hope it's all for nothing."

Chapter 12- Ease and Comfort

A revelation never comes on command. It must be sussed out, and then when you are about to give up... BAM!

The next morning, I gathered my notes and thoughts in my tinker room. I wanted to be sure I had everything prepared for Constable Weston this evening so I could enjoy tea with Lord Thetford without my nagging thoughts interrupting us. I wasn't sure what I was looking forward to more: Miro's new secret invention or conversing with my friend again. It has seemed an age since I had seen him in person. I hoped that he would not feel slighted by having waited this long to do so.

After writing a few more observations about my interaction with Mrs. Squires, I put my notes away and observed my table of creations. I felt the excitement bubble up about the Bergenhalt festivities soon approaching. Lady Bergenhalt had informed me that she would announce the theme at the beginning of the season, which was just a sennight hence. I had made her a brilliant headpiece in the shape of a snake that would shine in the gaslight like the sun itself. I fingered the red jewels that formed the snake's eyes. I wondered if Jaime would uncover the theme before the reveal. I knew he would be enraptured, and I wanted to share my pieces with him. I hoped that the lack of actual feathers wouldn't dampen his spirits, but I figured he would find a way to incorporate them anyway.

I sighed at the thought of last year's event. The beautiful costumes, the gorgeous decor, and the amazing refreshments all led me to an entrancing dance I could never forget. The silent promises that Luke and I had made seemed like a foggy dream. I thought about the phoenix necklace I wore that evening and felt like I was still trying to rise from the ashes of my past.

At first, the anguish and turmoil we had gone through was a binder, bringing us closer together. Now it seemed that the very thing that had bonded Luke and I was driving us apart. There was a need inside of me to continue this work, to help people, and to solve the puzzles no one else could. It appeared there was a need inside Luke to shelter me somehow, from the atrocities of the world. While this was a sweet sentiment, it was simply too late. I had already been through it, I had already dealt with it. Perhaps the fault lay in the fact that he hadn't dealt with it.

For my part, I have found that no one knows when their time is up. To live your life in fear of it being your last, every day, is not sustainable.

I heard the click, click, click of nails on the floor outside my door. I stood up and walked toward the noise. Opening the door, I was greeted by a chuff. I looked both ways down the hall and let Purgatorio in. The mechanical manticore had become so dear to me. He was a combination of fierce protector and temperamental house cat. His mane was made up of smooth brass sections secured to his head by steel metal rivets. Purgy's head didn't rise above my knee. His body was about the length of a loaf of bread with metal plates encasing his internal components. A clear window panel showcased the main power core that emitted a slight buzzing sound when he was recharging. Two butterfly screws held a lower hollow compartment closed on his undercarriage. This I could use to have him quickly dispatch messages if I could not make a trip myself.

His legs, though strong and hinged, moved with great flexibility. Purgy's back flowed into a pair of sturdy leather encased wings. They had a batlike quality, with pointed tips. His segmented tail led to the scorpion tip that rotated with retractable spikes. He slipped into the room and took residence in the corner cushion I had set up for him.

I knew he didn't require a cushion. He was a machine, but I couldn't help treating him as a most beloved pet. He had saved my life. I knelt and stroked under his chin, and he closed his eyes and vibrated out his brassy purr. It calmed my nerves and set my insides to rights. I felt better for it. The clock on the wall began to whistle out steam as the hour struck two. Tea time had come. I needed to confirm my appearance was acceptable and make my way down to the drawing room.

"Come on, then. I am sure he'll want to see you too, Purgy," I said.

We stopped at my bed chambers, and I took a glance at the looking glass. My curls were not too out of place. My skin was fair but not too pale. My eyes had lost some of their light this past year, but I hoped to change that. I adjusted my bodice and fluffed out my half skirt. It was navy blue with golden yellow cord detailing. I had a yellow ribbon strung throughout my hair with a small, blue feather just off-center to the left. I pinched my cheeks and smiled. Perhaps this tea would be the beginning of some normalcy seeping back into my world. I didn't think I could take too much more at my current trajectory.

Purgatorio took flight down the stairs, and I followed, gliding my hand along the polished wooden rail. I looked down at my navy blue slippers and made sure not to trip on the last stair. Entering the drawing room, I saw Jaime looking over the desserts and giving some last-minute instructions to our new servant, Lily. She bowed and smiled at me on her way out of the room. I walked to Jaime and took his hands in mine.

"It looks wonderful, cousin. I cannot say how glad I am to have you home again. I missed this. I missed you. Hopefully, we shall get back to normal for this coming season. I felt quite out of sorts this past few months," I confided.

"Yes, my dear. I must admit it has been a trying time. I daresay this will be the start to a new age for us. Although, I do hope you will set aside time for just us. I do love our conversations," he replied.

"Of course!"

A knock on the door, and Stewart introduced Lord Miro Nassar, Earl of Thetford. I held my breath as he entered the room. He walked with a silver cane now. His leg, broken in the motorcar race last year, had given him a permanent limp. The cane was ornate and contained images of Greek gods along it. The top was Atlas holding up the world. I could see the resemblance to the man holding the cane. It must have been quite the struggle for Miro to take over his brother's portion of the business as well as deal with the aftermath of his family's transgressions. I smiled as he bowed, and he smiled back with that cat-like smirk.

"Welcome, Lord Thetford!" Jaime greeted, shaking his hand. "How long it has been. I daresay six months at the least. You are looking quite recovered and a bit more dapper with that extraordinary cane. Please, do come in and sit down," he said, ushering Miro towards a chair.

"Thank you, sir! And please call me Nassar or Miro. I fear that the name Lord Thetford has still not become familiar to me yet. You both look quite well also," he replied.

His eyes lingered on me as he walked to join us.

"It is good to see you, Miro," I said, sitting down in a chair opposite him. "I want to thank you for your continued correspondence. It has been of great comfort as of late. I do enjoy you sharing with me the latest findings on your water treatment process for the Boroughs. I saw a few in action the other day, and they are quite remarkable," I said.

"You did? Pray, what brought you to that part of town, Miss Annabelle?"

"Ah, well it was another investigation I am entangled in," I replied. "One involving Nathan's old orphanage. It was called Second Chance Orphanage, have you heard of it?"

"Aye, I've heard of it. It is a troublesome spot, indeed. Sometimes I don't believe they want our help. They have other things in play that will only come to light if people are about," Miro said.

"You know some of these other elements in play then?" I asked.

"I've only heard stories from some of my workers in the area. They claim Chancey Street is not a place to find welcome. A rough crowd there, indeed! Do be careful, but I am sure you already are. You also have Purgatorio, I see, ever by your side," he said.

He smiled at the mechanical wonder he had gifted to me. The manticore sprang up beside him and nudged his elbow with his delicate leather nose. Purgy chuffed happily as he got the desired reaction when Miro stroked back his smooth metallic mane.

"Ah, one of my better contraptions, I'd say. I have sold a multitude of these to the motor racing park, but none has bonded to a person as he has. Simply extraordinary!"

"He truly is, sir. I cannot thank you enough. I find that he has become quite dear to me, " I replied.

"Just so, how would I go about getting such a creation, Lord...I mean Nassar? I find that I am quite jealous of my cousin, and believe it would be quite beneficial to have one of my own," Jaime inquired.

"Do you think so? Miro asked. "Do you think that society would be interested in personalized mechanical companions? I must say, it had crossed my mind, but after what had happened, I wasn't sure that the opportunity would still be open to me."

"Oh, yes," Jamie assured him. "I think they would be very much in demand. I believe your time of penance has long since been up, and that society can no longer punish you for the sins of your family, as it were. I say you should, and I'll be your first customer. Something with feathers, I think."

I looked at Miro, and we both laughed.

"Yes, well, I suppose I am quite predictable," said Jaime.

My cousin blushed a bit as we tried to contain our amusement.

"Oh Jaime , you are anything but. However, feathers will always be your Achilles heel I think," I replied.

He smiled at that and nodded. Then the door swung open, and Lily entered with our tea. She moved swiftly across the room and tried not to splash the tea about. Setting it down, she curtsied and turned to leave.

"Lily, one moment," I called after her.

Yes, Miss Sweeting?" she said, turning around.

"Did the cook make any of those delicious tarts?" I asked.

"I believe she did, just this morning. I will go check it at once, miss."

"Thank you."

"A new servant, then?" Miro asked.

"Yes, she is quite an amiable girl," Jaime replied. "She is the daughter of one of Lady Whipley's maids, and I credit, a sharp girl to boot. I think she will do quite well here. It is always so nice to have new and interesting people about, you know? Some would say servants are not interesting, but they have such fascinating tales, I rarely find want for entertainment," Jaime said.

"Many of my servants left after the incident with my brother. I am just starting to find my way back to a healthy crew. If you have any recommendations, I would dearly appreciate it."

"What posts do you need, sir?" asked Jaime.

"I will make you a list if that will suffice? I shouldn't want to bore you with the domestic drama today," Miro said.

"Yes, send it 'round when you are able," Jamie replied.

"Now, Nassar, do tell us what this new gizmo is that you have cloaked in secrecy?" I interjected.

I took a sip of my tea and looked over the edge at Miro, waiting for his reply. He grinned and looked down. His green eyes lit up with that inventor enthusiasm I had missed so much. There is something about creating that makes the spirit soar.

"Oh, I was wondering how long it would take before you asked," Miro said. "You lasted longer than I anticipated, Miss Annabelle. I shant tease you any longer though. I know how you hate to wait," he quipped.

I felt comfortable there, with my cousin and the new Lord Thetford. It felt like we were all on familiar terms with no tension at all. I was quite overcome with the ease of it all. It had me smiling, and it felt good to smile.

"What is that look for?" Miro asked, trying to read my face. "I see you are off somewhere again. Perhaps, you are trying to guess what it could be?"

"You do have a habit of catching me in thought, Miro," I replied.

"Ahem," Jaime said.

I looked at him, and his brow was raised in question. I found myself blushing. Perhaps I hadn't taken his advice to heart as much as I had thought.

Chapter 13- Tea and Transports

Inventions are our dreams becoming reality. We need only to believe in them enough and never give way to doubt. Piece of cake, right?

We watched as Miro unpacked a flat satchel and laid the contents on the now cleared table. His eyes darted between us in delight and anticipation.

"Yes, well. Here is the drawing I have. You might remember, Annabelle, when I took you to my place of business, the room at the end of the corridor?"

I smiled warmly at the memory. It had been an evening that could have changed the direction of my life. I remember the amazing gizmos and devices in the room. Robotic appendages, airships, and flying parcel carriers had been set up at different stations along the walls. Each one with a multitude of uses that could change the city for the better. My cheeks flushed as I remembered the ending of our outing. A soft kiss in his hangar-like invention room.

"Yes, sir, I do," I replied.

"These are the diagrams for the parcel machines I was working on. Your ideas about helping people in quarantined places got me thinking bigger."

"Bigger, sir, what could be bigger than that?" I asked.

Miro sat on the edge of his seat and pointed down at the table.

"You see this sketch here?"

Jaime and I inched closer to his drawing. The lead markings on an off-white velum looked striking. Rotors and steam plumes were depicted, but the one that captivated me was in the very center. It was a dual-fan system with three wires and hooks extending from a circular frame on the bottom. The fans led to a balloon on the top. It was like a tiny hot air balloon, without the use of fire.

"How will it run? How will the fans move?" I asked.

I searched his eyes with excitement. He had come across a new technology, and I had to know how it was done.

"Quite clever, yes, the fans will move causing air to fill the balloon here. The fan will be run by the same design as Purgatorio here. While a trade secret, I will give you a few notes. This centerpiece here has a power source that can be re-energized by friction. The more the fans move against the inner coil the more friction is produced, and in turn the more energy is stored to keep the fans moving. The trick is to get them moving in the first place. Now that was a struggle," Miro said.

I couldn't help being caught up in his excitement once again. His passion for creating was contagious. I had forgotten how much joy I had when I created a new mechanism for my baubles. Sure, I had created a vast amount of embellishments of late for the upcoming dance, but they were all of the similar elements, nothing new, nothing progressive.

"So, how did you get it to start? Don't leave us in the lurch, good man!" Jaime pressed him.

It was quite clear that Jaime was as much invested in this new development as I was.

"The key was momentum," Miro said, pointing to the drawing. "You see this spot here? Well, what I did was take a complicated element and try to make it simple. If I turn it on its side, what does it look like to you?"

He pulled out another diagram with the dual fan contraption depicted on its side. "It looks like a wheel," said Jaime.

"Think simpler," Miro hinted.

"Hmmm, perhaps a platter on its side, or the track of a bicycle. Like a place you could put a chain," I guessed.

"That is a good guess too, but what I came up with was a child's toy," Miro said. "I can see you are quite confused, so I will not prolong the suspense any further. I used the mechanics of a bandalore! I thread the strong rope through here," he said, pointing to a hold on the edge of the frame. "Then I pull here, and the friction gives the core enough energy to run itself!"

"Brilliant! Oh, but how do you shut it off?" I asked.

"Yes, very good. That was quite the week in my workshop, I assure you," Miro replied with amusement. "I put in a switch, much like I did for Purgatorio when he had the optic capture in his eye. It can be turned off and on by a separate control located at my workshop. They have a homing beacon, like the pigeons that deliver missives. I have a large signal amplifier attached to the building now, so I can reach anywhere in the city. Like right now," he looked at his timepiece, "please go look out your front door, sir."

Jaime's eyes grew large, and he jumped up and headed toward the main entrance. Miro and I followed him out. Stewart came to the hall raising his brow in question.

"Is something amiss, sir?"

"No, Stewart, but there very well may be something at the door. Make way, man!" Jaime exclaimed.

Stewart skittered out of Jaime's path and joined our parade to the front door. Jaime flung the door opened and gasped at the balloon hovering on his doorstep. Neighbors were gawking on both sides of the street as the bright yellow balloon fluttered and hummed with the dual fans flying. I noticed Miro had retrieved a panel from his pocket and hit a button on it. The hooks on the bottom of the frame attached to the balloon opened, and a parcel fell squarely into Jaime's arms. The gizmo zoomed up into the sky and headed back to where it came from. Jaime turned around beaming.

"You've out done yourself man! How amazing!"

"Wait until you see what's inside the parcel," Miro replied.

He looked at me with a sly smile and bumped my elbow. I smiled back, even though I had no idea what was in the package. Jaime rushed back to the drawing room and proceeded to open the box on the table. He shredded the paper like it was Christmas morning and I giggled at his unconstrained joy.

"This can't be," Jaime exclaimed.

"What is it, cousin?" I asked, fairly humming with the excitement of it all.

"You are not going to believe it, Belle. I think he might be a magician," he replied.

"Show us, show us!" I begged.

Stewart edged forward, along with a few other servants, having found their way to the drawing room as the uproar continued. Finally, Jaime pulled out an object with a brass and green patina that had strange metal feathers adhered to it. I moved forward to get a better look.

"Press the center of his head three times, good sir," Miro said.

Jaime did as he was told, and the contraption came to life before us. It sprang onto its talons revealing itself to be a most stunning mechanical peacock. The tail feathers sprawled out in quick succession, and the bird stretched a pair of sturdy copper and nickel-plated wings. It pranced about the room for a moment and returned to flutter its eyelashes at Jaime.

"Nassar, I don't know what to say, it is beyond any vision I could have imagined," Jaime gushed.

"You have been a friend to me, both of you, when friends were scarce, and people were cruel. Bestowing this gift is the least I can do to show my gratitude. I hope that, as time goes on, we shall see more of each other again?"

"Yes, Nassar. You need not buy our affections, though. We esteem your association and are glad you have been washed clean of the "ton's" tarnish. Please let this afternoon be the beginning of many more engagements to come," Jaime said.

"I second that notion," I added. "It has been far too long since we've had a good gathering. Perhaps we should throw another luncheon, cousin?" I asked Jaime.

Just then, a knock at the door halted the conversation. We all turned to find Constable Weston standing awkwardly by the entrance.

"Pardon me, the front door was ajar, and I thought you might need aid. I see I was mistaken," he said shyly.

"Come in, Constable! Come see what I have just acquired from Lord Thetford. It is quite something, indeed," Jaime said, inviting him in.

The shining peacock squawked with appreciation. It liked to be fawned over just as much as Jaime.

"Thank you, sir, but I do not wish to intrude," Luke replied. He looked at me with sad eyes.

"Do come in, Weston," Miro said. I have not seen you in an age, and Miss Annabelle refuses to give me reports on you in her letters. I fear I haven't known you for some time. I have longed for good conversation, besides these beasts," he continued, pointing at the peacock.

"Yes, Mr. Weston, do come in," I said.

"Miss Annabelle," Lily said from behind Luke.

Luke walked towards the table and looked down at the peacock.

"Yes, Lily?" I asked, turning towards her.

"The tarts are here. I brought three, but should I go fetch another?"

"Yes, please do, and another cup and fresh tea, please. Make it the India Black, it's the constable's favorite. Now, tell us, Constable Weston, did you see anything odd in the sky?" I said.

I looked at Jaime and Miro, and we all giggled a bit. Luke looked at us, confused.

"No, miss, I can't say that I did. What was it that I should have seen?"

I smiled at Miro and nodded. Luke looked between us and grimaced.

"Well, Mr. Weston, it is a new invention I have just launched," Miro continued.

He proceeded to show Luke the outlines, and as Lily brought in another two tarts, I watched the two interact. I was about to ask Lily why she had brought the fifth tart, when Nathan squeaked past her and sat down beside Jaime. He put a finger out toward the mechanical bird, and it took a peck at him. Purgy roared at the bird in a scolding manner. The peacock edged closer to Nathan and laid its head on his knee in apology. This is what I had longed for. A moment in time with friends and family. I looked at Luke, and when he caught me staring, he smiled back. A bit of the spark was still there, but would it last?

Chapter 14- The Case Before Us

The truth about things is rarely seen by those who live it. They only know their own perspective.

Tea came to an end as Miro had to dash to make sure his delivery prototype made it safely back to the hangar. We were all smiles as we promised to plan another gathering soon. Jaime had tried to pay Miro for the mechanical bird, but Miro said his payment would be from Jaime demonstrating it to other members of his acquaintance. Perhaps it would show them how the addition of such a device would add to their lives. Miro hoped the word would get around and perhaps enable him to contract more productions.

"Miss Annabelle, a pleasure," he said. He took my hand and kissed it. I thanked him for coming and looked forward to our next meeting. I turned to find Luke behind me, watching the whole of the conversation. He looked curious, but no longer sad.

"Are you quite well, Constable?" I asked him.

"Yes, I was just thinking. Lord Thetford is quite changed. He was always so over the top, but. I found him quite amiable today. There is something different in his manner, more respectful. I find it appealing. I think perhaps I was mistaken in his overall character," he replied.

"That is very generous of you, Mr. Weston. When we can look past our own prejudices and see fault in our judgments, we too are growing. It is not an easy skill to master, I assure you," I said.

"So, I am learning. Shall we depart then? I was thinking about Claymore's; do you have your notes?"

"Let me gather my things, and yes, Claymore's will be fine," I replied.

I started up the stairs and looked back down at him. He turned away from me as Jaime invited him to the drawing room to wait. I rushed back to my room and decided to change into my warmer brown dress with orange ribbon accents. It had a white lacy collar and sleeves. Gold buttons were stamped uniformly down either side of my corset. A floral pattern accentuated the center panel, leading to a long brown skirt. Matching boots and a hat completed the outfit. I gathered my observations from the tinkering room and walked back downstairs.

"You think it's too late, then?" I overheard Luke ask Jaime as I was about to enter the drawing room. At his words, I hesitated a few steps outside the door.

"I think you need to talk to Belle. I think that you must take what you learned about Lord Thetford today and apply it to your relationship with her," Jaime replied.

"How do you mean, Jaime?" Luke asked sincerely.

"What I mean is, take away the expectations you have, and just see what is in front of you. If your heart still agrees, then you have your answer," Jaime said.

I didn't know exactly what that meant, but I didn't want to be caught eavesdropping, so I stepped loudly the last few strides to the doorway.

"Constable Weston, are you ready? I believe we have a lot to go through," I inquired.

He nodded and said his thanks to Jaime before following me out of the room.

"So tell me, how did your lead pan out?" I asked, as we turned towards the hall.

"Not as well as I had hoped, but it gave me some ideas. Will Nate and Purgatorio be joining us at Claymore's?"

"No, Nathan has been sent on a task this evening," I replied.

"Indeed?"

"I shall explain more at dinner. As for Purgatorio, I have sent him along after young Starling to keep watch. Something tells me that we need to tread lightly right now."

"That is very wise," he agreed. "Shall we be off then?"

I nodded and followed him out to the hall. Stewart had my short coat waiting for me, and I shimmied into the sleeves while he held it for me.

"Thank you, Stewart."

"Of course, Miss Anabelle, do be careful out there tonight. I hear it is a full moon," he warned.

I reflexively rubbed the ankh that One-eyed Whitmore had gifted me and nodded.

"Yes, I always try to be. Do keep an eye on Jaime, I fear he will be up all night toying with that new companion of his," I said.

"Yes, miss, I think you are right."

Stewart nodded and opened the door for us. We walked down the steps to the waiting motor. Luke guided me to the passenger side of his vehicle, and I opened the door myself.

"I got it," I said.

"I can see that," he quipped.

I sat down and waited for him to enter the driver's side. The motor was rough to start, but once it purred to life, we were on our way.

"I feel like we need to clear the air," I suggested.

"Oh, how so?"

"I can see you no longer like working with me on investigations, and I have made the appropriate efforts to rectify this by changing partners, but shall we discuss the other elephant in the room?" I said.

"I'm not sure what you are referring to?"

I could tell he was toying with me, and I couldn't help thinking, *this is not the time for coyness*. Perhaps my feelings were stronger than his, and if that be the case, we should deal with it now so this last investigation could go smoothly and quickly.

"Luke, you know very well what I'm referring to. I don't know what game you are trying at, but it is quite vexing and a little insulting, to own the truth," I retorted.

"Belle, I was merely trying to diffuse the growing tension. It seems my words and actions of late have been anything but hitting the mark. My apologies. I gather from your serious tone you are talking about the turbulent turn our current personal relationship has taken, yes?"

He looked over toward me, and I nodded.

"I think that there are some things that we need to clear up, and I don't want to make any more mistakes, so let me think on that for a bit."

I looked at him in confusion.

"Let us focus only on this case for tonight. I fear mixing the two facets of our lives has been precisely the reason we are in this position as of late. Does that suit?" he asked.

"No, not particularly, but do I really have a choice with you lately?" I asked. "I wish we could go back to our first few puzzles together and figure out where the deviation came from. We are a solid team, and I had thought in every aspect, but you are methodically shutting me out of areas of our relationship that I find unreasonable. I will, as you say, let the subject rest for now, but this is in no way over," I said.

"Yes, well…I just want to say, my feelings for you have not changed. I just need to find a better way to explain what I am about, apparently. Please allow me a few days to do that."

"Very well, Mr. Weston," I replied.

"Very well, Miss Sweeting," he parroted back.

We rode in silence the rest of the trip, both battling internally with all that was left unsaid. As we entered Claymore's my stomach growled in reaction to the delicious aroma permeating the room. We found a table towards the back with good lighting and fell into the rhythm of unpacking our notes until the servant came to take our order.

When the lad left we sat down and stared at each other for a few moments. The world around us faded as we progressed through the details we had collected so far, only stopping to enjoy some meat pies and tea when they arrived.

I was surprised not to be scolded as I told him of my trip to the orphanage and the alley where we met Gwennie's brother. He jotted a few questions down as I talked, to ask me when I had finished. As he inquired about Mrs. Squires, I told him of our meeting outside this very eatery, and how she had tried to rob me of my observation journal.

Luke told me he would have one of his contacts from the Brass Boroughs begin watching the foundling home and the superintendent. It was strange to me that Mrs. Squires should know about my visit to the orphanage, as I never made it inside. I didn't think Byron would say anything, but I didn't know him that well. This is why I sent Nathan back this evening to inquire. I hadn't told Nate, but I sent Purgatorio to watch his back. If anyone was harming the slum dwellers on purpose, Nate would be a very tempting target. Sometimes it came to mind that Nathan Starling had a vast more bravery than he did common sense. It was risky, but we needed to know more, and he was in the best position to get real answers.

Luke revealed to me more information about a few parcels they had intercepted. I wasn't wholly surprised to find out they contained more organs packed in ice. Some were pigs, but some were human. I had a very real suspicion that they were tied into the Greenwich Grave robber case, but I didn't want to ruin the evening by bringing up that debacle again. Well, not just yet. Not until I had more proof that could in no way be disputed. We were finally on a roll, and the trepidation of the past seemed forgotten as we poured our combined efforts into the riddle before us.

Chapter 15- In Hysterics

The clues that seem black and white are most often shades of grey. Much like flirtation signals, no?

I glanced toward the window of Claymore's storefront and saw a most unexpected sight. A young freckled face was smushed against the glass, hands on either side to block out the exterior reflection, and two large eyes scanning the interior until they halted on mine. A surprised expression was replaced by an urgent wave to come outside.

"Luke, I am being beckoned," I said.

I directed him toward the window and the face of the rather impatient urchin, Sadie.

"I'll be right back," I said.

He nodded and followed my path to the front door with his eyes. I opened it and held the door tighter as a gusty breeze threatened to steal it from my hands.

"Sadie, what are you doing here? Are you okay?" I asked, standing in the doorway.

"Ah, miss, I wasn't sure where to go, but I ran into Nate, and he says you was here, and I just needed to tell someone not at the dungeon," she exclaimed.

"The dungeon?"

"Ah, it be what we call the orphanage sometimes. It can be terribly medieval there, if you catch my meaning."

"I see."

"Somethin' horrible has happened, miss!" Sadie exclaimed.

"Come in, come in. Let us get you warm and set you up with a hot meal, my dear. Then you can tell us all about it," I replied.

"Us?" she asked, hesitating.

"Yes, my friend Constable Weston is inside, and we are working together to help uncover what happened to Gwennie," I said.

"I don't trust no bobbies, miss," she replied.

Her eyes darted back to the door I still held open. I had to make her stay, but what would convince her?

"Well, Sadie, I trust this one with my life and so does Nate. Let us help you," I said.

She still looked skittish, but I could see her need to release the current anxiety, and the promise of food was winning her over.

"Well, I guess," she said, "but the first sign that he is going to drag me down to the Yard, and I am a ghost, POOF!"

"Deal," I agreed.

We walked back to the table where Luke was waiting.

"Constable Weston, this is Sadie, from Second Chance, she says something has happened and I thought it best if we both heard it at the same time," I started.

"Nice to make your acquaintance, Miss Sadie. You can call me Mr. Weston or Luke, no need to be throwing that constable part about. It tends to make people nervous," Luke smiled.

"I'll say," she agreed.

While they made their introductions, I flagged down the servant lad and ordered another meat pie and warm cider for the girl.

"Now then, what is the news you have for us?" I looked at her with an encouraging expression.

"Oh, it has been dreadful, it has," Sadie began. "Mrs. Squires has been on a true rampage all week. She is all dodgy, thinking we are all out to get her. Even slapped Byron right in the eye, she did! He's got a fat shiner, for sure. The Missus was still having Jane and me taking packages, you know?"

Sadie looked suspiciously at Luke, and I nodded to let her know it was okay to continue.

"Yea, well…she was being real hush-hush and not telling us wheres we was to take them until it was right before we was leaving."

Luke interrupted, "Is that not normal?"

I looked at her confused, wondering the same.

"No, usually we have a whole day to scout the area, like the older kids showed us. We needs to slip in and out like a fog, you see? Without being noticed, because the Missus doesn't like her business being entangled with. I think that's the words she uses," Sadie said.

She lifted her cap off her head, scratched it for a second, and then shook away the thought.

"Anyway, these recent trips were causing us more run-ins with the big caps," she looked accusingly at Luke. "They are after somethin' in the boxes, I guess. Even though we don't knows what it was. Not sure why they be needing to take Mrs. Squires' dirty clothes bundles anyway," she huffed.

"Why do you think they are dirty clothes? Did you open one?" I asked.

"No, it's just we are usually delivering them to the launders work-house over on the East End. I hate it over there, you see? Full of rats, and not just the ones with tails either," she shivered.

We took a reprieve from the questions for a few moments as her meal arrived, and she quickly tucked into the food before her. We had to tell her to use the utensils as she attacked the meal with her hands at first, causing the other patrons of the eatery to look our way with a mix of concern and disgust.

Children of Sadie's heritage were often considered beneath the notice of the social elite. Not only beneath their status, but with no connections, or obvious value, they were discarded like the weekly rubbish. It made me realize how different our family was in the country. Although we were neither rich nor ranked highly among the "ton", my parents made an effort to provide food for the local children's home. Giving to the unfortunate what we could, we were told, was what God wanted from us. Now, having been to church in London town, perhaps their catechism class had different lessons than ours.

She finished her meat pie and looked up at us almost guiltily.

"Do you want another?"

She nodded.

"Okay, I will have them bring you another, but first, please tell us the original news you were going to relay with such urgency. I fear we were derailed by the tales of your package deliveries," I said.

"Ah, sawrry, miss. I have been quite taken away with it all myself. So the news is, Janey girl is missing! She took the last task from Mrs. Squires yesterday afternoon, and no one's seen her since. We weren't supposed to, but we've been sharing our routes of late. Since the Missus ain't been right in the head, we didn't want to get snatched up. I was supposed to follow her, but I was held up at the station," she said.

A cunning smile crossed her face as she sneaked a look at Luke. Something told me it was the same situation that I met Nathan in. It was a shame that the urchins had to resort to begging and stealing when the city was on the rise and starting to thrive. There was a definite disconnect drawing its line through the center of town.

The smile on Sadie's face faded as she continued, "I told her to wait for me, but she said that Mrs. Squires wouldn't let her. She didn't want to get beat like Byron, so she ran off to Tapers Grove. I haven't seen her since."

She wiped her eyes and turned away so we wouldn't see her in a vulnerable state. Jane must have meant a lot to her for this weather-battered urchin to show such emotion. I hoped Jane was caught up by the law and not anything more drastic.

"Where is Tapers Grove? I don't believe I've heard of the area," I inquired.

"Tapers Grove is where they make all the candles in the Brass Boroughs. All the fancy to-dos don't realize they be getting their sticks from the gutters. But that's the case with most goods these days, I suspect," Sadie shrugged. "It's hot there, all that wax. Stinky too; sometimes the perfumes are worse than the rubbish in the streets. I can't stand when we have to deliver there, but Mr. Fieldworth oversees the workhouse there."

"Mr. Fieldworth? That name sounds vaguely familiar," I said.

"He's a beadle, miss. I think he reports to the church over in Greenwich."

"Not St. Alfege Church?"

"That's just the one," Sadie confirmed.

"Don't even suggest it, Miss Sweeting," Luke warned.

"You seem to have suggested it for me, Mr. Weston," I said.

"That case is closed, and we don't want to rock any more boats," Luke said, looking at me sternly.

"Well, I did talk to Chief Farthing on the subject, and he thinks I should do exactly that. I am going to follow the clues wherever they may lead. If that is an uncomfortable thought to you, you need not come along. I have no qualms about seeking the truth no matter the patronage that a person may claim," I stated.

Luke let out a breath, scrubbed his hand through his stubble beard, and closed his eyes for a moment. I couldn't tell what he was thinking, but I was prepared for the worst. If recent events had any indication, I would be on this path alone. I wasn't afraid. I knew there was more to this story than they claimed to have solved. It was frustrating that no one else was willing to see it. Finally, he looked up, almost in defeat.

"Fine, we will do it your way," he said. "I don't know why I thought we could do it any other. I fear fighting you will only lead to more chaos. Now, Miss Sweeting, what do you suggest?"

I sat there speechless. I didn't know how I should feel, victorious or insulted. I was happy for him to join me, but I also didn't want it to be against his will. Perhaps if I were to show him the validity of my claims once again, we could get past this current barrier between us. I decided to take this as a victory. I felt like this was going to be the beginning of whatever our story was leading to, good or bad.

Chapter 16- Getting Nowhere

I find a fruitless clue is like an annoying itch. It never really leads to relief, just more irritation.

Sadie was finishing her second meat pie when the door swung open to a very concerned looking Nathan. A screech from behind him announced Purgy's arrival as well. I watched as they rushed over to where we were seated.

"Did she tell you about Janey, or has she just been stuffing her face?" Nathan demanded.

"That is quite unkind of you Nate, and yes she has told us. What else is afoot, you are quite unkempt?" I inquired.

"Pardon, Sadie, I just know from Byron, you aren't always forthcoming until you get your payment first. Byron is a right fright, half his face is black and blue, and the other rats are all nervous as a cat in a bag. Mrs. Squires is beside herself and has the older boys searching the Boroughs from top to bottom, but no luck yet, I heard," he huffed.

Sadie made room for him and offered Nate a drink of her cider. Nate took it gratefully and sat down. Purgatorio clicked his claws over and fluttered to perch on the back of my chair. He chuffed at me, and I scratched his chin in greeting.

"Did anyone see you, approach you while you were out? Anything suspicious?" I asked Nate.

"Naw, miss. Just the regular crew moving about the slums. I stopped in some places that I heard she liked to hide when the heat was on, but no luck," he said.

"I think she's still in Tapers Grove, no where else you could hide so well," Sadie said.

"Luke, do you have anyone in that area you can trust to be discreet?" I asked. "Maybe Tallon?"

He nodded and moved to grab a piece of parchment from his book. He wrote down a quick missive and flagged down a servant to have their runner take it to The Yard post haste. Luke slipped him a coin, and the lad ran to the back of the eatery to get the note on its way.

We needed to find the girl fast. The darkness of the night seemed overwhelming, but I hated to wait until morning to begin our own search. Propriety dictated that this was the correct course, and we made plans to meet up and get the report from Constable Tallon before we made our way to the Brass Boroughs.

I didn't want Sadie to travel to the orphanage in the dark, so I invited her to join Nathan and me back at Bread Street and when we got there I set her up in the room off the kitchen. She resisted at first, but when I promised her a tart, she yielded instantly. We said our goodbyes to Luke and made our way home. We were in the entryway when Sadie spoke up.

"I just hope the Missus don't beat me black and blue when I return," she said.

"I won't let that happen, and you need not return there if you wish. I am sure I can find you a position if you are willing to do an honest day's work."

"You should take her up, Sades, she ain't lying. I don't like what I saw tonight. There is a storm brewing at Second Chance, and if you return I think you'll be dead in the center of it," Nate exclaimed.

Sadie gulped and looked at us both with huge, worried eyes.

"I don't want to die," she said quietly.

I grabbed her and held her close to me. She stood stiffly for a moment before she buried her face into the side of my skirt. I could feel her body quivering and stroked the back of her head to calm her.

"This will not be your fate, just stick with us, okay?" I reassured her.

She looked up with shining eyes and nodded.

"Nate, set her up with water and a tub. I'll go see if Lily has any small clothes she doesn't need anymore. We'll get you a proper bath, and a warm bed, and hopefully some answers on the morrow," I said.

I walked to Lily's quarters and knocked gently on the door. I heard movement in the room before light could be seen under the door frame. Quickened steps came, and a concerned Lily opened the door to me in question.

"Miss Sweeting, what is amiss? Are you okay? Is it Master Nethersby?"

"No, no, calm yourself, Lily. I am in need of some smaller clothing for a young girl I have brought home, in desperate need of a bath. I was wondering if you had anything on the verge of being discarded that she could use? I will, obviously, be making you a new outfit to compensate for it," I said.

"Oh, well, let me see," she said.

She scurried back from the door and left it open for me to follow. Her room was nice and tidy, and she had fresh flowers on the table beside her bed. She shuffled through a few drawers and then went to her closet.

"Ah, ha! Found it!"

She whirled around, and there was a faded pale blue dress with silver trim in her hands. It would be perfect. I inquired about a pair of pantaloons to accompany the dress, and she pulled out a gray set that was nice and thick for cool evenings.

"Thank you, Lily. These will do perfectly. Pray, what is your favorite color? I will be going to the shop for this season's fabrics soon, and I will pick up some for the promised outfit I owe you."

"Awe, Miss Sweeting, that is very kind. You need not do that. I am glad to help, and it was not in use at all," she said shyly.

"Nonsense, what is it? From your frocks and the flowers, I am going to say yellow?"

"Yes! You are quite the sleuth."

"Wonderful, I will add it to my list. Now, I am sorry to have disturbed your sleep. Please have a pleasant evening," I said.

"Wait, miss. Don't you need someone to run the bath for the little miss?"

"That is quite kind of you, but Nathan and I have it covered."

"No trouble at all, miss. I would be happy to help. It is lovely to see such kindness from you and your cousin, I will come directly and help the young girl," she replied.

I thanked her and led her to meet Sadie. The young urchin was shy at first but took a liking to Lily when she saw the dress she had gifted her. Lily brought several soaps and scented flowers and hurried Nathan and I out of the room. Purgatorio yawned and stretched his feline body, letting his barbed tail flex over his back.

"Yes, it is quite time for bed I would say. Nate, thank you for taking the risk today. We must be very careful on how we proceed next. I don't want us to get in the trap that seems to have befallen these girls. I know you are strong and quick witted, but take my warning to heart, yes?"

"I will, miss. I know better than to disregard one of your inklings. I almost want to say we should search out the sage, but I'm afraid of getting too deep into that realm," he said.

"Yes, that had crossed my mind as well. Why did he lead us to Gwennie just to disappear? And better yet, what else does he know about what is happening in the Brass Boroughs? Yes, Nathan Starling, we need to find One-eye Whitmore, indeed."

Chapter 17- Finding Solace

In the depths of our doubt, we find those that counter the dark or make us snort uncontrollably.

I found myself rising earlier than usual. The previous night's events weighed heavily on my mind. I dreamt of long tapered candles hanging from drying dowels in various colors. Walking through a drafty room that held them, I stopped as I reached muted yellow ones. They shone like a beacon in the darkened space, and I reached out to take one in my hand. As I slid the smooth, warm taper from its resting place, a gap between the candles revealed the back corner of the crowded room. Although cloaked in darkness, the retrained light from a small window penetrated just enough to reveal a pale form on the ground. I dropped the candle to the floor and jolted awake from the dream.

I lay awake for several hours before my mind eased enough to return to sleep. The recaptured peace didn't last long as the room materialized again within what seemed like minutes. I hoped it wasn't a foreboding vision of the future, but my heart knew otherwise.

I put my clothes on like armor. Piece by piece, reflecting what I might need to face before the day's completion. Dark leather breeches with a black belt pouch covered my legs, leading down to my hard-soled black boots. My white and brown vertical striped blouse frilled at the wrists and neck. The top, encased in a brown leather waist corset with arm straps, gave me a slim appearance. The buttons were dark in color and had almost no shine to them. I put the bracer I had received from Whitmore on my right arm. I had fiddled with the casing to try and add the leather cord and ankh charm to it, but it didn't suit. Instead, I added the charm to a set of pins placed securely on the left arm of my cropped jacket. It almost had a militia aspect to it.

I curled the hair around my face and put the rest into a high bun. I fixed the bun with the hairpin Nathan had created for me all those months ago. It was the same one that had saved my life against the deranged former Lady Thetford in the motor park. Somehow, having these things upon my person made me feel safer. They were reminders of a time when odds were against me, but I pushed through and conquered those who sought to destroy me. I couldn't help but feel stronger for it.

I snatched another belt pouch and laced it on backwards. Here I could store a few items that I could quickly access from my lower back if needed. I also grabbed my investigative goggles and let them dangle around my neck. They had several different lenses and could detect things through the color spectrum much more readily than with my eyes alone. I felt prepared.

A knock on my door directed my attention away from my looking glass. I strode across the wooden floor to see who had arrived. Purgatorio sprang to life as I opened the door to find Lily waiting.

"Good Morning, Lily," I said.

"Morning, Miss Sweeting. I thought you should know that Miss Sadie is up and helping in the kitchen this morning. I also wanted to ask if it was okay to take her with me to the market to gather provisions. I wasn't sure of the circumstances in which she found herself here. What I mean to say is…" she hesitated, "well… is she hiding, miss?"

"That is a valid question. No, she is not hiding, and yes, she can go to the market with you. Lily, she is of a type that you'll need to watch carefully, though. She has been raised to steal, do you understand?" I asked.

"Oh, yes, Miss Sweeting," Lily replied. "I know a bit about the street rats from the Boroughs. My cousins were caught up in that before my mother and I were able to get them in the foundling hospital over on Briar Street. It seems such a shame that so many should be living in poverty, especially as we are entering this great time of invention. Surely there is something we could do to equalize the status quo?"

"Perhaps there is, but let us take one problem at a time. Let us help where we are able now, until a more suitable plan is in effect by our leaders. We are just cogs in the wheel; we must do what we are able with what we can. And so we are, by helping the good people we meet along the way," I said.

"Yes, miss, you are very right, indeed. I shall do my best to follow your example," Lily said.

I wasn't sure if I liked that idea, for most of the time, I hardly knew what direction I was going in. My father had always told me to let my morals be my guide, and so I tried to do just that. Hopefully, it was enough, although it never could be when so many people were suffering. Today's problems were ahead of me though, so I must lay the anguish I felt aside for another day and focus on the task at hand. We needed to find Jane and get some real answers from Mrs. Squires.

I headed toward the breakfast room with Purgy in tow and went about preparing my meal from the sideboard. Jaime was not down yet, but it was clear that they expected him any moment. A steamy pot of hot chocolate sat at the ready next to his seat at the table. The newspaper lay folded perfectly on the corner ready for his perusal. They did have such affection for him, and how could they not? My cousin had a way about him that made me strive to be as generous. It was a gift that we were able to come together at this time.

I heard him before he entered the room. He was whistling a jovial tune. I couldn't help but smile.

"Cousin, you look ready to slay a dragon in that attire. Have I missed a call to arms?" he asked cheekily.

"Jaime, you have indeed. Another girl has gone missing, and I fear the worst. I wanted to be prepared for anything as we make our way to Tapers Grove," I replied.

"Ah, I see," he said, sitting down. "Well, in any case it looks quite good on you, quite fetching. I wouldn't want to take you on for anything. I understand we have a new resident in the servant quarters as well? Another stray, I assume?"

"You know very well I cannot leave a child out in the dark when all this chaos is about us. Lily has taken her on as a kind of apprentice, so perhaps with a little training and some shining up we could find her employment among our acquaintances?" I asked.

"I do love how you are always thinking of others, my dear. Yes, very well. As long as it doesn't interfere with Lily's work, I see no issue with it, " Jaime said as he began eating.

"Well, I learned how to take care of others from the best, you know?"

"Oh, indeed? And who, pray, is this wonderful patron saint, I wonder?"

"Are you being modest, or simply obtuse?"

"You are suggesting I inspired such gallantry, dear Belle? I cannot fathom why. I have always taken inspiration from you. Perhaps we are reflecting our own actions back to each other?"

"Now, that is a wonderful thought indeed. I am rather pleased by the idea," I said.

We shared a smile, and I couldn't help but feel my mood lighten by the conversation. Maybe I was doing something right. The words of my father must have penetrated my actions more than I had realized.

I hoped that to be true, for it made all the worry worth it.

Jaime shook out the paper and looked at the front page news. He gripped the edge of the paper tighter as something of interest caught his gaze.

"Belle, you will not believe it!"

"What is it, cousin?"

Jaime brought the paper down to just below his chin and grinned over the top at me.

"One of the Cosswald girls is getting married. It's just been announced! And…what's this?"

He scanned the article closer.

"They are going to set the season off with her wedding to Lord Bonan. I am not familiar with the chap; I will have to make inquiries. Lady Whipley will be sure to know. Oh, what news!" he gushed.

"Cousin, you seem overjoyed?" I said, questioningly.

"Why of course. Now I shan't have to dodge both of them at assemblies any longer. Just the one, I suppose."

I couldn't help but chuckle at his response. Those two sisters had been chasing him for several seasons now. Jaime had been able to dodge their obvious pursuit the majority of the time, but I knew it had been quite trying for him at times.

"Does it say which sister it is?" I asked.

"Mmmm, that is strange. It doesn't. How peculiar. What do you think it could mean?" he asked, folding the paper and setting it aside.

"I had the most provocative thought right now, but surely it could not be true."

"Do tell!" he prompted.

"What if they left it out on purpose to cause a buzz, and make everyone want to come to the wedding to find out which one it is? Wouldn't that be ghastly?" I said in mock disgust.

"Or ingeniously devious," Jaime replied. "Everyone loves a good mystery, as I am sure you can attest, dear Belle. Why, we can't seem to keep you away from them. I have long given up on the subject, but I fear your suitor has lasted longer than most. How are things going in that arena, pray?"

I gave out an exasperated huff as I took a sip of my chamomile and mint tea. The herbal floral notes soothed my nerves as I chose the right words to describe our current relationship.

"Honestly, I don't know yet. We were able to work quite fluidly last night going over the details we had collected," I explained. "We are set to meet shortly at The Yard today as well, to head out together in pursuit of the missing girl. Mr. Weston has told me himself that he was giving in to my methods on this one, and I am not sure if that is good or bad. I am going to take it as a good sign, but we shall see how this all plays out, no?"

"Very interesting developments indeed. Do keep me abreast of anything new," Jaime said.

"Why must I always be your source of entertainment? I want to hear something of your doings with Charles Kaplan. I have not heard you speak of him since you left for France. Has that door been shut, or are you holding out on me, cousin?"

Jaime's face took on a pained expression, and I feared the answer was an unpleasant one.

"In truth, I wasn't sure how it happened, but we just found ourselves heading in very different directions. I won't deny I had hopes of some sort of relationship, but it seems distance did not make his heart grow fonder. Alas, I must start anew, and for now live vicariously through you, my dear."

My shoulders sagged a little at his revelation. It was most disappointing and I hoped he wouldn't feel cast down for too long. It seemed neither of us were having much success in matters of the heart.

"Oh, I am sorry. I was hoping you were having better luck than I. It is quite trying lately. Do you think it is us?"

"Belle, I shudder to think! How can we be to blame? We are patron saints after all!"

His declaration sent me into a fit of giggles. He joined in, and before we knew it, we had grown quite hysterical. It reminded me of when I had just arrived at his home; it felt like a renewal of something between us. A renewal to my soul that I hadn't known I needed.

"No matter what, dear cousin. We shall always be able to lean on each other. Of that, you can depend," I said.

"You are very right. I second that most ardently."

I kissed Jaime farewell on the cheek and collected Nathan from the kitchen to head to The Yard to meet Luke. Whatever this day was to bring, it would not take this morning's joy from me. Of that, I would make certain.

Chapter 18- The Search Is On

The path to discovery is neither comfortable nor easy, but the results are often worth the trouble.

I walked into the corridors of The Yard and looked for Constable Weston. Nathan and Purgatorio stayed by the street's edge, weary of the officers that walked about. I couldn't help but feel guilty that they never came with me to see all that Scotland Yard's inner chambers had to hide. Etchings lined the walls of famous men that once claimed respect within these halls. I often wondered if anyone remembered them, or if they had just become ghosts of a lost past to be looked at and fantasized about. I slowed my pace as a particular picture caught my eye. It was of a man with a familiar face standing next to a slew of young children in front of one of the foundling hospitals. I leaned closer to see if I could pick up any more details when a throat cleared behind me.

"Well, Miss Sweeting, I see you are back for more then? Couldn't stay away from the murder business, hey? It is quite enticing, as I, myself, have found. What is it you are looking at there?"

"Doctor Cannish, good morning. I was just trying to put a name to this familiar face, and as I look at you before me, I can't help but to see a likeness," I replied.

"Ah, yes, that was my father. He was very fond of helping the less fortunate. The living ones, anyhow. He had helped gather donations for several children's homes in the area. Although, when he passed it seems the quality of those homes has sadly decreased. I could never really stand the sticky little cretins, although young Nathan has grown on me a bit," he admitted.

I smiled at his confession and looked back at the picture.

"Yes, this very subject seems to be breaching the case we are working on," I told him. "These poor children have gone missing or are being found dead. I am not sure what to make of it yet, but I am hoping we can find answers soon."

"Well, I shan't detain you, Miss Sweeting. I believe you can find Constable Weston in the courtyard."

"Thank you, Doctor. Have a good day, sir."

He nodded his farewell as he headed to the morgue. I wondered what sadness was to be found there today. Best not to dwell but to try and help stop any more from entering his doors. I walked toward the entrance leading to the courtyard and swung the door outward. I heard a huff behind me as it collided with something, or rather, someone on the other side.

"Oh, my apologies, sir. Oh, it's you, Tallon. How are you? I mean besides me trying to knock you unconscious."

"Ah, Miss Sweeting, just the lady we were waiting for. Come, come, I have some news. The sooner I relay it the sooner I can get some rest. The night was not pleasant by half," Constable Tallon said.

I quickly followed him to the bench where Luke was waiting. He wasn't dressed in his uniform but rather a run-down set of plain clothes. Although rough and distressed, they looked good on him. I feared they would not pass for pauper's clothing, as they were too well fitted to his form. He looked down from the branch of a tree he was fiddling with and smiled as I approached.

"Miss Sweeting, you look ready to wage war. Quite dashing, indeed," he said.

"I thank you, sir. I suspect your outfit is an attempt to fly below the airships?"

"Does it not suit?" he asked.

"I think it suits very well, a little too well, actually," I admitted.

A knowing grin flitted across his face, and I blushed at my own admission. It seemed that our attraction was not as easily buried as I thought.

"Okay, you two, save that conversation for later, I have news and then I must dash," Tallon interjected.

"Of course, please proceed," I said.

I tried to cover my embarrassment by focusing on the seriousness of the current situation.

"I ran the streets of Tapers Grove all night and couldn't find any claims of seeing the young girl," Tallon started. "I did, however, catch wind of a package that was dropped off at the beadle's early this morning. It is clear they are still running whatever it is between the orphanage and the parish official. I haven't sussed out the connection yet, but it feels off. Miss Sweeting, I suggest you take this handkerchief with you, it is soaked in lavender oil. The smell in that part of town will rob you of your senses if you are not careful," he said.

I took the offered cloth gratefully.

"I'm sorry. I don't have more to go on, but many were abed when I made my tour of the area," he finished.

"Thank you, Tallon," Luke said. "That will give us a start. Did you have someone post outside the beadle's dwelling like I requested?"

"Yes, sir. A young officer Caleb Quincy is there now."

I could see Luke physically jolt at the name. He was to be my new liaison once this case wrapped up. I wasn't sure what his reaction meant, but it clearly wasn't one of happiness. He recovered quickly, though.

"Good, good. Thank you. Off to bed with you then. I may call on you this evening," Luke said.

"Very good, sir, miss."

Tallon bowed and left us to find his sleep sanctuary. We turned to follow him and headed towards the front entrance. My foot caught a crack, and I slipped sideways, momentarily, before Luke's hand caught my elbow and steadied me. I smiled up at him, and he smiled back. I grabbed the offered crook of his arm, and we proceeded to leave The Yard and meet up with Nathan and Purgy.

***

"Where do you think we should start?" I asked.

I turned to Nate as we entered the slums of Tapers Grove. I looked along the roads and recoiled as the first waft of cooked animal fat hit my nostrils. You would think the odor would be savory, but it smelled old and rancid. I gathered the handkerchief Tallon had given me to my nose to cover the assault to my senses and was thankful for his forethought. My eyes watered a bit, but I was able to muster through with the lavender-scented cloth.

"This way, Miss!"Nate directed.

Purgatorio took to the sky and circled us as we proceeded down the road towards a row of rough-looking shacks. Luke kept his head on a swivel as people peered out from their steam-filled windows. Their faces were dirty and drawn down in what appeared to be permanent frowns. I felt my lips mimic the look as the sadness of the residents overwhelmed me. Nathan slowed his progress and reached to hold my hand.

"It's okay, miss. I know it seems rough, but it ain't all bad. These folks at least have a way to feed themselves. Now come this way, I think I know a chap we can talk to," he said.

We continued to hold hands as he led Luke and me down a side road to a little nicer area of town. You could tell that these people took pride in their small yet tidy homes. Little wax flowers gave the rustic wooden window boxes a cheery look. We stopped at the farthest house on the left, and Nathan knocked on the door.

"Who is it? I'm busy you know, orders to fill!"

An older gentleman with wild bushy hair came to the door and peered out suspiciously. He looked at each of us, then stopped and squinted when he spotted Nate.

"Well, I'll be a toadie's tongue. Is that you, Starling? You're quite a strapping lad now. You've got a new buyer for me then?" the man asked, eyeing me up and down.

"Mr. Penzy, sir, good day to you!" Nate said in greeting. "I'm actually here on a different line of business, hoping you could help us with some information, yes?"

"Well, that's as lucrative as any, I'd say. Come in, come in," Mr. Penzy waved us in as he opened the door wide.

The room was set up in small stations, each a step in the candle-making process, laid out before us. The smell wasn't as strong in his home, which was strange since we were so close to the materials that made the candles. He smiled, revealing a few gaps in his teeth, and ushered us towards a small table in the corner. There were not enough seats, but Luke and Nathan let me take the other seat provided.

"You fancy folk want a drink? I don't have much, but I have a nice wild mint tea I've been saving for a good conversation, and this seems as good as any," he grumbled.

"That is very kind of you, sir. It is unnecessary, however; we do not wish to impose," I replied.

"Well aren't you a right fine lady, with such manners, and kindness. Now I definitely need to break out the china!"

He chuckled a little as he moved around the room collecting the cups he had strewn about and setting the pot onto his wood stove to boil.

"Now Nate, who are these fine people and why are you looking for information in this part of town? Nothing happens here but candles and death," Mr. Penzy said.

"Well, since we ain't here for candles, it's the other thing we be trying to discover, sir, Nate replied. "This here is Miss Annabelle Sweeting; a right fine lady but no stranger to the Brass. This gent is Mr. Luke Weston. He is a tad on the uppity side, but does good in a pinch." Nate replied.

Luke looked at Nathan with a raised brow but didn't interject. I covered my mouth to hide a smile.

"We come on sleuthin' business, we have," Nate said.

I noticed more and more, as we delved deeper into the Boroughs, that Nathan's accent began to revert to when I first met him. Harsh and wild, and not altogether clear, but it seemed to put the people we met at ease.

"Ah, I see. Some fancy to-do go missin'?" Mr. Penzy asked curiously.

"Nah, but little Janey Thatcher," Nate told him. "You know the girl with the long braid from Second Chancey?"

"I know that girl, always fluttering about where she ain't meant to be. Why would you all be caring about that little sprite? Not sure anyone cares about any of those orphans anymore," he replied.

"Well we do, so have you seen her lately?" Nate said, his face turning red. "She twas to have been here last she was seen."

"Hmmm, let me think a spell," Mr. Penzy said.

He poured the steaming brew into the cups and handed us each one.

"I'm afraid no sugar, but the mint has a very nice flavor, I'd say," he said.

We each took a sip, and the aroma was wonderful. I was surprised by the rich flavor of the wild herb and thanked him for sharing it with us.

He tapped his chin a few moments and put his finger up in the air in triumph.

"Yes, I remember now. The child was outside that sleazy beadle's office up on Cabbage Street. He's always lurking about, trying to get donations. Like we have anything to spare out here."

We all nodded in agreement that it was unpardonably unjust.

"Anyway, she was dropping off another one of them poorly wrapped boxes. It looked like a child wrapping a bundle of old carrot stems, but that's not what you want to hear about, I'm guessing? No, what happened next might be worth some coin," Mr. Penzy said.

"Of course, how much do you think it's worth, sir?" I asked.

He issued a price, and I put out double what he asked. His eyebrows raised, and he smiled that gap toothed grin again.

"Well then, she started yelling at Beadle Fieldworth and telling him that Mrs. Squires wasn't going to like it if she returned with half the promised fee. He wrestled the package right out the young girl's hand and kicked her down the stairs. She stumbled a bit, looked back and hissed just like a rat, then ran towards Galley Street. That was the last time I saw her," Mr. Penzy finished.

I couldn't afford to let the rage that swirled inside me at the poor girl's treatment take hold. This beadle would definitely be inquired about, and I could tell by Lukes stiffened pose that he felt the same. I needed to remain calm and collect all the facts if we were to find Janey.

"What is down Galley Street?" I asked, taking a slow breath afterward.

I glanced between Mr. Penzy and Nathan as they shared an uncomfortable look.

"Nothin' good, miss," Nate said. "It's the bottom of the barrel for this area. Rough crowd, rank tempers, and even worse candle practices. I heard horrible stories about it. Never go there at night or you might end up in the candles, if you know what I mean?" Nate hinted.

"Young Starling, are you suggesting they use people in the candles down there?" Luke asked, looking horrified by what Nate had implied. A determination to stomp out such evil seemed to awaken in his gaze. My heart skipped a beat.

Nate and Mr. Penzy nodded in unison, and an eerie quiet filled the room. We sipped our tea thoughtfully as the possible horrors played with our imaginations. I think we were all bracing ourselves for the next move. Meeting each other's eyes, we felt the impending weight of the expedition to an even darker side of town. I smiled bravely at Nate, and he nodded in return. I heard a screech outside the door and got up to see what Purgatorio was raging on about.

"What in the monarch's menagerie was that?" Mr. Penzy exclaimed.

Mr. Penzy followed me to the door. I flung the door wide and found Purgy on the ground with a dent in his side shoulder. I looked around the area and saw two urchins with rocks running down the lane toward us.

"Halt, you wretched beasts!" I shouted "Come no further. This creature is my companion and you will do him no more harm!"

The children skidded to a stop before me and looked with raised brows.

"But miss, he's a demon he is. Sent to snatch us up. He's the horror that's been takin' my mates!"

"Yeah, get him," the other, smaller boy yelled.

Luke and Nate moved out the door and stood by my side as I blocked the urchins from Purgatorio.

"How many of your mates are missin'?" Nate asked.

They looked at each other wearily, not sure if they should answer or flee.

"Three, so far. They were at the workhouse all week then poof, one by one they be gone. No sign of them nowheres. Papa said it's a demon, and then we saw him and knew it had to be true," said the first boy, pointing at Purgatorio behind me.

"I'm sorry about your friends, but I fear Purgy had nothing to do with it," I replied.

Purgatorio chuffed and shook out his mane. He fluttered up to perch on my shoulder and roared at the two boys, causing them to step backward.

"It seems you have caught him in the shoulder while in flight, you must have very good aim," I said.

"Yeah we do, we help the beadle keep the rats away from the provisions. He gives us two apples for every four rats we kill," the smaller boy said proudly.

"Shut up, Terrance!"

"So you work for the beadle?" I asked.

Terrance nodded while the other boy scowled.

"Ain't none of your business lady, we are just trying to find our friends," the taller boy said.

"We are trying to find our friend as well," Nate chimed in.

The boys looked Nate up and down and nodded in some silent agreement.

"Well if it ain't that thing, then what is it?" Terrance asked, pointing accusingly at Purgy.

"We are thinking more of a "who" than a "what," Luke said. "We need to go to Galley Street, you lads know the area?"

"Yes, but we don't go there. It's a bad place."

The larger boy grimaced with the thought. His eyes squinted in suspicion, looking at each of us a little closer.

"Come on, Petey, what if Glenn is there?" Terrance urged.

"Who's Glenn?" I asked.

"It's Petey's brother. He's also missin'," Terrance said.

"Perhaps if we all went together there would be less of a threat?" I suggested.

The lads looked between each other, then over at Luke and I, and then Nate and Purgy. They leaned their heads in close to each other and started whispering.

"Fine, but don't say I didn't warn ya!" Petey shouted.

Petey turned away and ran down the street. Terrance stood there unsure and put the rock he was going to throw at Purgy in his pocket. He wiped his hand off on his rather dirty breeches and held it out to Nate.

"Name's Terrance Harper."

"I'm Nathan Starling, and this here is Miss Annabelle Sweeting and Mr. Luke Weston. They are real good at finding people. Are you coming with us then?"

Nate shook Terrance's hand firmly. Apparently, there was a code amongst the street boys that we were not privy to. It was said that such a thing existed, but for once I was glad that Nate had experience in that world.

"Yeah, it appears I care more about Glenn than his own brother," Terrance griped.

He wiped his sleeve against his nose and nodded towards Luke and me.

"Let's get to it then, I suppose," Luke said.

"Wait just a moment there!" Mr. Penzy called from his doorway. We turned to find him with his jacket on and a dark wooden walking stick. He had a satchel slung over his arm with a few candles poking out of the top.

"Oh, Mr. Penzy, we couldn't ask it of you to come with us," I said.

"You didn't ask, I am offerin'. Besides I have a cousin down there I've been meaning to check on. I was hoping to convince him to come back with me, so now is as good a time as any, I'd say," he said.

"Very well, let us be off, and try to stick together. The shadows have a way of taking over the light in Galley Street," Nate said.

I checked on Purgatorio's shoulder to make sure the rocks that dented him hadn't done any real damage to his mechanisms and then launched him back in the air. We headed south toward where heat and even more intense smells radiated. I stroked the charm Whitmore gave me and followed our little group down the street. I sent up a silent prayer to keep us all safe from harm.

Chapter 19- Counting Corpses

The battle between good and evil is often found in religion. It is when the religious are found guilty that true horror is revealed.

We walked in silence, only our breathing breaking the quiet around us. We listened– I'm not sure for what. Perhaps for some unknown monster to jump at us from the shadows. Why were we allowing rumors and ghost stories to rule over our rational thoughts? It was mind-boggling. I shook my head and smiled.

"This is ridiculous. There is a line between being cautious and being downright paranoid, and I believe we've crossed it gentlemen," I said.

They all turned to me in surprise as I walked to the front of the group and started quickening the pace towards our destination. We turned the corner to a row of run-down shacks and piles of refuse. I covered my mouth again with the lavender-scented cloth and continued down the road. I could see women in the alleyways leering at the men of our party with greedy eyes, and half-dressed children chased each other with what appeared to be sticks covered in wax. We had almost reached the next intersection when I stopped dead in my tracks.

I turned to the left and stared at the shack on the corner. Its knotted weather-worn wood warped along the roof and led to a crooked door with a rope for a handle. The windows were shuttered closed, but light peeked out from the cracks. I found myself drawn to the door and unpinned the charm from my left shoulder to hold. The others behind me were asking me something, but I couldn't hear them. I could only see this eerily familiar door, and I knew what I would find. Luke grabbed my shoulder and turned me toward him.

"What's wrong, Belle? You're practically white. You are unwell, we should go back," he said.

The worry was etched over his face, and I am sure if I had a mirror I would be concerned by my reflection as well. I couldn't turn back, however; knowing what I knew was behind that door. The dream that plagued me all night was becoming a vivid reality.

"Mr. Penzy, do you know who's dwelling this is?" I asked the candlemaker.

"Can't say that I do, miss. Everything okay?" Mr. Penzy asked, concerned.

"You said your cousin lives about these parts?"

"Ah, yes, just a street or two over," he replied.

"Nathan and Terrance," I said, turning to the boys, "would you be so kind as to accompany Mr. Penzy to his cousin's and bring him back here? Perhaps he knows the house better," I said.

Luke watched me suspiciously, but Nate nodded and walked away with the two Tapers Grove residents in tow. Luke rubbed my shoulders up and down with concern flooding his features. I wanted the boys out of range when we entered this shack. I didn't want them to witness the horror I somehow knew was waiting for us inside.

"What is it?" he asked.

I let out a whistle and put my arm out. Purgatorio screeched from above and dove down to my outstretched limb.

"Luke, you may think I am crazy, but I dreamed of this house last night. This very place, and if I am right we are not going to be happy with what we find inside," I admitted.

A look of shock washed over Luke, and he shook his head.

"Belle, a dream is nothing more. Any run-down shack can look like another. I am sure you are just imagining things. Let us go knock and put your fears to rest," he said.

"Just the same, I am going to send Purgy to lead Constable Williams back to us. I know you don't believe me, but you will."

I wrote a quick note and tucked it in Purgatorio's undercarriage compartment. I whispered the urgency in his lion-like ear, and he chuffed with acknowledgment. Taking flight, he spiraled up into the air and took off north.

"Lead the way, Constable Weston," I said with resignation.

He shook his head in disbelief and turned with determined strides towards the crooked door of the corner shack. No smoke could be seen coming from the stack, but a faint light peeked through the openings of the misaligned boards. The urge to run clawed at my mind, but I wouldn't leave her there.

Luke knocked several times with no answer. He looked at me and shrugged his shoulders. I straightened my stance and plunged into action. Pushing past him, I shoved in the door with little effort. The room was dark except for two fading candles in the far right corner of the room next to the wood stove. A cot lay beside the stove, and a tattered rug covered the dirt floor. The other half of the room was taken over by wax and candles. My eyes followed the path of the different colored drying candle tapers, straight to the yellow ones. They dangled there innocently, and I wished that Luke was right, that it was all but a dream.

I pointed to the yellow candles, and Luke walked in that direction.

"Here? I don't see anything," he said.

"Pull the yellow taper down, Luke," I whispered.

He looked back to the candles and then at me. He took a few tapers from the top rung and showed me there was nothing behind it. I walked up beside him and grabbed a large handful of the yellow candles below it. The tapers hung, two candles to a wick, with the wick bracing the weight as they dried. I slowly pulled the tapers from the middle rung, and the hollow eyes of Janey stared up at me, just visible in the weak candlelight from across the room. I stared down at her, willing the view to be my imagination, but when Luke gasped beside me, I knew it wasn't. My eyes began to water, and I turned from the heart-wrenching sight.

Luke looked at me in astonishment. "How?"

"I don't know, but we mustn't linger," I replied.

He took me in his arms and held me close. I shuddered in the small comfort of his embrace. I heard a creak at the door and peered over to a shadow crossing the threshold.

"Miss, we're here. What's happened?" Nate came up to us with concern in his eyes. I pointed to the gap in the candles, and he walked over to see Janey on the floor. Before I knew it he was dragging all the draped candles off the rungs and throwing them to the floor.

"Nathan, what is the meaning of this?" Luke demanded.

Luke grabbed the boy by the shoulder but stopped when he saw where Nate was pointing. On the floor beside Janey were two other children. A couple of boys, both with shaggy brown hair, and glazed-over eyes.

"Glenn! No!"

Terrance ran past us and kneeled next to the boy on the far left. He tried to shake the deceased boy awake before Mr. Penzy came in and pulled him away.

"He's gone, son. He's gone. Come outside with me, we'll have a talk," he whispered.

Mr. Penzy nodded at Luke and I with sad eyes and led the boy outside.

"We can talk about my dream later, Luke," I said. "Right now we should get to work and have things prepared for when Williams joins us. I'd said that this just got a whole lot messier."

I straightened my jacket and unbuckled the pouch on my front belt. I had Nathan ask Mr. Penzy for a few of his candles, as I didn't want to touch any in this shack. I didn't think I would ever look at a yellow candle the same. I walked towards the small bodies and began to write down the details of their positions and conditions. I poured myself into the routine. It was the only way to help them. Solve the puzzle and find the criminal. That was the only way to make these atrocities stop. I could feel Luke's eyes on me as I worked. I looked back at him and saw his clouded expression. He tilted his head to me and took out his own tools of detection. Whatever qualms we may have were brushed aside in the pursuit of this adversary. They didn't stand a chance.

Chapter 20- What Can Be Done?

I watched a lark fly so free among the clouds above. I wished a moment that lark was me to escape the grasp of woeful love and rid myself of melancholy.

I walked out of the shack to get some air but found only the oppressive smell of wax and boiling fat to welcome me. I looked about myself and found Mr. Penzy and the gentleman that must be his cousin sitting on a wooden box a few houses down. They were talking to poor Terrance and trying to calm the now weeping boy. The hardships these people endured were only amplified by this current trauma, and it made me angry. I walked over to where they sat.

"Mr. Penzy, is this your cousin?" I asked.

"Yes, miss, this here is Alan Swinley. He says he knows the chap that lives there, but hasn't seen him in over a fortnight. A man by the name of Viktor Barnes. Not too vicious, right?" He turned to his cousin for confirmation.

"Naw, not a bad man, not like some others along this street," Mr. Swinley said. "A lady like you is quite daring to venture so deep in the Boroughs, I am surprised that my cousin would allow it," he said.

"Cousin, don't be rude. I have no influence over the young lady, nor would I claim to negate anyone who is willing to help these lost souls on our wayward streets," Mr. Penzy said. "I wish there were more like her willing to go where none else will venture. Now apologize to the young miss and go collect your things, we must leave this place soon."

"Apologies, miss. I meant nothin' by it, I swears. Just be careful is all," Mr. Swinley said.

"Before you go, sir, can you tell me where you saw this Viktor Barnes last?" I inquired.

"Yes, it was at the provisions line over by Beadle Fieldworth's place. We stood in line for about three hours for a bag full of half bad potatoes and stale bread. It's the way of things so we are to be grateful, but it down right stinks," he said.

"Thank you, sir," I said graciously. "Perhaps your cousin and you can make a go of things out of Galley Street?"

"We'll have to start bringing our wares to the market. Now that Alan here will be able to haul it back and forth for me, I think that will be a greater possibility," Mr. Penzy said.

"I will keep an eye out for your stand there," I replied.

The gentleman's eyes lit up. "Thank you, miss."

Mr. Swinley left his cousin to tend to Terrance as he ventured to his house to collect anything he wanted to keep for the journey back to Penzy's home. I wasn't sure what took them so long to team up, but I had a sneaking suspicion Mr. Penzy didn't want to travel through this part of town on his own. It was quite unsettling.

A roar came from the sky, and Purgatorio started his descent towards me. I lifted my arm, and he landed on my bracer. He gently butted his head against mine in greeting. I looked down the street and saw two bobbie motors making their way over the rubbish-filled cobblestone streets. I watched as the people walked from their homes and alleys to see the motors enter. They sneered and pushed each other out of the way. It was as if a parade had arrived, and they all were jostling for the best position to see.

I could see Constable Williams directing them to get out of the way, and his frustration as they moved at a snail's pace to get to us. Finally, they parked and cut a path to our location.

Luke exited the house and ordered the other officers to bring in stretchers for the children. I inquired if Doctor Cannish was with them, but they said he was waiting at the morgue for their arrival. He would have everything prepared for our return. It was quite jarring watching their small bodies carried out of the run-down shack, and it sent Terrance into a fit of crying again.

Mr. Penzy waited for his cousin to return, and then they left; taking Terrance with them to the other side of Tapers Grove. I watched them depart and wondered what had happened to the other lost boys Terrance had mentioned. I also wondered who the other boy was found next to Janey and Glenn. Would someone be missing him as well? The thought made me terribly sad.

I caught Nathan's eye, and he came over to me. I patted him on the shoulder, and he took my hand and patted it gently. We were in the midst of something we didn't fully understand, but I could feel a crest on the horizon. It felt like once we reached the summit of our current course we would be able to see farther into this puzzle. It was just the waiting, the anticipation of getting there, and the fear of more children dying before we did, that was excruciating. I bent down to meet Nate at eye level.

"We need a plan, and quickly. I can not explain it, but I need you to find Whitmore. I know he set us on this path, but I feel his part is not played out. Do you think you can find him?"

"It might take some doing, but I'll find him. Miss, I think we should bring in Byron. What I mean to say is, he'd be a great help. He is all by himself now, with Gwennie gone. It's better to move in groups and scatter when danger comes, than to be a lone duck on the pond, you know?"

I tapped my chin in thought as a vision of a lurking monster sprung from the depths of a pond and swallowed a small duck whole. It sent shivers down my arms, and I quickly nodded my agreement.

"Yes, I think that is an excellent idea. I think you should gather some of your friends and find Whitmore, then meet me at Kaplan's," I replied.

"The smithies? Why there, miss?" Nate asked.

"I have an idea forming, but it isn't complete yet. Let us meet there and hopefully it will be whole by then. I will accompany Luke to meet Doctor Cannish. I think I will send Purgatorio along with you, as I fear you are more in danger on this one than I. Send word with him when you have found our quarry, and I will meet you."

"What if he needs to recharge?" Nate asked, concerned.

"Then find a safe place to bunker down for a few hours. We need to be smart, and stay safe this time around, Young Starling. I feel we are in a game of chess that we didn't know we were playing."

"Who are the kings?" he wondered aloud.

"That is a very good question, a very good one indeed. Now make haste, and send word when you've found him."

I pulled Nate to me with a fierce hug, drew back and scooped his face with my hands. He smiled bravely, and I smiled and nodded back. He turned and ran in the direction of the orphanage, and Purgatorio leapt from my shoulder to follow. I watched their path until a hand gently touched my elbow and turned to find Luke looking at me in confusion.

"Are we ready to leave then?" I asked him.

"Where is Starling going?" he asked in reply, ignoring my question.

"I sent him to gather some forces and to find Whitmore. We are going to need a little help from the Brass I'd say, and it's high time we got some answers about what One-Eye knows. The world is terribly dark right now. Let us bring them in to help join our light," I replied.

"But won't that lead to more riddles, and dead ends? That charlatan has brought us nothing but grief," Luke said.

"Constable Weston, he has done nothing but be a victim to this city's social expectations. He is, I admit, quite strange and compelling. But are we not all this way in some capacity? I have just recently uncovered a queer characteristic about myself that I have not fully absorbed yet. I think no matter the personal grievance you have for the man, we must utilize all the weapons we have in our arsenal against this unknown foe. His riddles tend to lead to answers, and right now I am thirsting for answers, aren't you?"

"Yes, of course I am. Perhaps I am just letting the past influence my judgement. I seem to be doing that a lot lately," he replied.

"We will not progress if we do not move forward, no matter how uncomfortable and unnerving it might be. Neither will this case. Let us move together, wisely of course, and I will take a note out of your book by not rushing head first into the fray. Does that suffice?"

Luke smirked at me and pulled on a loose curl by the side of my face.

"Yes, Miss Annabelle, it will suffice,"he said. "Let us go now and get this horrid examination over with."

We joined Constable Williams as the officers loaded the last of the contents of the shack and headed back to The Yard to meet Doctor Cannish. I watched as the streets went from a sea of sullen and dirty faces to the pristine homes and gizmos of the elite. How could we make everyone prosperous? The daunting question nagged at me. It would have to wait, however, until this investigation was solved.

Chapter 21- The Scars Within

We must not squelch another's hope merely because they have less than us. Let us, as a people, support those that would enrich our lives but haven't the means to accomplish it.

It took us time to make our way out of the Boroughs and back to Scotland Yard. As we arrived, a very harried Doctor Cannish made his way out of the front corridor. I had never seen him in such a state.

"They are here then, the wee ones?" he asked.

We nodded. The officers opened the back of the motors and brought the stretchers out toward the back room where Doctor Cannish had tables set up. We followed in a line that reminded me of the Celtic funeral processions I had read about. The dead are carried by their loved ones and community to a mighty pyre and set ablaze for their spirits to return to the stars they were once a part of. Those occasions were meant for closure and relief, a showing of love. This was not that kind of procession.

I feared what Doctor Cannish would have to do. To analyze a man who had lived his life was one thing, but to examine the body of a child that had barely experienced life's joy was harrowing. Some would say these children hadn't and wouldn't know joy in their state of living, but I think that to be untrue.

The bodies were placed on the tables one by one, and the men took their hats off and bowed their heads as they left the room. Cannish straightened his spectacles and his spine as he walked to the first table.

"Yes, well, best to get to it then. No sense in waiting for some miracle to banish such evil. We, I suppose, must be that miracle," he mumbled as he lifted the sheet off the unknown boy.

"Hmmmm, you found him in Tapers Grove, you say?" the doctor asked, to no one in particular.

"Yes, Doctor," Luke replied. "Do you recognize him?"

"Let me clean him up a bit to be sure, but I am afraid I do. I believe this is the young servant boy that has been missing from Claymore's."

"What? Truly, sir?" I asked. I moved in closer to get a better look at the boy's face.

"Yes, when you and I met the other night, I had a conversation with the owner before you arrived. And look here, in his pocket. Yes, it is him. It's a missive from the proprietor himself, this is his seal," the doctor said.

"Should we open it? Perhaps it can tell us where he was heading when he was taken, or am I jumping to conclusions? Can you tell if he was murdered sir, or was this some horrible accident involving candle fumes?" I asked.

Doctor Cannish looked at me and then at the young boy before him.

"Miss Sweeting, this was not an accident. See here, by his head? He has been bludgeoned," Dr. Cannish replied.

He quickly pulled the cloths covering the other two children and checked their heads for similar markings.

"Hmmm, this boy was killed the same way, but the girl, the girl was strangled. You can see the bruising around her neck here and here."

I moved in closer to see, but Luke held back with a stoic look on his strained features. I watched as the doctor washed the grime from Jane's face and neck. The bruising was more visible as the dirt slid from her face. Someone had closed the girl's eyes before we came here, and I was happy about it. There is a hollow when you peer into the eyes of the dead where a light once flickered. To see the flame of someone's soul missing hurts your own in such a way, I could hardly describe it.

"Yes, she is different. It looks like she fought back. These other two, it doesn't seem like they saw it coming at all. How fortunate for them," Dr. Cannish said.

I brought out my journal and jotted down what the doctor relayed. He was gruff as he pointed out several old scars from each of the children. The hardships and pain they had endured growing up without family were evident on their small bodies. Luke didn't move from his spot in the corner, and it reminded me of how much he hated these examinations. I sidled up beside him and nudged him with my arm. He looked down at me but said nothing.

"Luke, let us make these the last of the lost children, yes?" I implored him.

He nodded once and looked back at the three laying out before us. He reached out for my hand and held it firmly. I gave a gentle squeeze back. He turned to speak, but the door flew open behind us, and a man walked in.

"There is a crazed mechanical peacock in the courtyard! I heard you were here, Miss Sweeting. I figured you would know what it was about, since that other beast often accompanies you," the officer said.

I released Luke's hand and nodded.

"Lead me to it, please, that is my cousin's new pet. I hope nothing is wrong," I said. "Constable Weston, please continue with Doctor Cannish. If you could take notes for me, I would appreciate it."

Luke nodded and took the journal from my hand. I followed the officer out of the room and toward the sounds of excessive chirping. We entered the courtyard, and the beast visibly calmed when it spotted me. It strutted over to me in an almost comical fashion. It reminded me of a royal court attendant about to announce something of great import with all the pomp and circumstance that it entailed.

The peacock bowed to me with its long, graceful neck, and I stroked the shiny feathers upon his head. On the side of the base of his neck was a tube. I reached for it and popped open the side to find a parchment rolled up within.

"What do you have for me here?" I asked.

I unrolled the parchment to see the familiar writing of my cousin.

Dearest Belle,

Do come home. We have need of you and that constable of yours. Your most recent charity has gone astray. Lily is beside herself, and I fear the young girl's absence was not of her choosing.

Yours,

Mr. Jaime Nethersby

P.S. Do bring Andre back with you, please.

"Andre?"

The bird squawked.

"Oh, I see. Thank you, Andre. Let us find Luke and be off then. Come with me, dearest," I cooed. Andre preened and followed me into the corridor.

I tried not to let the vexing news of Sadie's disappearance overwhelm me. I needed to stay calm, collect Luke, and make it to Bread Street to get all the details. I couldn't let the horrible images racing through my mind take hold. I wouldn't fall apart without knowing all the facts. I would be useless to her if I did. Walking quickly, I made my way back to the examination room. I relayed the news to Doctor Cannish and Luke, and we took our leave. The doctor promised to get us news of any other discoveries he made during the rest of his examination. I hoped that Nathan was faring better than I.

Chapter 22- Taken

Half of an investigation is spent finding what is lost, whether it be the clues or the people that left them behind.

I could only imagine what Nathan had been up to since we parted in Tapers Grove. I hoped that he had not found himself in a risky situation. I also hoped that as Luke and I rushed to Bread Street, we wouldn't find Sadie in a worse predicament.

Upon arrival at my cousin's house, we exited the motor and headed toward the door. Andre flew up to an open window on the second floor. We made our way through the front entrance and were directed to the drawing room, where Jaime was pacing before the fireplace.

"Ah good, the feathered phenom found you then! I will ring for Lily. It is best you hear it from her, as I am sure I will jumble some crucial detail," Jaime said.

"Oh cousin, what a trying affair. Thank you for sending your bird. I hope we can find young Sadie. Are you sure she didn't run?"

"Yes, yes, we went over that. Do be patient. I know you want to start the search now, but you must hear her story first," he replied.

"Calm yourself, Belle. Remember not to rush in," Luke whispered.

I took a big breath and let it out. He was right, of course. We needed the facts before we could make another move. My heart raced as we waited for the maid to come. I heard the rustling of steps outside the door before she rushed into the room. Her face was tear-soaked, and she held her hands together, wringing them in distress.

"Lily, come here please," I said.

She nodded and slowly walked toward me. I gathered her in my arms while another wave of sobs took over her body.

"It is not your fault, whatever you might be blaming yourself for. But dear girl, we must know what happened, and quickly, if Sadie is in danger. Can you speak?" I asked gently, but as adamantly as I could.

She drew back from my embrace and wiped the tears from her eyes with her sleeve. She looked at us and nodded.

"Yes, miss, I can," she said.

Lily worked hard to subdue her powerful emotions and took a cleansing breath.

"We went to the market, just as I said we would," she continued. "She was being quite helpful, and I kept my eyes peeled for mischief on her end, like you directed. Sadie was chatting away about how glad she was to get out of the Second Chance dungeon and how she hoped she could stay on like Nate. I told her that she needed to put those pesky lessons from the urchins behind her if she wanted a chance. She was being amicable and pleasing. I watched her go to the vendor for the produce we needed. The girl was very courteous and I was quite proud. But then she saw something, or someone to the right. Her face went ghostly pale, and I rushed to complete my purchase at the table a couple stalls down. I turned to pay the vendor and when I looked back, she was running away from whatever had spooked her, miss."

"Did you see what was chasing her?" Luke asked.

"I ran to the produce table and followed her path as she bolted. I turned the opposite way to see where she had been gazing. There I saw the back of a black coat disappear behind the stalls. I thought it better to chase after young Sadie, than to pursue some unknown ghost," she said.

I nodded at the wise choice and told her to continue.

"So, I started running down the path that I saw her take. I caught a glimpse of her by a bridge that led back to Bread Street. She was about to cross it when she stopped and looked below it. I tried to catch up but was too far away. I could make out a couple of other kids below and they were shouting to her. She was just about to join them, but a large dark carriage came up beside her. The door flung open, and a dark figure snatched her up inside. She screamed, but no one seemed to care. I ran and ran, but the carriage took off back toward the Burroughs, and I couldn't think of what else to do but come back here and tell Mr. Nethersby straight away," she began to sob again.

"You did the right thing, dear," Jaime assured her, consoling the young maid. "No point in putting yourself in danger, you would not help her that way, now, would you?"

"What do you think, Constable Weston?" I asked.

I looked to Luke for direction. Perhaps he heard something I did not that would give us a lead.

"Did you see any markings on the carriage, Lily?" Luke asked.

"I did not, sir. Although, it did have a crucifix hanging from the window," she said.

"Lily, what about the children below the bridge?" I asked. "I wonder if perhaps they had a better look. Did you by chance talk to them?"

I looked at her hopeful, but she shook her head no.

"Sorry, miss. I didn't think to do that. I just ran back here as fast as I could," she replied.

"Then I think our best bet are those children. Did you get a good look at them?" I prompted.

"Hmmm, well there was a boy with jet-black hair and a blue handkerchief around his neck. The other one I think was a girl, as there was a bow on her jacket. I'm sorry. I didn't see much more than that."

"Oh, that is very good, Lily. Very good, indeed," Luke praised.

I patted my dress in search of my journal to add the descriptions to my notes, but it was not there. A spike of dread filled me before Luke produced the missing volume. I snatched it up in relief and held it to my chest. I had forgotten I had given it to him while in search of Andre. I opened it up to the string and moved it to a blank page. I would review the notes Luke took later, but for now, I needed to write down everything that Lily relayed before I forgot.

A thought occurred to me, and I went and fetched a piece of parchment.

"Jaime, may I impose upon you to send Andre to Miro with this missive? I had a thought and I want to know if he might be able to help us," I said.

"Yes, of course. Whatever you need is at your disposal. Lily, go fetch Andre, I believe he is in the library. I set out a little cushion for him there."

Lily nodded and raced from the room, happy to be useful in the stressful situation.

"Constable, I think we need to find the children under the bridge," I said to Luke. "Let us head to the market now and see if we can get lucky. Do you concur?"

"Yes, Miss Sweeting, that is a sound plan. Then perhaps you can tell me of your idea that would involve Lord Thetford," he said.

"Yes, indeed. Ideas are coming quickly, but we must move, let us talk on the way."

As we headed for the door, I turned to Jaime. "Thank you, cousin, for your summons. Let us hope we find her safe and sound."

We departed and moved swiftly into town. I filled Luke in on part of my idea, of using a multitude of Miro's mechanical beasts in the search for missing youth. I, however, had another part that I wasn't ready to expose yet. I needed to be sure before I brought Luke in. If I was wrong, it would only drive a bigger wedge between us. I knew that Lord Thetford would not question my actions, as I had proven a worthy ally to him. But for some reason, questioning my actions was all Luke Weston seemed to do as of late. This common ground we had found would not be disturbed unless absolutely necessary.

Chapter 23- The Lost Ones

Mischief is best done by the small; they are so much better at going unnoticed.

The market was bustling as vendors shouted out about their available wares. It reminded me of the first time I had met One-Eye Whitmore – the excitement of gizmos flying about, the leather and metal rivets glistening in the afternoon sun. Nate had been with me that day. I hoped Nathan was gaining purchase in the pursuit of the missing sage, although I feared what Whitmore might have to say when next we met.

We shuffled through the crowd, Luke still in his common clothing, not receiving the same desired reaction as he did with his official attire. We located the stand Sadie had run from and peered down both directions of the line of vendors. I could make out the bridge on the left of us from this viewpoint, but it was still quite a ways off. I pointed in its direction, and Luke followed me as I progressed. The crowd became so dense that I grabbed his hand and pulled him behind me. I didn't want to be separated in our haste. He moved to catch up with me, bobbing and weaving between people with their baskets and packages.

Luke caught up to my pace and intertwined our fingers, pulling me to a stop. I felt the warmth and strength that his grasp conveyed and grinned. I couldn't help thinking that this is where we belonged – in the heat of the chase, together. A force, when not battling each other, that could take on the most despicable foes of humanity. I turned toward him and smiled broadly.

The return gaze I received was both warm and intense. A reflection of my own emotions staring back at me.

"You look like an arch angel right now, sent down to smite those who would do harm. I am quite in awe," he said.

I blushed at his description and squeezed his hand a little tighter.

"A pair," I muttered.

"What?"

"We are a pair of angels. Our greatness lies in our teamwork, otherwise we only see half the problem," I replied.

"You are too modest by half, Belle. I am sure you could solve many a puzzle on your own."

"Perhaps, but never in time, and I doubt in an orderly manner."

He laughed at my reply. It was good to see the lightness return to his stormy eyes. We moved together again, and the conversation faded as we neared the bridge, noticing movement below.

"There, do you see?" I pointed.

"Yes, let's split on each side, and box them in," he replied.

"Alright." I followed Luke's lead and made my way to the west side of the bridge. We signaled each other and descended the embankment in unison. I felt like we were about to confront the troll beneath the bridge that would eat wayward travelers that couldn't solve his riddles.

I saw the young man first. He appeared to be around fifteen. He had a startling appearance, like a dark elf, fierce and angular. He moved to shield the girl behind him as I lowered my head under the bridge's support beam. I could see Luke peeking in from the other side but didn't want to give his position away, so I addressed the young man.

"Hello there. I didn't mean to startle you," I said softly.

"You ain't supposed to be heres, miss. You best be leaving. We were just about to leave ourselves, we was. Just taking a rest from the sun," he stammered, trying to move past me.

"Actually, young sir. I was hoping you might be able to help me find a friend of mine. I understood you might have seen her this morning," I replied.

"Sassy Sadie ain't got no friends," said the girl. She appeared to be around ten or eleven.

"Shut it, Marcie," the boy scolded.

"I dare say she is quite sassy, Marcie, but I can assure you I am certainly her friend," I said. "She has found herself in a tough spot, and I aim to help. Can you tell us what you saw?"

"Us?" The young man looked behind me in confusion.

"My friend, Mr. Weston, is there behind you," I replied.

They turned around, startled, backing towards me.

"Nothing to fear I assure you; we just want to know what the carriage looked like that took her," he said calmly.

"How's you know about that?" the boy asked in surprise.

They pointed a glare at Luke and then at me.

"Well, you see, Sadie was helping our maid with some shopping, and ran at the sight of someone. Then our maid saw her being hauled off in the carriage. She also saw you yelling at Sadie. Can you tell us what it was about?" I asked.

The young man jumped slightly when he saw how closely he had backed up toward me. He calmed a bit when I made no movement to grab him.

"Well, come on then, Adam. Tell the lady. You know it wasn't good. At least someone cares," Marcie said.

Adam looked down into the pleading face of his companion, and his resistance cracked.

"Very well. There have been terrible things happening of late. Many a rat has been lost to the cheese, I would say," Adam said solemnly.

"Rat?" I asked.

"Yes, that's what they call us lost ones. The children that have no home, no family. We are rats among the gutter, stealing our meals and begging for everything else. Ah, don't give that pitying look, miss. We get by well enough, me and Marcie. Loners like Sadie are the ones that are getting snatched," Adam said.

"And what, pray, is the cheese that is drawing the rats to the trap?" asked Luke.

Adam turned to face Luke as he answered.

"A promise of a warm bed, a good meal, and the escape from the workhouses and vile foundling homes that are infesting the Boroughs. They are naught but a scheme to brutalize the rats in a different way, under the guise of charity."

Adam spat toward the ground as if the very thought of these places was a curse.

"I understood from our maid that Sadie did not go willingly," I replied.

"No, that she did not. We tried to warn her off, but she wouldn't listen. We told her they were coming from the other side of the bridge, but she said the beadle was in the market. She said she needed to cross to get to safety, but the carriage was already clambering across."

"The beadle? He was the man in the market, then?" I asked.

"That is what she told us," Adam said. "Had her scared to death, it did. I know he has something to do with the Missus over at Second Chance. Maybe she was afraid he would haul her back there. Mrs. Squires is known for her switches."

I winced at the vision of a child being hit with a branch. The overall thought was appalling. I wanted to take a stick and hit that woman senseless.

"Steady on, Miss Sweeting," Luke warned, seeing where my thoughts had taken me.

"You're Miss Sweeting?" Young Marcie asked with wide eyes.

"Yes, you know of me?"

She nodded fervently. "Adam's friend Nathan Starling talks of you often," she replied.

As if being summoned from the ether, I heard a screech in the world above the bridge and knew that Purgatorio was near.

"What was that?"Marcie yelped and held on to Adam.

"That would be a beastie. A helpful one, but a beastie nonetheless," said Luke.

I took a lens from my goggles and reflected it off the light from the water. It refracted the light toward the sky, and I aimed for the shiny gold object floating above us. I heard some crunching of rocks to my left and turned to see a group of kids scurrying down to where we were.

"Adam, you here, you bloody rascal?!" Nathan pulled up short when he saw me standing underneath the bridge.

"Well, miss, what do you do here? Pardon my words just now, but I am gathering my crew like you said to. Are Adam and Marcie okay?"

He moved around me to check for himself, and I heard him release a sigh at seeing them whole and in good form. Three more girls and a boy followed him to shake hands with Adam and Marcie.

"Your crew, hey? Since when am I a part of that?" Adam said, grabbing Nate's cap and pulling it down over his eyes in jest.

"I'd say since it's open season on snipes and we are the most cunning of them all. They'll be sure to have it out for us soon, if not already. Wouldn't you say?" Nate replied.

"Yeah, Adam. Don't yous know anythin'? The Missus on Chancey has done gone mental. Whatever scheme she got involved with the beadle has backfired, I'd say," said the tallest girl.

"Is that so, Nancy Pinth? You seem to have a lot of opinions when no one asks," said Marcie.

"How dare you talk to me that way, pipsqueak? I'd pound you flat if it weren't for your protector here," Nancy yelled back.

"Enough!" Nate yelled. He looked at each of them in the eyes one at a time.

"We do not have time for this. Friends are dead, family," he looked at Byron, who had entered unnoticed sometime after Marcie and Nancy started arguing.

"We are not weak; we are the strong ones. The ones who survived. We are still lost, but not helpless. We need to work together with Miss Sweeting and Mr. Weston here. A plan must be hatched, and I trust only the most cunning of snipes to see it done. There is no betrayal here, no one is favored among us."

Nate continued, addressing each child in turn. "Now, Adam is the oldest among us, and strongest. Byron has the best aim. Nancy can talk her way out of most situations, and Rose is the fastest runner I'd ever seen," he said smiling at a thin short girl.

He turned to another girl on his right and said, "Penny here has an apt sense for when a situation is no good. Marcie, you are small and can fit into tight places. I'm not sure how these skills will be tested, but I know together they could be very useful," he huffed.

There was a look of pride from each of the children as he listed their strengths.

"What about me, Nate?" The youngest of them, a small boy, no older than six yanked at his arm.

"You, Simon, are the piece de resistance," he replied.

"What does that mean, why are you so fancy to-do with words now?" Simon asked.

"It means you are the key piece. I need you for your cute aspect. No one can turn down those dimples, my boy," Nate smiled.

"You forgot to list your strength, Nate," Adam said.

"It's probably getting you guys to come together," he muttered.

"Nope, that's not it. It's being cunning as a fox, clever as a general, and brave as a mouse in a lion's cage. So, what is the plan?" Adam said.

"Miss Sweeting, you're up," Nate said, trying not to look too abashed by the compliments he just received.

All the faces turned to me, hope in their eyes. If this was going to work, I had to have it precise and down to the letter. I couldn't risk anything with these children, they already risked a lot to be here now. I looked at each of their faces and ingrained their strength in my memory. A flutter behind me announced Purgy's arrival, and he perched on my left shoulder.

"Fine, yes fine. Let's get to work."

Chapter 24- A Plan Is Hatched

The most cleverly laid plans often lack variables. Let us hope for better luck than those destined to fail.

"Hey, what are you all doing in there?"

A voice roused us from our conversation. Luke peered up behind himself at the face of a bobbie.

"Oh, officer, nothing of consequence. The lady dropped a most beloved trinket, and the children were helping us locate it," he replied smoothly.

A moment of recognition crossed the officer's face before he responded.

"You sure everything is good then, sir?"

"Yes, quite fine. Thank you for your inquiry," Luke said reassuringly.

The officer nodded and turned to head back up the embankment. They held their breath until the bobbie was out of range.

"That was a close one, mister," said Nancy. "They take any chance to capture a crew like us."

Luke looked at me and winked. I hid a grin and looked back at the group before me.

"I think it is best if we find a better spot to work this out. However, the first part of business must be attended to. Nate, we need someone to go in search of One-Eye Whitmore, and another to find the parish official and follow him. That would need to either be a pair of you or one very sly. He, I believe, is the key. I don't want to risk any of you being caught, so we must move cautiously."

"Agreed," Nate said. "Nancy, take Penny and go find Whitmore. Ring the bell when you find him. We'll meet at the spot," he directed.

"Adam, I want you to watch the beadle. I think you have the best chance with an altercation, if one arises," he said.

"Can't do it, Nate," Adam said, shaking his head. "I need to stay with Marcie, I made a promise."

A knowing look passed between the two boys.

"Ah, yes, of course. Then, Rose, it will need to be you. Stay a far away distance but keep an eye. I would even say go above top. Run at any sign of danger," Nate said.

Rose nodded and tightened her bonnet ribbon. The courage these children possessed amid current affairs was beyond compare. I couldn't help feeling responsible for them, though we had just met.

"Please, do take care," I said.

"Tain't nothin', Miss Sweetin'. We've lived this way our whole lives, that we can remember anyways," said Rose.

She tipped her finger to the brim of her bonnet in farewell and turned to leave. Nathan was not exaggerating when he said she was fast. She had disappeared into the crowd of the market in a matter of moments. Nancy and Penny took their leave next.

"What now?" Nate looked at me for further direction.

"We need to get back to Bread Street. I am waiting on a response, and once that is confirmed the real plan falls into place. Luke, can you go talk to Doctor Cannish and find out if he discovered anything more about the found children?"

"Yes, of course, but what is the plan, Miss Annabelle?" Luke asked.

"I need a few more clues before it's finalized, and they are out getting them. Once I have them you will know all," I responded.

To be honest, I couldn't tell him my whole scheme, as it involved a very touchy subject between us. He bowed and left to return to The Yard for my inquiries. I waited until he was quite far away before I placed Purgatorio on the ground and leaned into the remaining group.

"Okay, this is where it gets risky. Anyone who doesn't want to participate, please walk away now. What I am about to ask you is highly irregular and challenging," I said.

I watched as they looked at each other and then Nate. As Nate nodded to each of them, a resolve took over their faces, and they all agreed it was in their best interest to participate together than to be on their own.

"Why didn't you want Mr. Weston here?" Nathan asked.

"Do you remember the grave robber case, Starling?" I said.

"Yes, miss."

"Well, I think they are connected, and if I tell him without proof, we will lose time, and I fear he won't believe me," I confessed.

"Adam and Marcie, I need you to go to church," I said.

They both looked at each other and back at me in confusion.

"Church, Miss Sweeting?" Adam inquired.

"Yes, specifically St. Alfege Church. I need you to keep watch over Father Gaverty. He is a good friend of a Lord Daven, do you know him?"

They all shook their heads no.

"We don't make the acquaintance of many Glimmers, miss," Adam quipped.

The others started to giggle.

"Yes, well he is apparently an important man in society, and if he catches wind that I am looking into the priest again we are sunk. So, we need to do this very slyly indeed," I said.

"We can be sly, miss, just like foxes," Marcie said smiling.

"That is what I am hoping. What I am looking for is some connection between the priest and Mrs. Squires."

"Mrs. Squires, that old witch! Gave me this black eye, she did," Byron said.

"Yes, I am sorry that happened to you, Byron. I do need your help with her, if you are willing?"

"What did you have in mind?"

"I want you to stick close to Mrs. Squires. If she is still transporting packages back and forth, I want you to follow one and find where it is dropped. When you have this information, I then need you to snag one and bring it to me," I said. "This is a very dangerous request, Byron."

"I understand, miss. You think she had something to do with Gwennie?"

"I do."

"Then I am in," he said.

I bent down and stroked Purgatorio's brass mane.

"Purgatorio will watch you from the sky. If you have need of him, let out a whistle, yes?"

Byron nodded and ran out from under the bridge towards the Brass Boroughs. Adam and Marcie said their goodbyes and headed toward their mission.

"What about us, miss?" A wide-eyed Simon looked up at me. He looked so tiny it broke my heart.

"You and Nathan are coming with me. Your tasks are not ready yet. Let us leave now, and hope that time is on our side. I fear Sadie is depending on us," I said.

"Sadie?" Nate asked, concern on his face.

"Yes, Nathan, she was taken this morning."

"That can't be, I just saw her when I went to fetch Byron and Simon. Mrs. Squires was making her scrub floors," he said.

"Are you sure?"

"Yes, miss. All the rats were prattling on about how she was dropped off in a carriage and thinks she is something special now," Nate explained.

"I was there!" Simon said, animatedly. "It was a big black one, and it had the letter D on all the wheels and a silver crucifix dangling in the window. Some cloaked man pushed her out right in front of the steps and told her it was her last warning. I'd never seen her so scared."

"We need to get back to the house now, let us be off," I said.

We dashed up the embankment and moved swiftly over the bridge toward Bread Street. I had a feeling that Sadie still needed our help. Whatever Mrs. Squires' involvement was, it was causing her to lose her hinges and become volatile. I tried to keep up with Nathan and Simon as they dashed through alleys and streets. After a few moments, I lost sight of them around the corner and tried to hasten my pace without drawing attention. My heart raced as I weaved my way back home, and turning the corner, I ran into a most unexpected gentleman.

"Father Gaverty! I apologize, in my haste I did not see you there," I said.

"Miss Sweeting, are you not accompanied?" he asked.

I looked around us and noticed how thin the crowd was. The boys were completely out of sight, and I was quite out of fashion without an escort.

"I fear my traveling boy has dashed ahead of me to make preparations, and I have lagged behind most abominably, sir. It's not two blocks hence though, so I will make sure not to have any further interruptions before I get there."

"Nonsense, I will attend you. It is my duty as a clergyman to set an example, after all," he said.

"You are all kindness, Father. It is truly unnecessary," I replied.

"Nonetheless, it shall be done," he said with no more room to argue.

Father Gaverty bent his arm to me, and I took it. We moved at a snail's pace, and I tried to catch my breath.

"Miss Sweeting, will you be attending church this week? I have planned a rather lively sermon on propriety and the wisdom of maintaining it. I think you would gain some vastly beneficial notes from it."

My mouth gaped open in a most unattractive manner as I tried to gain my composure at the clear cut he had just delivered me.

"Perhaps where there are no emotions, propriety may well be preserved, sir. I will attend your mass. If you have found a way to conquer having no feelings, then you are truly a saint in the making," I retorted.

After a brief silence, I asked, "Father Gaverty, are you familiar with many foundling hospitals?"

He looked up sharply, "Why do you ask?"

"I've just been noticing the poor conditions of the children of late, and the stories being reported recently are quite sad, don't you agree? I felt perhaps I could offer some sort of help, if you knew about them," I replied.

Father Gaverty physically relaxed and patted my arm.

"That is a most Christian feeling, Miss Sweeting, and I quite approve. Yes, I know of a few places. We are always in need of donations."

"Do you by chance know a Mrs. Squires? She is the guardian of the Second Chance Orphanage in Chancey Street."

A slight narrowing of eyes and thinning of lips flashed across his face before his serene countenance returned. Clearly, he had not conquered his own emotions now, and I tried to hide my grin at this revelation.

"I don't believe I have had the pleasure, although my parish officer, Mr. Fieldworth, does charity and oversees that area. There is an orphanage not far from our church that I would think would be much more convenient for you, Miss Sweeting," he replied.

"Oh, Mr. Fieldworth, the beadle, yes? I have heard of him. Mayhap you could introduce us at the next service? I find for some reason, perhaps divine intervention, I am drawn to the Second Chance. We cannot ignore God's will, now can we, Father?"

He smiled at me, but it did not reach his eyes. We turned the corner to Bread Street, and I could see Jaime's house down the lane. I wasn't sure if I wanted to continue the conversation or rush to get home. I, however, couldn't help myself.

"Father Gaverty, I must inquire, how is your friend Lord Daven? I understand he has been ill recently," I said.

"That is quite thoughtful of you. He is quite well now. An illness in the family has made him absent, but all have since recovered. All shall be well, God willing. He has been a dear friend since boyhood, I am glad you harbor no ill will toward him for having you dismissed from The Yard, miss. Lord Daven is very protective of me," he said reverently.

"It is wonderful to have such connections. A friendship like that is worth its weight in gears. I am not angry, and no longer dismissed from my post," I said.

"What?" He looked at me with a mix of shock and confusion. I pretended to not understand which reference shocked him.

"Anger is not an emotion that serves me well. I would think you would be congratulating me on my capacity for forgiveness?"

"No, not that, Miss Sweeting. You are continuing to investigate calamities? That is not a proper female pursuit, nor do you have cause to further inquire on such delicate matters. The case, in which you so brashly accused my involvement, has been solved. What could they need your assistance for?"

We stopped in front of my cousin's house, and I stared at the obtusely rigid man.

"Father Gaverty, did not God create man and woman? Are we not both in his image? Should women hide our minds and talents if they would serve God's will? I cannot fathom anything more Christian than the pursuit of ending the evil in this world. We must, as mortals, help where we can. If we lay complacent, for the sake of the current society's expectation, we invite wrongdoing, no?" I asked.

"Miss Sweeting, am I to understand that I am under scrutiny again, then?"

"Father, as you said, that case has been solved. We met by happenstance, and I have learned my lesson on such matters," I said.

A clear relief washed over his face.

"Very well, then. Good day to you, Miss Sweeting,"

"Good day to you as well. I shall see you at the next mass," I replied.

He bowed and took his leave. I was convinced, now more than ever, that his part in the crime was not fully complete. I worried my lip with my teeth as I reflected on our conversation. A whispered beckon broke me from my thoughts, and I turned to find Simon and Nate hiding by the servants' entrance. I quickly moved toward them, and we entered the house. Whatever the priest's involvement, it would have to wait. Sadie was in need now.

Chapter 25- Miro's Machines

It's a frightful burden to have a great mind of invention. It can breed such pleasure or wreak such havoc.

Instead of a return missive, as I expected, I found Lord Miro Nassar Thetford waiting for us in my cousin's drawing room. Jaime paced by the fireplace, and his peacock mirrored his action by the window. The sight was beyond humorous, but I knew his anguish was not, so I kept my mirth at bay. I walked quickly to where Jaime stood and took his hands in mine.

"Calm yourself, cousin. We are well, and we have word on where Sadie is. I believe she is safe for the time being, but we must move swiftly. When we are done here can you send Andre with a note to Constable Weston for me?" I said.

"Of course, Belle. Where is the girl?" Jaime asked, concern still etched across his face.

"Nathan found her back at Second Chance. Nate can you fill Jaime in on everything that you know?" I asked.

"Of course," Nate responded.

I moved over to where Miro sat. He reached for his cane and stood at my approach.

"Lord Thetford, you received my missive then?" I asked.

"Yes, Miss Annabelle. I must say I was quite shocked, but given the circumstances, I see how my devices could be quite useful for someone that doesn't want to be detected. I will help you in whatever way I can," he replied.

"Thank you, I knew you would understand my intentions," I said.

I smiled at him and moved to shake his hand. He held onto it instead and turned my hand upward, placing a kiss on the back.

"The prototypes are at your disposal, Miss Anna," he said, looking up at me with intense green eyes.

"Thank you, sir."

A blush crept up my neck, but it wasn't from a thrill, more from a sense of wrongness. Although it would be easier with Miro, as I could see his support at every turn of our acquaintance, my heart would not yield to his charms. It was as stubborn as my determination to solve a puzzle. I slid my hand from his and drew back slightly. I could see Jaime from the corner of my eye nod his head once. If that was any indication, I suspected his original perception of my true feelings concerning Luke had been accurate.

"Thank you, sir. I will send Nate along with you. Nathan, come here please," I said.

Miro straightened his jacket and looked a bit put out.

"You will not be accompanying me?" Miro asked with a tinge of hurt in his voice.

"No, sir, I am needed elsewhere, if this is to take shape accordingly." Turning to Nathan, I said, "Lord Thetford has agreed to let us use several of his parcel prototypes. They have the capacity to communicate long distances, and I have tasked him with applying a visual recording mechanism on some of them. They are also capable of picking up items, is that not so, sir?"

"Yes, Miss Sweeting, it is in fact so. I have a tower from my workshop that can relay messages to them. I only have a few working now and was able to quickly add the visual aspect to two of them. I hope they will suffice for your needs," Miro said.

"Very well, indeed. I am most grateful. Nathan do make haste and go along with Lord Thetford. I want you to send a parcel prototype with a lens to Mr. Fieldworth's residence. I want to intercept one of the packages," I directed.

"I thought you had Byron on that mission, miss?" Nathan said.

"I do, but in case he is unable, I need an alternate course of action. I must see what's inside one of Mrs. Squires' boxes," I replied.

"What is it that you think is in them?" Nate asked.

"Not Mrs. Squires' dirty laundry, that is for certain. I also need one of your prototypes with visual capacity, and the ability to fly around Lord Daven's residence. Mainly if you could maneuver it through his stables and motor park," I said, turning to Miro.

"What do you aim to find? I would not want to get on his bad side. He has quite the reputation for retribution, Miss Sweeting," Miro said.

"Yes, I well know it. I was so unfortunate to feel it when I interviewed his friend, Father Gaverty, on our last investigation. That is why I have a suspicion he is somehow tangled in it all. I cannot emphasize how much this needs to remain a secret. Until we are certain, we cannot let anyone catch wind of our designs," I said.

"Okay so the motor park and stables?" Miro confirmed.

"Yes, we are looking for his carriage, I have an inkling that it will strike a resemblance to one of recent events. Do a scan of the exterior of the home as well, just to be safe. I understand from Father Gaverty that a family member was quite ill. Do either of you know who it might be?" I turned to Jaime and Miro in question.

"Of course, cousin," Jaime replied. "If you were not so neglectful of your church going you would know that his wife is laid up. It's been in the sermons for months. As I understand it, the lady has been to all sorts of herbalists, doctors, and charlatans in the pursuit of some remedy. Something regarding the inner workings of her body is failing. It has been kept quite hush-hush on how dire the situation is, but I fear without some sort of miracle she will not recover," Jaime said.

"Oh, that is quite shocking! I had no idea. I wonder, perhaps, if Dr. Cannish has been consulted. Although he did say he prefers the dead, he has skills that are beyond compare," I suggested.

"That is not an option, I'm afraid," Jaime continued. "The Lord and Dr. Cannish are not on speaking terms. There was a falling out, I understand. It was quite the gossip when it occurred, although I am not sure of the details now. I will consult with Lady Whipley on the manner if you think it to be useful?"

"Yes, I think I would very much like to hear about it," I said.

"I will be meeting her for tea this afternoon. I shall inquire then," Jaime smiled.

"Thank you, Jaime."

"What is it that you will be doing, miss?" Nate asked.

All four faces turned to me. My plan was starting to gain momentum. Pieces were sliding into place, but another concern had been plaguing me for a while. I hoped to kill two birds with the proverbial stone.

"Simon, this adorable well-manner boy here, and I are needed elsewhere. Not to worry though. We shall be quite safe. We will be dropping off some of the accessory pieces to Lady Bergenhalt. She had been expecting them earlier this week, but I have been quite wrapped up with the current situation," I replied.

"You must be off now Nate. Miro, please send word if you uncover anything strikingly out of the ordinary," I said.

"What should we be looking for?" Miro asked.

"A crucifix in the window of a carriage and a letter "D" emblem stamped about it," I replied.

Nathan's eyes glinted in realization, "You think he snatched Sadie, Miss Anna?"

"That is what we need to find out. It is just a suspicion I have. One that will either prove true or false. It is best to know either way, now is it not?" I quipped.

"Yes, but why would he lower himself to such a task?" Nate said.

"That is what we need to find out. Let us get the answer to the first question before we jump to the next, young Starling," I said.

"Very well, Lord Thetford, would you be so kind as to show me the way?" Nate asked.

"Of course, Starling. Let us go solve a mystery, shall we?" Miro smiled.

They left the room, and as the door shut, I felt a sense of relief. Parts were in motion, and I merely had to wait for my hypothesis to be right or wrong. I kept Simon with me as I couldn't risk putting him in any sort of danger. The small lad was such a darling, and I thought, perhaps, he might help with a different task I had recently taken an interest in. Miro and Nathan left the house and I turned to my cousin standing next to the fireplace in thought.

"Lady Bergenhalt is to announce the theme of her soiree at the Cosswald girl's wedding. Have you guessed yet what it is?" I asked.

Jaime's eyes lit up at the question. I could tell he had been mulling it over for several days. I couldn't help but wonder if he was ready to share his thoughts.

"You think you are quite clever," he smirked. "I think, however, I have solved your little riddle, cousin. It is to be a Roman theme, I believe. It's clear that the Tiber is longer than the Thames, the three shadows are the three domes atop the basilica of Vatican City, and of course, it leads to the glorious, beautiful halls of St. Peters. Come now, I am right, aren't I?"

"That is a good guess, but it is incorrect. I must give you compliments on your reasoning. It was very well thought out," I said.

"Come then, tell me what it is?" he begged.

His face was crestfallen at the defeat.

"Perhaps later. Right now, I must dash. The wedding is to occur at this week's end. You did answer the invitation, did you not?" I asked.

"You know I did. We could hardly be anyone at all if we were to miss it, Belle. Lady Whipley and I have been working on the dress. It has all been quite hush-hush," he said.

A look of mischief fluttered over his face. Some scheme had entered his mind, and I was delighted to hear it.

"I happen to know which Cosswald sister is to be married. They are indeed keeping it a secret until the day of. Do you wish to know?" he said, with an excited mirth.

"Oh yes, do tell," I pleaded.

"Perhaps later, when you are free, you do have to dash after all," he quipped.

"Touché! Well played, dear cousin. A secret for a secret is quite fair, indeed. Tonight then?" I said.

Jaime nodded, and I took my leave, leading Simon out of the drawing room and up to my tinker room. There was a secondary reason I was visiting Lady Bergenhalt, and I hoped for its success. I wanted to pick her brain about the current state of affairs with the orphans of the city. A woman of influence and generally liked may have some ideas on how to make it better. Perhaps a fundraiser for the poor dears, and who better to plead their case than the small darling boy beside me? We gathered the individually packaged accessories in a sturdy leather bag. I saw a brass scarab on the table, and it reminded me of the first hat I created for Nathan. I took the small bug, affixed a pin to its backing, and attached it to Simon's jacket front. He looked up at me in question.

"For luck," I said.

"We sure could use some of that, miss!" Simon replied.

"We certainly could. Let us be off then," I said, heading for the door.

"We have much to learn, and an ever-ticking clock to compete with."

We headed down the stairs and out the front entrance. I didn't want to take the time of walking so far, so I attached a small side cart to my motorbike and had Simon sit inside. He placed the leather satchel beside him, and I started the engine. I looked at him and nodded. He returned the gesture, and we headed off into town.

Chapter 26- Curious Conversation

Sometimes we forget the small things, but in the details lies the important bits we cannot do without.

The season was upon us now. With the Cosswald wedding to launch it off, it felt like a renewal of sorts. The winter had been solitary and quite jarring. I was glad to see signs of the town coming back to life in such a way. We rode with ease through the streets, enjoying the bustling of the shop owners as they altered their storefronts with the latest material goods. A city so full of promise and even more secrets. It had become like another living thing to me. A friend that I visited daily. I smiled as we passed the blacksmith's shop and waved to Kaplan through his open door. He waved back with his hammer in return.

Men and women were about town shopping for the season's fashions. Struggling maids hauling packages and hat boxes could be seen shuffling after their charges. The new debutants of the season would have their chance to shine amongst the "ton". It really was a hopeful time for young ladies and their fussing mamas alike.

I wondered what it would have been like to have had that life. I cherished my freedom, but I often thought of how different my life might be if I was counted amongst the young ladies that duty demanded to find good marital matches. Dressing in such amazing gowns and finery was definitely a draw, but to only be looked on to marry well, seemed a vast disservice to the possibility or promise of a young lady. It felt somehow like having half a life. I shook my head at the thought. Such progressive thinking was sure to be frowned upon.

I took a left at the corner and drew up in front of the Bergenhalt's massive home. Lord Bergenhalt, I understood, not only came from a rather prosperous family but also owned a successful shipping enterprise. His vessels were often sought after by traders receiving and sending goods throughout Europe. It clearly had been quite lucrative for them. Simon brushed off the front of his clothes and looked up in amazement at the home before us.

"Grab the satchel, Simon. Follow me this way, please," I directed.

He tore his eyes away from the view and quickly followed my instructions. Hauling the large bag, he looked even smaller. Perhaps my plan was a bit manipulative, but for a good cause, I thought it could be overlooked. Ringing the front bell, we waited outside for the butler.

"Miss Sweeting, you are expected. The lady is in the front parlor. Please follow me. Angus, take the young lady's coat," the butler directed.

I allowed the other servant to remove my cropped jacket but grabbed the charm from its sleeve and attached it to my belt. Simon stayed close to my side as we were led to the parlor. I could hear gasps from him along the way. The grandeur was more than he had likely seen before in his young life. I admit I was still taken aback by its impressiveness. The lady of this house surely had a lot of sway when it came to the direction of its maintenance. Is that what the dream of a debutante was? Such a life is surely quite fulfilling. I, however, could not imagine myself in such a role. A stronger force called to me. Peculiar, though, it might be.

"Lady Bergenhalt, how wonderful to see you! You are looking remarkably well today. I think the improvement of the weather has us all feeling a vast more lively, don't you?" I said in greeting.

"Oh, Miss Sweeting. Good day, indeed. I thank you for your compliments. I dare say you are quite right. The turn of weather has been ever beneficial. And pray, who is this mite you have with you?" The lady turned to inspect Simon.

"Ah, let me introduce you to young Simon here. He is an orphan at the Second Chance Orphanage and has generously aided me in the task of bringing your orders today. Simon, greet Lady Bergenhalt," I replied.

The young boy placed the bag on the ground and approached the lady. He produced a gallant bow, I had not known him capable of, and greeted her sweetly. As he straightened, the scarab on his jacket caught the firelight.

"What is this, young sir? It is quite striking," Lady Bergenhalt inquired.

She leaned down and brushed her fingers along the back of the embellishment.

"A gift, mi lady. From Miss Sweetin'. She is so very generous in taking me along, you see. I had nawt expected it at all. Then she just pinned it on me with nawt a thought about it. I assure you it's nawt even my birthday," he said.

"Yes, I see. She is very kind indeed. You seem to be a good boy though, so I think you must have deserved it," she praised.

He beamed up at her with a heart-melting smile. She turned to me and gushed.

"I dare say he is the sweetest little thing. You know, Daniel and I tried for a child for many years, but alas it was not to be. If it had, I would have wished for just such a boy," Lady Bergenhalt sighed.

A wistful look washed across her features. I could tell she was replaying those times in her life.

"I did wish to speak to you on a manner pertaining to dear Simon.

Do you have some time to spare?" I asked.

"Oh, of course. Let me call for tea, my dear. And Simon, are you hungry?" she replied.

"Always, mum," he said.

Lady Bergenhalt gasped in reaction.

"Well, let us remedy that at once. Ashley, please take young Simon down to the kitchen and have the cook fix him up anything that he might require," she directed.

"A scrap of bread will do. I don't want to be a burden, mum," he said shyly.

Simon looked at me and then back to her, nervous he had made a mistake of some kind.

"Simon it is okay to accept Lady Bergenhalt's invitation. You have done me a kindness today. A reward is indeed in order," I said.

He smiled broadly and nodded in excitement.

"Yes, miss. Thank you, mum!" Simon beamed.

He followed the servant out of the parlor in search of a hearty well-deserved meal. I could see Nathan was not wrong about the young boy's charm. The endearing way he called Lady Bergenhalt "mum" was not lost on me.

Tea was served. Lady Bergenhalt and I took our seats near a window. "Now then, what is it you wish to speak of, Miss Annabelle? And do call me Diana," she said.

"I thank you, Diana. I understand that your husband and you are quite popular within society," I started. My nerves eased at her encouraging smile. "I am looking for a way to excite an interest among the "ton" into the very dire circumstances that the orphans of the Boroughs are currently facing. I wanted to inquire if you perhaps had any ideas on the subject? I do not know how to approach it without being passed over for something more amusing," I admitted.

A knowing smile flitted across her face, then a furrowed brow, as she thought over my quandary.

"Ah, I see. Well, I plan events. I am not sure what good I may be," she replied. A sad look crossed her expression. "You are saying, young Simon is without a family? He did look rather thin. The orphanage is struggling then?"

"He is alone in the world, yes. Nathan Starling had brought his plight to my attention, and after meeting him I could not help but be interested," I said.

"I can see why," she agreed.

"The real problem, you see, is that the orphanage he resides in seems to be mixed up in nefarious dealings. I fear the children are being taken advantage of. I need to find a means to generate interest to help put rights to the current wrongs affecting them. It is a daunting task, I know. I thought that with your creative mind, and my determination we could come up with a viable solution," I said.

"Yes, you are determined. I will indeed give you that, my dear," Diana agreed. "A thought has just occurred to me. It is quite an undertaking, and I daresay if you can get your cousin to help we may just pull it off. We shall need a trusted group of children to see it through, however."

"What do you have in mind?" I asked, excitement and hope warring inside me.

"The masquerade ball, of course! We could have the children incorporated in some way. Servers perhaps?" Lady Bergenhalt suggested. "We could have them dressed in gold suits with turquoise and red detailing, and of course each must have a darling scarab like the one on young Simon's lapel. Yes, indeed," she said.

I took out my journal and turned to a fresh page to write down her ideas. My graphite flew across the paper with haste at the wonderful and detailed designs she had in mind.

"That is a brilliant idea! How clever you are, Diana!" I exclaimed. "Would there be a way to raise money for their plight without it being crass, do you think?"

"Of course! We can auction off the attire I had made up for the party, along with some of your baubles. Proceeds to the Justice for Children charity that I will have my dear Daniel form on the morrow. What do you think, Annabelle?"

"I knew I asked the right person. You have truly an amazing mind. I will start producing the scarabs post haste and request my cousin to start the small ensembles. He will be glad to be included, he has been an admirer of your gatherings for years," I replied.

"Truly? I thought Lady Whipley was having your cousin assist with the servants' attire already, is it not so?" she asked, surprised.

"No, she takes it on herself. She does not include Jaime in the crafting at all," I said.

"That is surprising indeed. He is quite an accomplished tailor in his own right. Perhaps this will give him the push he needs to strike out on his own?" Diana suggested.

"You think he favors such an idea? I mean to say, striking out on his own is a desired course of action?" I asked.

"Miss Sweeting, anyone who apprentices for as long as your cousin is dreaming of their turn. That she hasn't given it to him can only mean one of two things. One, that she loves his work so much she can't bear to part with it, or two, that she is jealous of his designs and doesn't want to compete with him," she divulged.

"I had not thought of that. I am quite happy then. You have managed to solve several problems with one afternoon tea, Diana. I don't know how to thank you enough."

"It was quite amusing, actually. Perhaps there is some merit to offering my council?" she said.

"I daresay. That would indeed be an honorable pursuit. There are many a lady that could benefit from your experience and decorum," I replied.

"You flatter me," Diana said. "Now let us see these anticipated pieces for the ball. We can finalize your compensation and the plans for the party afterward. I am quite in suspense."

Chapter 27- A Willful Girl

It suits us all to be daring and eager. The world would be quite boring if not for a willful girl.

I left Lady Bergenhalt's with a lightness to my body. I hadn't felt it since I first arrived in town. The idea of making things better had me giddy. Simon smiled along with me. His belly was full, and he was so charming that Lady Bergenhalt invited him along the next time I visited. I didn't want to visualize such a happy ending, but I couldn't help but think he would be a great addition to their family. Could one dare to wish for such joy? I would keep it a secret wish for now.

We rode back to Bread Street, and I directed Simon to Nathan's room. He could rest there until Nate returned. Tomorrow was church. I wanted to discuss attending with my cousin and clue him into the plan regarding the ball. I couldn't help but smile at the thought of bringing him joy at the hands of Lady Bergenhalt. I could scarcely believe I had not picked up on Jaime's desire to flourish in his own shop. I had thought he was happy in his current situation. Looking back, I could see his contributions and attempts at achieving more.

I walked into the library to find him and Andre sitting by the fire. They hadn't heard me come in, and they were in a deep conversation, on my cousin's part at least. As far as I could tell, squawking and chirping were the only things coming from the mechanical peacock. I chuckled at the pair as Jaime was discussing the finer attributes of a dove feather compared to a pigeon. It was quite riveting. As another chuckle escaped my lips, a startled Jaime turned to find me standing there.

"Cousin, what do you do there? An eavesdropper in my midst? I daresay, I thought you outgrew that little hobby of yours?" Jaime teased.

"Yes, well it would have been quite rude of me to interrupt such a diverting conversation. I am happy your companion is to your liking," I said.

"Come sit down then. I must hear about this theme now. I have waited quite long enough. I can then tell you of my meeting with Lady Whipley."

"Very well. The theme this year is 'Land of the Pharaohs'. She will be holding it at the Egyptian Hall. It will be quite lavish, and I haven't told you the best part. You will be responsible for some costumes as of today!"

"What? Do I understand you to say that Lady Bergenhalt has requested my services? I scarcely believe it, Belle. Cordelia Whipley has always been the one to provide the wardrobe. She has not given me word of this when I met her just this afternoon. How did you come by this information?"

"I saw Lady Bergenhalt for tea this afternoon. I told you I was dropping off my pieces, yes?"

He nodded.

"Well, I had made a request of her that she fulfilled amiably, and it ended up involving you," I said.

"Belle, please tell me you did not beg on my behalf. I would be utterly mortified," he replied.

"Nothing of the sort. I had recently been taken aback by the travesty of the current state of that orphanage. It has been weighing heavily on my mind, you know?" I said.

"Yes, I had noticed that," he replied, giving me a tender look.

"Well, I thought, who better than the inventive Lady Diana Bergenhalt to ask about creating a frenzy to help the struggling youth? She was brilliant. The answer seemed so obvious once she had freed it from her lips. She offered to allow some trustworthy orphans to serve as an example at her gathering, and she wants you to create their costumes. She suggested you specifically. They are to be gold with touches of turquoise and red. I am to provide you with a scarab pin for each. Is it not exciting?" I inquired.

"Oh dear, and only a month away. How will I find the time? We will need the children here immediately for measurements. Oh, and I must make sure to get the fabric on order. She asked for me directly? Yes, my dear Belle, this is quite exciting, indeed!" Jaime gushed.

He moved across the room and embraced me. Just like when I first arrived, he spun me around in his glee. I laughed at his exuberance. He set me down and kissed the top of my forehead.

"Now, you must hear my news. It is to be Whitney on the marriage block. She is quite bursting at the seams that her parents will not let her tell. It seems unfair to her that her sister, Cara, is receiving such attention when she has nothing to do with it. They have been seen around town of late stirring up a flurry of excitement. She is to have seven bride's maids, seven! I can scarcely believe Lord Cosswald is much too happy with the expense. The mother is all pride and peacocking about," Jaime said with annoyance.

A squawk of admonishment filled the room. We turned to find Jaime's mechanical companion staring at us with accusing ocular lenses.

"I do apologize, Andre. I merely meant she hasn't the foundation to strut as you do. She is making a show of herself unduly," Jaime explained.

The bird turned his back on Jaime and continued to, I guess the only way to describe it is, pout.

"Do stop carrying on. You may leave if you are to continue on so," Jaime huffed.

The bird fluttered his metallic wings about and moved to the cushion in the corner. He powered down, and a hum of the recharge cycle filled the room. Jaime stretched out his arm and directed me to take the seat across from him by the fireplace. We sat down and he called for tea. I felt the tension leave my body as we settled in.

"There now. Where was I? Oh, yes, the woman is quite the pompous braggart. Now onto the other news I meant to divulge. I heard from Cornelia about the curious happenings between Lord Daven and Doctor Cannish," Jaime wiggled his eyebrows. I chuckled at his gossipy nature. He did get such provocative information.

"It is my understanding that they were childhood mates at Eton," he continued. "They shared a dormitory and got into some scrapes there, but never with each other. When they left school, Cannish went off to pursue the medicinal field while Daven prepared to take over his father's estate. Their paths would cross again several years later in London. Both attended an invention fair showcasing a wide range of tools and mechanisms. That is where they met Miss Eloise Bridgemont. She was a most sought-after young lady who had the heart of society at the time. I guess a rivalry was formed, and poor Cannish ended up the vanquished. I dare say that would explain his current disposition," he said.

"Oh, that is a tale indeed. So, then is the former Miss Bridgemont the current Lady Daven? The one who is ill?" I guessed.

"Yes!" Jaime confirmed.

"This does put a new spin on it. Perhaps that is why he does not wish to ask for Dr. Cannish's help. Lord Daven cannot bear to ask his rival to assist in the aid of the woman they both loved. It is quite tragic," I said.

"It is indeed," Jaime agreed.

We both sat in silence for a spell staring at the flickering flames and mesmerizing coals before us. The pride of a man was something that I could not quite understand. If one truly loved, would they not turn every stone for the solution, no matter how wounding it may be to one's ego? A question for another day, I supposed.

"Cousin, I aim to free Sadie from that home tomorrow. I am not sure what may come of it. Either we shall take her on as a servant or be forced to adopt her. Normally they wouldn't care if a child had been sheltered, like we had done, but she is special. Whatever she is involved in is necessary to them. I just know that while she stays there, she is not completely safe," I said.

"Yes, there is something quite surprising about what happened," Jaime agreed. "So many children go about without a person noticing. She was sought out. I believe you are onto something, Belle. Take Weston with you. I feel like his presence is warranted in this event. I have been making inquiries about Mrs. Squires as well, since you brought her to my attention. She is not at all liked, and I fear being caught up in something that is far out of her depths," he said, tapping his chin in thought.

"The poor woman had started out with good intentions, but the patrons of the home abandoned her and had stopped sending funding," he said. "It is my understanding that living in the Brass Boroughs forced her to take unseemly measures to survive. The children were in need of food and clothing, not to mention her own needs. One of the wards she took in showed her a purse full of coin he had taken from an aristocrat, and she was hooked. Her goodness was stolen away by the poverty and turmoil of the situation. One can hardly blame her," Jaime said.

"How devastating! Perhaps whatever scheme she is wrapped up in, it is not too late to get her out?" I suggested.

"If children are winding up dead, and she is involved, it is definitely too late," Jaime said, resolutely.

I knew he was right. It saddened me, but we all make our own choices. There are certain lines one can never come back from. Jaime and I parted ways for the evening with plenty on our minds. I lost myself in my workshop and worked far into the night. When exhaustion finally forced me to quit, I went to bed and didn't dream.

Chapter 28- Too Much Information

Sometimes a well of information can produce too many details leading us in the completely wrong direction.

I woke to a curtain being pulled open. Cringing, I pulled my blanket over my head.

"Do get up, Miss Anna. I need to speak with you most urgently," Nate whispered.

I bolted upright and gawked at him.

"I'm not properly attired, Nate. Do wait outside, and I will join you momentarily," I sputtered.

"Sorry, miss," he blushed. "It's just that I needed to move swiftly, and there weren't time for proprieties."

The blush continued to spread across his freckled cheeks. He shifted from one foot to the other in nervous agitation.

"What has happened?" I asked.

"You were right about the carriage, it was just as you suspected. Adam confirmed it when I met with him. He had followed Father Gaverty to Lord Daven's home and they met. While they were inside Adam hid in the motor park and couldn't help but look at the fancy vehicles about. He stumbled on it quite by chance and I had the Nassar Navigator sending back images from the very spot," he said.

"Nassar Navigator? Is that what he is calling it?"

"Yes, Miss Anna. That's not the biggest news though. We were hovering about and around the mansion and what we picked up was quite extraordinary. The beadle was admitted as well, with many parcels! He didn't go into the main entrance but a side building near the greenhouse. I could see a woman in a wheelchair there among the roses. She did not look well at all, miss. I am not sure what it all means, but it must mean something," he said.

"That is all valuable information, but I daresay it could have waited for me to be properly attired. Is there more?"

"Oh, yes. Perhaps I should have relayed it first. Sadie, miss, she was accompanying the beadle!"

"What could this mean? Could you tell from the device if she was in distress?" I asked.

"I couldn't. It was all quite fast," Nate said.

"Okay, do get out and let me dress. Do not leave here yet, I need you for something first."

"I can only stay a moment or two, I heard the church bell signal on the way here, so I must meet with Nancy soon," he said.

"I will hurry," I replied.

He left my room, and I threw off the covers, bolting to my wardrobe. I quickly put on a full torso corset with leather strapping and gold buckles. It was a gift from Jaime last year. I donned a deep burgundy skirt with gold trim. I quickly braided my hair to the side and wove a matching burgundy ribbon through it. I stepped into my short black half-boots and exited the room. Nathan was waiting in the hall for me.

"You did all that in five minutes?" Nathan questioned, astounded.

"If the need arises, I can move with haste, yes. Now we must discuss the parcels. Have you been able to snag one?" I replied.

"No, Miss Anna. It's like they are moving underground. I am not sure if our one Nassar Navigator will be enough to complete the task as the other one is still at Lord Daven's. We have it waiting above the orphanage now, but nothing has been seen coming or going," he said.

The frustration was evident in his address. I, too, couldn't help but feel it. We needed to be sure. If the parcels from the orphanage were just ordinary packages, then we were chasing down the wrong lead. Something about Tapers Grove nudged at my subconscious. Mr. Fieldworth did dwell nearby, but there was some other mystery there.

"Tell me, have you heard from Rose yet?" I inquired.

"No. Adam didn't see her either when he was at Lord Daven's. It does not do well to worry. She knows where to meet when the church bell tolls. If she is not in hiding, then she will seek us if something has happened. Rose is quite clever," he said.

I felt he was assuring himself more than he was me. I bit my lip in worry at the prospect of one of the team being caught or worse. Perhaps I should make a symbol for them to wear that the bobbies could distinguish. This would remove at least one set of pursuers from the game. It really was quite vexing to me how hard they must work to simply move about the city.

"I am going to Second Chance today. I mean to speak with Mrs. Squires about Sadie and I will check up on Byron. Purgatorio should be there. I hope that we can figure this out soon. I daresay the pieces are not falling together as I had hoped. True, some are, but the clear picture is still evading me," I admitted.

"I understand. I must go now. I can't be late. I will find you when I have more news," Nate responded.

He ran down the stairs without a backward glance, and I felt a most unpleasant sinking sensation. I needed to find out whether Sadie was a victim or an accomplice. The thought that she had deceived us turned my stomach. It felt off, somehow. I fought the wave of panic and forced myself to eat a light breakfast. I needed to find Luke and see what he uncovered. Hopefully, he would have some opinion on the matter. The hour was early, so I went to the kitchen to find a few morsels and headed out into the predawn city. I didn't find Luke at The Yard, so I traveled to his apartments on the other side of town. He answered the door himself after three knocks.

"Belle, what do you do here? Is something the matter? Young Starling?" Luke searched my face for some indication of what was amiss.

"No, sir. All is well, as well as it can be. What I mean is, Nathan is fine, as am I. There have been several developments that I need your opinion on. Now then, may I come in?" I asked.

"It is quite improper I'm afraid. You shouldn't be out alone," he said.

"She ain't alone sir! I have accompanied the miss, and she is well enough, I'd say," squeaked Simon from behind me.

I moved aside for the young boy to be seen. Luke looked down at the brave boy's face and scratched his chin in thought.

"You'll do, I suppose. Come in then," Luke directed.

He swung the door inward and directed us to a sitting area in a very comfortable room. The chairs were worn from use and many books laid about, it was quite a splendid sight.

"I apologize for my lack of tidiness. I rarely get company, so I let the maid from my aunt's house come every other day for some extra coin. It serves us both quite well," he said.

"It is quite alright, sir. It is a most comfortable, pleasant place, I assure you."

"I shall make us some tea, and then we can get down to what has happened," Luke said.

He left the room, and I was tempted to see what volume lay by the chair most adjacent to the fireplace. I stood up and took a turn about his space looking at all the portraits and furnishings. It reminded me of home. My father and mother led a simpler life. One of tending the land and the love of the hearth. Not wealthy but happy with what they did have. A couple with gentry birth that gave up the city to pursue a country life.

"I've been meaning to get a piece for above the fireplace commissioned. I know not of what yet, perhaps a landscape. What do you think?" Luke said from behind me.

I turned to find him setting down a tea service and Simon attacking the biscuits that were laid out. I smiled at the boy's enthusiasm.

"I think you should commission a landscape. Perhaps, a calm sea? Those always bring such reflections of serenity," I replied.

"That could be useful indeed. Serenity is much needed," he replied.

"Simon, do take care, you don't want to give yourself a stomach ache," I chided.

He looked up at me with guilty eyes. I couldn't help but soften his expression.

"Yes, miss. They are quite tasty, sir. Thank you ever so much," Simon said.

Simon excused himself and set about tidying up.

"What is he doing?" Luke asked, puzzled.

"Ask him." I suggested.

"Young man, you do not need to clean. You are my guest," Luke said.

"That's alright, sir. You've been needing to talk to the miss, and I am needing to be useful. 'Tis no bother," he said.

"I thank you then. I shall reward you for your services when you are finished," Luke replied.

Simon's eyes lit up, and he returned to his task with gusto.

"Now then, let us have it. What did you find out?"

"I would rather you divulged any news from Doctor Cannish first. It might soften the blow to what I must tell you," I said.

He eyed me suspiciously, then nodded.

"Have it your way, though it is quite a strange one, I admit. Doctor Cannish did in fact find something of use. It was quite queer and altogether unsettling. A cross had been burned upon the bottom of each of the children's left heels. He of course looked back at Gwennie's and found a very faint one there as well. So faint he quite overlooked it for just another scratch," Luke said.

"A cross? Did it have any telling markings?" I said, searching his eyes for insight.

"It did have the burning heart where the cross intersects. I don't think that is very common, but I cannot say for sure," Luke responded.

"I must confess something now, and you should not get mad at me, as your clue does coincide with my line of thinking," I said.

"You are scaring me, Miss Annabelle. Out with it," he said.

"I have had Father Gaverty followed. Before you scold me, let me tell you what has occurred. You remember the carriage that abducted poor Sadie, yes?" I asked.

He nodded, and a stern look clouded his face.

"The carriage had a crucifix hanging from the windows and the 'D' emblem on the wheels. It led me to the idea that only an older, highly ranked family would still use such a transport. A whim of the wealthy. Lord Daven fits the description quite nicely," I implied.

"Oh, please tell me you didn't. You are batting at a bee's nest," Luke scolded.

"Let me finish, Luke!" I retorted.

"Very well, although I doubt it will get much better," he said, folding his arms across his chest.

He really could be quite infuriating when he put his mind to it.

"As I was saying, I requested the use of some of Lord Thetford's prototype aerial devices. Do you remember the drawings at tea?" I waited for him to nod before continuing on. "I had him outfit a couple with an optical recorder so we could get a bird's eye view without Lord Daven knowing. I also didn't want anyone to be at the location for fear of him becoming excessively mad, as we know him to do."

Luke scoffed at that. "An ocular lens like the one Lord Thetford used to spy on you by inserting it in that beastie of yours? I suppose you always did make something positive come out of such rakish behavior," he said. Luke's face betrayed him, with his jealousy evident.

"I thought you had moved past such pettiness? Besides, it was a grand invention if put toward the correct application, no?" I reasoned.

Luke nodded. I waited for a breath and then continued.

"We captured a carriage in the motor park that had all the descriptions that the children we met below the bridge gave us. Also, unbeknownst to us, Father Gaverty was paying a visit to Lord Daven. Adam and Marcie were the children I had keeping an eye on the priest, and they hid within the motor park when he went in. Adam confirmed it was the same carriage that had taken Sadie," I said.

"Are you serious? What would he want with a sprite like that? This is getting into dangerous waters," Luke said.

"That's not even the most insane part of the story," I said. "While they were there, Adam saw Mr. Fieldworth, the beadle from Tapers Grove, arrive with a load of parcels. He did not enter the main house but went round back to a separate building. Lady Daven was seen from our aerial view in the greenhouse, so they were not quite sure what or who was in that back building. The children dared not attempt to sneak around longer. And who do you think was with the beadle? You'll never guess so I'll tell you. Sadie was helping carry the packages!" I exclaimed.

Chapter 29- Taking to Task

I find that neglect is created by one's own making- both to oneself and to others. Neither are acceptable.

Luke was just as confused as I by the turn of events. He did not like having to admit I had been correct in suspecting the priest. We did not know what capacity or what exactly was happening. We only knew that some of the people we suspected were meeting together. The only one not in attendance was Mrs. Squires. I didn't know if Sadie would have returned by the time we arrived, but I still planned on visiting the orphanage today. Luke agreed that he would attend me, and we set out for the Boroughs not long after.

Constable Weston dressed in his uniform for the visit, and I wore a very plain dress and long coat. I opted for a brown bonnet with rivets along the seam. I kept my bracer on my right arm and tied the charm Whitmore gave me around my other wrist. I would need to come up with a more permanent attachment for it soon. We decided to take the train to the station in the Boroughs that Nathan and I had visited when we returned from the last trip. It wasn't as stuffy or crowded, but the workday was not nearly over. We sat quietly, watching the city turn from shiny to dusty in a slow progression of streets. I saw a few of Miro's water purification tanks in the middle, but toward the end of the track there were none.

We climbed onto the platform and moved down the stairs to the street. People were wandering about aimlessly. I couldn't help but think they could be doing some small part to make it better. It is always easier from the outside looking in, so I focused on my current task.

Luke and I reached the orphanage just before tea time. I could tell that the woman was in as her shrill directives could be heard from the street. Several children loitered on the steps and looked at us as possible marks. I shook my head at them and they scurried up the stairs and into the front hall to announce visitors.

"Who is it? I don't have any appointments today. I had made sure of it," Mrs. Squires screeched.

"Nawt sure, Missus. Just some lady and a bobbie. You must be in for it now," said a scrawny brown haired boy.

"Oh, why didn't you say that first! I will deal with you later," she promised.

We heard her heavy booted steps as she came out of the parlor to meet us. She curtsied sweetly to Luke and then looked at me, surprise filling her eyes.

"Miss Sweeting? What is the meaning of this? I would hope that our little misunderstanding the other day would be water under the bridge. Do you mean to have me arrested then?" Miss Squires said, aghast.

"No, nothing of the sort Mrs. Squires. We are on orphanage business. You see, I have been talking to Father Gaverty," I paused.

I watched for the name to give some indication of recognition, and I was not disappointed. A flash of the eyes was all I needed to know.

"I attend his church you see, and had inquired about what was the best way to help the wee ones in such desolate circumstances. He had told me about another foundling hospital, but I felt drawn to yours, " I said.

"Oh, well, that is very kind of you, miss. We are always welcome to contributions of any kind to help get these children into good homes," she replied.

"I was wondering about one girl in particular. She has been quite helpful to my cousin's kitchen staff lately, but then I heard she had returned here. Is Sadie here by chance? I thought of offering her a few side jobs to help her to gain some references."

"Awe, you don't want nothing to do with that one, miss. A lost cause I would say," she said with her eyes darting from me to Luke. "She's been assigned to help with the beadle as of late. But my Abby might be a good candidate if you need someone," Mrs. Squires said.

"It is quite strange that she would leave in such haste. My servant Lily was quite concerned you see. If she is here can you call her down just so we can set her mind at ease. I know they had grown quite fond of each other in such a short acquaintance," I pressed.

"She's not here," she said abruptly.

I wouldn't let her squirm out of the inquiry that easily.

"Do you know when she will return, we can come back then?" I continued.

"As I said, she is working with Mr. Fieldworth. I am not sure when or if she will ever return. To own the truth, she has been a plague on me since her arrival six months ago," Mrs. Squires said with venom.

"Wait a moment, you are saying that Sadie has only been with your orphanage for six months?" Luke said, looking at the woman suspiciously.

"Indeed sir, and what's stranger is that Mr. Fieldworth himself was the one who brought her here. It is quite queer that he just up and takes her back again," she confided.

"Mrs. Squires, I must ask you a very important question, and you can choose not to answer. However, if you do answer it would clear you of all suspicion on a case we are currently working on," Luke said bluntly.

I looked at him in shock. He was going head first, a direction I have never seen him take. Always calculated, reserved, and patient in his pursuit for an answer.

"I'm listening," Mrs. Squires replied cautiously.

"We have been following the path of several parcels that have in their containment unsavory items. You know of what I speak?" Luke said.

She nods. Her face paling at the words.

"We also know that you are having parcels delivered back and forth with the beadle, yes?" Luke asked.

"I am," she said.

"Can you tell me what you are sending to him and why?" Luke demanded.

"I have done some things, sir, that I am not proud of. This is a hard world to live in and even harder with so many mouths to feed. An opportunity arose that seemed innocent enough. I fear that if I tell you what I know, I will end up like those poor children in Tapers Grove," she whispered.

We all looked at the door as Byron burst into the room and pointed his small determined finger at Mrs. Squires' nose.

"I knew you were an evil bitty, but you better tell them what they needs to know or I will take you out myself, I swears it. To think how Gwennie followed you about, saying you weren't so bad. Lot of good it done her," Byron said, accusingly.

"Okay, okay. I have done nothing wrong beside causing a distraction is all. That is what I was to do. The parcels are empty, you see? Some might be filled with old rags. The ones I've been sending anyway. I've heard stories about the other ones though. Whatever is happening you best see the beadle," she said through teary eyes.

"Who hired you to send empty packages using the children?" I asked.

"Mr. Fieldworth said the man that hired us was quite imposing. He never gave me a name, and I never met him," Mrs. Squires admitted.

A familiar screech from outside drew my attention away from the conversation. I left the room and went to look outside. Purgatorio was circling the dark alley. He saw me and dove down into the darkness. Whatever he had found he wanted me to see it.

I dashed toward the alley and stopped abruptly to give my eyes a few moments to adjust to the darkness. Walking slowly I couldn't help but notice my breathing sounded louder. Purgatorio would never knowingly put me at risk. I reminded myself of that and relaxed a little more, heading deeper into the alley. Squinting I could make out the red eyes of Purgy and a tall figure standing next to him. It was definitely not a child.

"Purgatorio, you aren't mad at me, are you?" I joked, uneasily.

He chuffed in the dark as I walked closer.

"Nothing to fret about Miss Sweeting. Just an old friend to see you," a man said from the shadows.

It took me a moment to recognize the voice, but when I did, I raced closer the last few steps.

"Whitmore! Where have you been? We've been scouring the city for you everywhere," I said.

"Yes, I am aware. The time was not right, my dear. I didn't know what you needed to know until now. I have found the missing link as it were. A Mr. Hillard is the man you seek," he said.

"Mr. Hillard? I've never heard of him!"

Chapter 30- Turning the Tide

Love makes us do crazy things. A heart in pain is far more dangerous than any common criminal could be.

"Pray tell, who is Mr. Hillard and how does he matter to my current investigation, Whitmore?" I asked.

The idea of another potential suspect in this mystery had my head spinning. It was bad enough with the ones I was already chasing.

"I don't know much but that he was ferried into the city in the dead of night by Lord Daven seven months ago," Whitmore whispered. "He's been seen at the apothecary a few times, but other than that nothing. I knew it would be of interest to you, but I had the hardest time discovering his name from the lass at the shop. She said he gave her the creeps, even more than I, apparently," he chuckled.

"Why do you think he has involvement in my investigation?"

"His association with Lord Daven, of course. I couldn't very well accuse the gentry of such goings on, but you, my dear, are a steam engine plowing down the track. A steady flame when all else would flicker in the face of such power," he said.

"Why didn't you just tell me he was whom you suspected from the start?" I said, irritation seeping through my words.

"What if I was wrong, what if you found a more reasonable culprit?. Nay, I couldn't cloud your findings with my own. I'm sorry I couldn't find the information in time to help those wee ones, but I am not allowed in society as you are. There are places I simply can not go," he said.

"ANNABELLE! ANNABELLE SWEETING, WHERE ARE YOU?"

I looked back down the alley where Luke's voice boomed, frantically searching for me.

"One more thing before you dash, Miss Sweeting. From what I understand Doctor Cannish has some prior entanglement with Mr. Hillard. The lass at the Apothecary shop said they had both happened to be in there at the same time and Doctor Cannish was not at all happy to see Mr. Hillard. He was quite rude and after telling him he should not be in such a shop he gave him the cut direct," Whitmore said. "Your friend is growing impatient, time for me to go."

He climbed the steel ladder on the opposite building's exterior and moved up toward the roof. His leather long coat flapped in the breeze.

"Do tell those children that we spoke, they were quite determined to pull me by my beard if I didn't do so," he winked.

"Wait, what do you know of Sadie?" I yelled after him.

He peered over the edge of the building. His white beard catching the fading sun.

"Don't trust the coggery, miss. No matter how cunning the delivery," he replied, cryptically.

Whitmore tipped his leather hat and disappeared onto the roof.

"MISS ANNABELLE SWEETING!"

"Here, Weston. I am here," I shouted back down the alley.

I could see his form blocking the light from the entrance and walked hastily towards it. Purgatorio took flight above me, and we reached the street in moments.

"My God, Belle! You scared me half to death. What were you doing down there?" Luke said, searching my person for any sign of injury.

"Collecting information. I am sorry I worried you, but when

Purgatorio signaled me, I felt it best to hurry," I explained. I could tell my reasoning didn't do anything to ease his concern.

Purgatorio chuffed at me from the ground by my feet. Then stole a sly look at Luke.

"So what did the little beastie have to show you in an almost completely dark alley where who knows what could be lying in wait for you?" Luke complained.

He took his hat off and raked a hand through his hair. A ragged breath escaped him, and he returned his hat to his head. I put my hand on his arm and looked into his eyes with remorse for having scared him in such a manner.

"It was One-Eyed Whitmore, and he has a lead for us," I replied softly.

I deliberately ignored his other comments and progressed into relaying what Whitmore had divulged. Purgatorio raised his tail in response to some sound behind us and we stopped our conversation to see what he detected.

"Come out, whomever you may be!" Luke commanded.

There was a moment where nothing occurred then a very embarrassed Byron appeared from behind the stair railing of the orphanage.

"That thing of yours has some good ears, miss. Rarely have I been sussed out," he said solemnly.

"Well, it serves you right for eavesdropping. Why not just come out and speak with us? We are, after all, trying to solve what happened to your sister, are we not?" I scolded.

"I suppose it's just in my nature. I won't do it again. Not to yous anyway. So you goin' after this Mr. H character then?" Byron asked.

I turned to Luke and searched his face. Convinced we were past the initial hurdle of concern I continued.

"First, we must speak to Doctor Cannish, I think that is something that needs to be done in haste. There is something not quite connecting. I fear we have overlooked a crucial element," I said.

"I agree with you on this. Byron, will you be okay staying here?" Luke looked at the tough little boy for confirmation. Byron rubbed the toe of his boot in the dirt and looked at the ground.

"Yeah, I'll be fine. Mrs. Squires and I have come to an agreement. I am not sure how long the truce will last, but I should be okay," he said bravely.

"Nonsense. Grab your things, Byron. I have need of you, if you can prove yourself trustworthy. And beyond that we shall see," I said.

The young man's eyes shone brightly at my proclamation, and he ran quickly to collect his belongings before I could change my mind.

"Miss Annabelle, what do you mean to do with the boy?" Luke questioned.

"There is an event I will need him to prepare for, and if he does as well as I suspect, I know a Lord in need of some servants. He is mighty young, but I daresay enthusiastic. Who could ask for more when one needs an apprentice?" I said.

"That is quite generous of you, indeed. I am not sure why I am still surprised. You are always making the best of unsavory situations," he winked.

"Thank you for the compliment," I smiled back.

The tension from the alleyway seemed to ease.

Hurried steps on the stairs made us turn our heads. Byron raced down with a blanket full of what must be his belongings.

"Oh good, you didn't leave," he said, trying to catch his breath.

"Don't be absurd," I replied.

"Miss, this ain't the first time someone's told me to grab my stuff only to be gone when I returned. Ain't no slight against you, but I'd be lying if I said I wasn't fearful of it happening again," he admitted.

I patted his shoulder as he remained with his hands on his knees gulping in air. Taking his chin in my hand, I lifted his face to meet my gaze.

"I am sorry that happened to you, but you can trust in my word. If you are honest, true, and can follow instructions, then you shan't be coming back to this place again. Deal?" I declared.

"Yes, miss, I promise! Oh, how I wish Gwennie was here. You would've surely helped her too, I just know it!" Bryon exclaimed.

I put my hand to my heart and took a step back. The emotion overwhelmed me, I needed a moment to steady myself. Luke's eyes shone with pride.

"I dare say you are right about our Miss Annabelle. Now, let's get to the train before it gets too full," Luke said.

I followed them in a daze to the station, and once there, was directed to a seat by the window. Purgatorio leaped into my lap making sure to keep his barbed tail spikes retracted so he wouldn't prick me by mistake. Byron sat across from me and watched as I fiddled with the manticore's whiskers. My finger brushed along the dents he received from the stones that hit him in Tapers Grove. Luke stood and held onto a pole above us, staring out the window. His eyes darted back and forth, looking for some unknown foe. I tugged on his sleeve, and he looked down.

"Sit a while. We have plenty to worry about without you looking for more villains to battle," I teased.

He smiled at me and sat down in the spot I made for him.

"I was just thinking about buttons," he said.

"Truly? That is never a thought I would guess," I said.

"Well, mainly your buttons," he said.

I raised an arched eyebrow at him, and he sputtered on.

"I meant the ones you take to every scene. You place them next to things you think are important. Such a simple item, but when they are not there it is quite striking. They are quite missed, you see?" he said.

He bit his bottom lip and pierced me with an intense gaze. I didn't know where this conversation was leading, but butterflies started to flutter in my stomach.

"I find that I do not wish you to work with anyone else. I might have been mistaken in my assessment of your contributions. I fear I let my ego outrank my sense and your wishes. What I said and wrote was deplorable. Please don't work with Constable Quincy. Let me work at redemption in some way," he said.

My mouth hung open. It was completely unladylike, and I daresay unattractive, but the moment called for it. I didn't say anything for a few minutes but stared at his anxious, waiting eyes. Finally, I pulled an object from my pocket and asked him to open his hand. Luke quickly complied. I placed a bright red button in the center of his palm and closed his fingers over it.

"This is so you never forget how the smallest of things can have the biggest of impacts, even words. If you truly mean what you say, we can meet with Chief Inspector Farthing when this case is concluded. I would rather not work with any other partner," I smiled.

He took my hand before I could pull it back and placed a kiss on my knuckles. Byron started to giggle. I blushed.

"You just wait until it happens to you, young man. See who will be laughing then," Luke admonished.

Byron gave him a horrified look, and we all laughed. We spent the rest of the train ride in pleasant conversation about the upcoming nuptials of Miss Whitney Cosswald. I laughed as Luke reported that his aunt had heard they would be using their pug as the ring bearer. It was all to be a glorious spectacle, and I was quite looking forward to the distraction. I couldn't wait to see what else the family had in store.

Chapter 31- Wedding Bells

"Happiness in marriage is entirely a matter of chance, you know," Charlotte Lucas- Pride and Prejudice

We were unable to meet with Doctor Cannish before the end of the week. He was called out to a village just outside London and would not be back until the following Tuesday. An illness had swept the town, and he needed to make sure that the sickness was no longer spreading. I didn't know the risks he took for his profession were so strenuous. I only knew the doctor on a superficial level. The talk we had at Claymore's was a rarity, and I felt I had somehow overlooked this aspect of our relationship. Clearly, there was much more to know.

Jaime had been buzzing around the house, barely containing his excitement for the wedding we were to attend. I wondered at his enthusiasm. Was it for the prospect of everyone being dressed in their finery, or was it for the final detachment from one of the most persistent of his admirers? One could hardly tell. One thing was for certain, I had never witnessed a person try on so many variations of dress as my cousin in the last several days.

Although I did look forward to the festivities, I also felt a nagging disapproval from my conscience for not attending to the investigation more diligently. To be consumed by it, however, wouldn't do myself or anyone else any good. It was wisest, as my cousin implored, to take advantage of such an event. It not only had the advantage of renewing my social connections but also revitalizing the reasons for which I fought for justice in the first place. If a show of love's undying devotion could not reignite the fire for which one endeavored such dreary tasks, I was not sure what could.

I decided to dress in lavender with silver trimming. My corset had a silver paisley pattern woven into it and heart-shaped latches down the front. I wore a full skirt with silver lace trimming on the bottom. My boots were dove grey with silver buckles and toe caps. I wore the beautiful hairpin Nathan had gifted me. It brought warring emotions from the memories associated with it to the forefront of my mind. That seemed to be the way of things, though, a mixture of good and bad.

I put the finishing touches on my appearance and went to the looking glass for one last glance. I pinched my cheeks to bring a bit more color to them and smiled. Purgatorio made a slightly annoyed huff from the corner, and I turned to see him stretching.

"I can't very well have you scaring the daylights out of the doggie ring bearer, you know? It would surely cause a scene, and I daresay reflect poorly on Jaime and I," I said.

Purgy turned his back on me and flopped down into his cushion. I didn't know a mechanical beast could brood, but that was the only word for what was occurring. It took quite a bit of self-restraint not to laugh.

"I shall tell you all the boring details upon my return," I promised.

I opened my bed chamber door and left to find Jaime. We would need to leave within the hour if we were to arrive at an appropriate time. I directed Stewart to have the motor ready, I couldn't take the chance that Jaime would be delayed and forget to do so. I chuckled at the image of the state of his dressing area with cast-off attire.

I held vigil in the library while I waited for him. I walked along the shelves and traced my fingers across the spines of the much-loved volumes. Some were of faraway places, while others were about our greatest military minds. It had been several weeks since I took the opportunity to look at such a tome, and I made a note to do so soon. The thought of a warm fire, a good cuppa, and an epic adventure had me yearning to miss the day's events completely.

Before I could fake an illness to do just that, Jaime entered the room. "There you are and how well you look! I must compliment you on your choice," he said.

"Thank you, Jaime. I do so love the color. I see that you have gone with the emerald green waistcoat. It is quite vibrant and perfectly you. Ah, and just one feather in your hat. You are subdued today," I jested.

"Yes, well I can't very well upstage the bride, now can I? Besides, I wouldn't want her to suddenly see me in all my glory and call off the wedding in pursuit of me," Jaime quipped.

I laughed unapologetically at that. He truly was a riot sometimes.

Now then, Belle, I think your attire does have one flaw," he said.

I looked down at my skirt, making sure no thread was out of place. I touched my hair to verify no tendrils had fallen from their pins. I looked at him in question as I couldn't find the fault he spotted.

"What pray is wrong?" I asked.

"Nothing wrong, my dear, simply missing," he replied.

Jaime then produced a beautiful, hammered silver bracelet that swirled in spiral formations in opposite directions. In the middle of the twin spirals were tiny amethyst stones. It sparkled brilliantly in the firelight, and I gasped as the present before me.

"Jaime, it is beautiful! Whatever did I do to deserve such a cousin as you?"

He helped me put it on my left wrist, and I turned it back and forth in awe.

"You like it then?" he asked, nervously.

"I adore it, and it matches the hairpin Nathan gave me. Thank you so much!"

Jaime's smile broadened so widely I could see one dimple on his left cheek.

"Yes, I had that in mind," he replied. "Now let us be off and see what outlandish decorations the Cosswalds have in store for us. Oh, did I mention the wedding is at St. Alfege Church?"

My head snapped in response to his words.

"Are you serious? Why had you not said this before? Is Father Gaverty presiding?" I interrogated.

"Why the shock, Belle? It is one of the most popular churches in town, and I thought you had read the invitation? Of course Father Gaverty will be performing the ceremony, could you imagine anyone else at the front of that church?" he jested.

I shook my head and stood quietly while the shock washed over me.

"Well, let us be off then, shall we?" Jaime said.

I nodded and let him lead me out of the library to where the servants waited with our coats and gloves. I felt wooden. How was I to enjoy the festivities now with the very man I suspected of having a hand in hurting innocent children presided over the altar? It would truly be a wonder indeed.

The trip across town was quick and not much conversation was had. I was too busy thinking about all that had occurred the past several weeks to be good company. We entered the church and saw every one of our acquaintances already in attendance. Lady Whipley and Luke were on the bride's side, sitting along with another gentleman I didn't know. A few pews in front of them were the Bergenhalts and Lord Thetford. Lord Daven was seated on the groom's side, which I thought was quite strange. Lady Cosswald was fussing over her dress and whispering to Lord Cosswald as each new arrival entered. It was a triumph for her to have most of polite society in attendance.

I looked around but did not see the rumored pug. I hoped they would produce one, otherwise Purgatorio would surely be upset with me for not bringing him along. The church was decorated with beautiful adornments of gold and blue. Ribbons and flowers were strung along the interior aisle leading to the altar. There the proud priest surveyed his flock. His eyes watched as the guest made ready to see the newest couple become husband and wife. His eyes stopped at me, and I realized I had been shamelessly staring. I offered a half-hearted smile and followed my cousin to find a seat.

We claimed a couple of spots on the bench behind Luke and his aunt and offered our greetings. Luke bowed over my hand and complimented me on my attire. Jaime did the same to Lady Whipley, and I couldn't help but see the symmetry in the act. We took our seats, as everyone else did, and waited for the ceremony to begin.

I felt a sudden tingle on my neck as the tiny hairs there gave me a warning. I could feel someone's eyes upon me and sought out the person from whence the feeling arose. I looked in front and behind me, then to the groom's side. I had almost chalked it up to my imagination when a pair of penetrating eyes and a most unkind scowl met my view- Lord Daven. I shivered at the unnerving man and wished he was not in attendance. Could he not be civil even at such an event?

A cough in front of me created the distraction I needed, and the lord's eyes moved to where Luke sat. I could make out his profile, and he stared back at Lord Daven in challenge. I looked back to see Lord Daven lift the corner of his mouth in mirth and turn to face the front. The act was dismissive, but I felt a small sense of victory was obtained by Luke. I was thankful for it.

The quartet was set up high in the balcony of the church and began to play. All eyes turned to the back of the room where the procession of bridesmaids and groomsmen entered, making their way down the aisle. The dresses were a shimmery baby blue, and I couldn't help but be impressed with their styling. While Lady Whipley was given credit, I am sure Miss Bethany had a hand in picking the fabric. She was the Cosswald sisters' favorite seamstress after all. Jaime leaned over the front of the pew and started whispering to Lady Whipley. A few hand gestures were made toward the dresses before a shush made them return to propriety.

I giggled to myself, and Luke smiled back at me conspiratorially. There was a shuffling, and we turned once more to the back, where a poor maid was trying helplessly to reign in a most rambunctious pug with a box attached to his neck. The little dog snorted, most unseemly, and several stifled giggles could be heard throughout the church as the guests tried to contain their amusement. The maid finally was able to tempt the dog with a morsel from her pocket and led it towards the front of the church. The time had come, and the crowd stood as the beautiful bride entered with her father. Her face shone brilliantly with joy, and her dress was immaculately styled with lace and pearl bead detailing. The light streamed through the stained-glass windows and made the scene even more magical. She truly was blessed on her day.

She walked slowly, keeping her eyes forward, nothing but her future husband in her sights. This was most certainly a love match on her part, and I felt her happiness. Whatever horrible things happened in the world, this made living worth it. I found myself stealing a glance at Luke. His deep brown eyes gazed back, and I lost my breath for a moment at their intensity. There was a longing in both of us, I think, to have such happiness. Whether it be fear or stubbornness that kept us from it was still to be answered.

We broke eye contact and returned our attention to Father Gaverty as he began speaking. Words of responsibility to God and each other were laced with moments of tenderness as the couple held hands. Cara Cosswald, the maid of honor, tried to stifle a few tears as she watched her sister marry before her. The couple said their vows and made tender promises in front of God and the room. Applause broke out as they filed down the aisle to the open church doors. The bells began to chime, and it seemed like nothing could get in the way of such joy.

Chapter 32- Revealing Reception

In the shadows of bliss lurk the melancholy, hoping to pull others down with them. Be steadfast in your joy; it is your greatest weapon.

The bells tolled high in their tower as the wedding ceremony concluded. The happy couple raced down the steps while flower petals were thrown above them. The wiggling pug could barely contain itself as its master rushed past him. The maid's face turned red as she held onto the manic thing for dear life. I laughed heartily at the sight, and Jaime joined me. The sun was shining down on us as we made our way to the Cosswald home for the celebratory banquet. Jaime was handing over his motor to the valet. Before he could walk around the front, where I waited in line at the entrance, a strong hand grasped my elbow and turned me toward them. I looked up into the barely contained wrath of one Lord Daven.

"Miss Sweeting, I am surprised to see you here. I would not think the Cosswald family would associate with one whom so easily spreads slander about. They seem the highest of the Christian community," he clamored.

"Lord Daven, it is nice to see you out on this festive day," I said, my voice dripping with sarcasm. "The Cosswald's are a most respectable family. As to my being here, I am fortunate to claim the bride and her sister as acquaintances. Fortunately, I fear that your assessment of my character is not felt by all. I can see this disappoints you, but I am sure you will find ample merriment inside. Now, if you will please unhand me I think it best if we part ways," I replied.

I steadied my breathing and turned to move away from him, but his grasp grew tighter. I winced at the contact. He leaned in closer to my face, seething. His voice was menacingly low when next he spoke.

"Whatever game you are playing at, you will lose, Miss Sweeting. Whatever you think you know, forget it. This is beyond you. It will not end well for you, if you continue. And stay away from Sadie," he warned.

"Is there a problem here?" Jaime joined me from behind and looked pointedly at Lord Daven's hand still holding my elbow. I looked around us as the other partygoers moved away from the scene that was unfolding. I flushed at the possible gossip rag headlines that this little production would produce.

"And if there is a problem? What is a little fop like you going to do, wave your ridiculous feathers at me?" Lord Daven sneered at my cousin with disdain. I heard a few gasps behind me, but I couldn't turn to see as I was still stuck in his stony clutch.

Then something I thought I never would witness again occurred. Jaime got livid. His whole body changed from nonchalant charisma to the embodiment of an entitled "ton" member. The relaxed posture morphed into a ridged, tall stance, and his eyes turned steely. He swiftly took hold of Lord Daven's middle finger on the offending appendage, lifted it, and twisted. A look of surprise and then pain flashed across the arrogant lord's face. Jaime grabbed my waist with his other arm and guided me behind him, never taking his gaze from his adversary.

He smiled deceivingly at Lord Daven. His voice was deceptively quiet.

"You. Will. Not. Touch. Her. Again." Each word was emphasized with another turn on the lord's finger. Lord Daven almost bent to the pressure but glared with hatred instead.

"Understood?" Jaime waited until Lord Daven nodded before releasing him.

I peered over Jaime's shoulder, watching as Daven's face grew flushed and his fist balled up at his side. His intention was clear. Before he could cock an arm back any further, Luke appeared. He came up behind Lord Daven and clasped him around the shoulders, pinning his arm down in the process. It made them appear, for anyone watching, to be the best of mates. The smile on Luke's face didn't quite reach his eyes, however.

"Lord Daven, how good of you to come to such happy tidings! I wish Lady Daven was well enough to attend. My aunt was telling me of how she loved such events so fervently! How does she get on, if you don't mind me asking?" Luke inquired, jovially.

Taken aback, Lord Daven turned to Luke and replied to the niceties as society dictated. Luke directed him to look at the decorations above the doorway, and with his other hand, motioned us to move on. Several stares and whispers followed us in, but we were saved from any more communication from the horrid man, for the moment. I could only hope the humiliating spectacle would not circulate to the entire wedding party, as we would not wish to dampen their festivities. Once we were quite clear of the main entrance and past the ballroom area, I took Jaime by both hands and drug him to an empty hallway.

"I can scarcely believe what we just encountered, cousin! And you were so bold and uncompromising. It was truly something! I daresay I haven't seen that intensity since your father's passing," I blurted out.

Jaime hauled me into a hug. It was so tight I could feel the breath of relief he expelled.

"Dear, only protecting you could cause me to rise to such emotion again. I do not like the feelings that the man provoked from me. He thought himself untouchable, I merely reminded him that he was wrong. I fear we will pay for this in future, but it was worth it. How dare he be so forward and grab a lady in full view of everyone! Let me see your arm," he demanded.

I pulled back from our embrace and showed him the reddened skin on my left elbow. I gasped as I noticed my bracelet was missing.

"What is wrong, Belle?"

"The bracelet you gave me, it is gone!"

"If that cad took it I will show him what I can do to his other fingers with a pair of shears," Jaime said.

"There you two are! Miss Annabelle, I found this on the ground near the entrance. I believe this is what you seek," Luke said as he strode toward us. "Mr. Nethersby, you took quite the gamble out there," he said.

"Yes, well did you see what he did to our girl here?" Jamie huffed.

Jaime gently took my hand and raised my now bruising arm to the light.

"If you hadn't of interfered I had half a mind to let him swing and then show him what for," Jaime said, enraged.

"He did this?" Luke growled.

I nodded and pulled my arm away in a sheltering motion.

"I merely wanted to avoid a scene. Had I known he had already assaulted you, I would have knocked in his teeth myself," he continued.

"Luke, he said something, about the case. He said I needed to forget what I thought I knew and that it was beyond me. He also warned me away from Sadie. I had not made a connection between them before now. I wonder how he could have known I was asking after her. He also said that…. that it wouldn't end well if I continued. My intuition tells me that he doesn't mean a slap on the wrist by society either," I said.

"He openly threatened you? This is beyond reproach. I should haul him in right now," Luke said.

"No, don't you see? We are close. The only time we get threats is when we are getting close to a secret someone doesn't want us to find. Let him alone. The way to best him is to take him down at the knees. Keep digging, until the secrets start pouring out," I smiled.

"Cousin, dearest, you look quite deranged at this moment. Perhaps we should skip the party?" Jaime said with mock concern.

I swatted his arm, and he laughed.

"No, Jaime," I said. Turning to Luke, I continued, "We need a night of levity, don't we Luke? If we are to battle monsters in the morning," I grinned.

"Mr. Nethersby, your cousin is quite right. Let us all have a pleasant evening before the hunting party starts tomorrow," Luke smiled.

"Call out the hounds, I dare say your prey is going to be a tricky conquest indeed!" Jaime joined in our unhinged mirth.

I took the arm of each man, and we entered the ballroom. Tonight would not be ruined by one abrasive lord. It proved to open a confidence inside my mind. I knew without a doubt I was on to something.

Chapter 33- Polite Society

I've heard that a tree makes no sound when it falls in the forest if no one is around to hear it. Can it also be said that the stars do not shine brightly for those who never look up?

The ballroom teemed with conversation as we entered from the side door. Everyone was excited for the season to start, and this was the most exquisite setting for the opening event. Lady Cosswald could hardly contain her glee as she glided across the floor, engaging with all her guests.

The bride and groom took the center of the room and bowed to each other. A flurry of violin notes pierced the air, and a beautiful melody took hold as the couple started to dance. I felt the moment in my heart, and a weight lifted from me as I watched their happiness in motion.

I felt a brush along my fingertips and found Luke's hand sliding into mine. Hidden from view, our fingers interlaced as we watched the remainder of the dance unfold before us. I felt my pulse race and my face flush. I didn't want to let go when the song ended, but I knew I must. We had already caused enough talk for one evening.

The couple was announced to applause before the floor was opened up for all couples to dance. Besides a few whispers as we passed by the ladies around the perimeter of the room, no other moments of concern arose. I danced nearly every dance, several with the constable. Jaime even danced with Miss Cara Cosswald. She was all a flutter as they glided across the floor. Jaime winked at me as they passed, and I couldn't help but laugh. We enjoyed a delicious meal, and Lady Bergenhalt was able to announce her party theme after the feast, to the joy of all attending. I felt overwhelming pride at the part that I was able to contribute to her upcoming ball. The fact that she would include the children had me more than overjoyed.

I hadn't seen Lord Daven the rest of the night after our scuffle. I wondered if he had left or merely went to the gambling room, as all unwilling dance partners did. I did see Father Gaverty at dinner, but he left shortly after. I was glad for it. I needed this evening to be a renewal of sorts. I wished that Nathan and Purgatorio could be here to enjoy the atmosphere.

Jaime and I took our leave and waited for our motor to be brought around. I looked up as the stars twinkled above me. Not quite as brilliant as they would be without the gaslights burning, but still shining bright nonetheless. I inhaled a breath of the cool evening air, and a memory surfaced of the night by the docks when Nate and I discovered Gwennie. The pocked-face man that Nathan had met with there had almost completely fled my mind. I wondered why he would reappear in my thoughts now. Questions started to assault my subconscious. Why was Gwennie's body at the docks, but all others were in the Boroughs? Why were they marked? The marking had to mean something. I just couldn't fathom what.

I was pulled from these introspections by a gentle touch on my right shoulder. I turned to find Luke standing behind me and smiled. His features warmed, and he took my hand in his and kissed it lightly.

"I fear I forgot to tell you how radiant you looked tonight, Miss Belle. Let me take the moment now to do so," he said.

His emotions were easy to read, and I couldn't help but wonder where this man had been for the past few months. It was good to see him reemerging.

"What about me, I was looking quite dashing too, wouldn't you say?" Jaime wedged in between us and waited for Luke's reply. A hearty laugh escaped the constable's lips, and he nodded in earnest.

"I must agree, Mr. Nethersby. Your fashion compares to no other. It's a wonder anyone else tries," Luke smirked.

"Well, I suppose that will do. You and your aunt were quite well outfitted also. Although one of these days I will get her to add a feather or two. Now I will stop interrupting and let you say your goodnights. Our motor is coming up next so do make haste, Belle," he said with a grin.

I swatted him with my fan, and he turned away laughing.

"Well, Mr. Weston, shall we meet again tomorrow to forge ahead on this most infuriating investigation?" I started.

"Miss Sweeting, I believe you were correct earlier. I fear we did learn a lot tonight about the illustrious Lord Daven. I also suspect that I may have been too harsh in the Greenwich Village case. Perhaps it was not as open and shut as we suspected. I should have known better than to oppose your intuition. However much trouble it seems to lead you in," he admitted.

I gawked at him in disbelief. Did I hear that right? I had to snap my gaping mouth closed. It made quite an unladylike sound, and Luke laughed.

"I am obviously astonished by your declaration. I thought you were set against my views on the case. But I must admit, I did go charging in like a bull. I have learned a few things this past month on patience. I guess I can thank you for that, although I didn't like the lesson at all," I conceded.

"Yes, well we both were taught some hard-fought lessons. I fear it almost created an irreparable rift between us, but I am glad to see that

I was wrong on that point as well. Let us start fresh tomorrow, yes?" Luke asked, hopefully.

I nodded and turned to leave. Luke grabbed my hand and spun me back toward him.

"One more thing, perhaps you should check your notes before we meet again. I think it best we have all the things we discovered fresh in our minds, don't you?" Luke said, almost insistently.

I watched as his lips kissed the top of my hand again, his eyes never leaving mine. The flecks of gold and hazel in his gaze flickered with intensity. I felt the heat rush to my cheeks and nodded wordlessly. I turned in a daze and was guided into the passenger side of Jaime's motor. Besides the tenderness and throbbing of my left elbow, tonight was the perfect night.

Chapter 34- Journal Entry

When we are overtaken by an emotion, it leads to mistakes and uncharac-teristic behavior; be it love or fear, and most certainly anger.

The ride home was a blur of steam and flickering lights. Jaime was prattling on about so and so's garments and embellishments, but I scarcely heard two words together. Later I would feel badly, but right now, I was exuberant in my own memories of the evening. I felt my heart keep time with the sounds of the city around me. I could feel the lopsided smile, that I couldn't contain, spread wider across my face. The thought of Luke and I finally finding common ground gave me hope. It seemed like he was willing to stay partners and rekindle our once blooming attachment.

I didn't want to raise my hopes too high, though. It wasn't too long ago Luke had thrown me to the proverbial wolves in Chief Inspector Farthing's office. I knew now it was because he feared for me. His fear got in the way of our relationship. I had proven myself helpful, hadn't I? The insights and details I uncovered were instrumental in helping our cases. His heart wanted to guard me from the horrible possibilities. I could see that now. Luke couldn't see that I needed to be part of the solution. I needed to help the world, not hide from it. It was this passion that brought us together in the first place. If tonight was any indication, he was finally reconciling himself to this fact.

Jaime pulled into the motor park with a yawn. He tousled his hair about and slapped his cheeks lightly to rouse himself.

"Tired, cousin?"

"Quite, Belle. And you were such a humdrum on the way home, I can barely make it up the stairs before I fall asleep," he pouted.

"My apologies. I was woolgathering about the night, and I didn't think to entertain you to keep you awake. Forgive me?" I pleaded.

"Always. Now I must dash. My pillow awaits and I daresay you have a big day of investigating ahead of you. Do be careful if I do not see you for breakfast," he said.

"I will, I promise. Good night."

We went our separate directions and prepared for bed. I brushed out my hair and pleated it into a side braid. I was just about to blow out my side table lamp when I remembered Luke's parting words. I patted across the room to my desk that held my journal and grabbed the book and a graphite stick. Plopping back down on the bed, I paged through my notes, looking for any clues I had forgotten.

I made my way through my observations and circled items that seemed important. Some things that jumped out at me were the markings, the white streak that was only found in Gwennie's hair, Mr. Hillard that I had yet to ask the doctor about, and the letter from the Claymore servant boy we never opened. As I read the description of the small bodies laid out that day, I noticed my notes stopped abruptly. I turned the page to find Luke's neat penmanship scrolled across it and remembered that I needed him to finish taking notes for me that day. Instead of observations, however, I found this letter.

Dearest Belle,

I can't help thinking I've made a terrible error. My intention to shield you from the horrors of this vocation was in vain as I see these children lying out before us. All this time, I've been trying to protect you, and you were the one to not flinch in the face of it. You gave me strength today. I had forgotten myself, and you brought me back.

I can scarcely think of how I discouraged you. I was coarse and unjust. I hope your heart is not completely turned against me, although I wouldn't blame you if it were so. Please forgive my foolishness. You are more than capable of taking on the darkness, in fact, your light is the flame that guides me. If you choose to work with Constable Quincy, I will not stand in your way, but I desperately hope you will reconsider and continue by my side. You are my equal in every way, and I was blind not to see it. I will wait upon your decision.

Yours most ardently,

Luke. C. Weston

P.S. Doctor Cannish has just told me that the letter from the boy from Claymore's was going to a Mr. Plitner. His face screwed up into a most amusing scowl, and he said he believes the man works on the docks. We will need to dig further.

I read the letter about fifteen times before I set it down. I felt wetness along my cheeks and hadn't realized I had been crying. To think that this had been in my journal all this time, and I had never known it. All these unsure feelings could have been banished, but for some reason, I wasn't completely upset. These tears were more joyful than anything. I realized that Luke's approval was what I was seeking. Somehow having it was the validation I needed. I know that one should be one's own champion, but where love is concerned, I daresay you crave their good opinion more than your own.

I shivered as the concept of love fluttered through my mind. I had known for a while how desperately I wanted things to work out between Luke and I. Even through the rage of being second-guessed and brushed off, I felt the need to stay close to him. My heart wasn't willing to let go, and perhaps my cousin was right. We would come out stronger for this. We would not let our connection fade into oblivion.

Knowing now how Luke truly felt about me gave new meaning

to our evening. A lightness took over, and I put the journal on my bedside table, blew the lamp out, and fell into a peaceful sleep. The monsters we were hunting on the morrow didn't stand a chance.

Chapter 35- New Beginnings

When propriety gets in the way of the pursuit of what is right, does it remain necessary?

I woke up to a racing mind. All the clues that had been bombarding me from the night of Gwennie's appearance to farther back seemed to collide in my brain at once. I needed to talk to Doctor Cannish. I felt it in my gut that he would have the missing pieces I needed.

I splashed water on my face and looked out the window to a still waking sky. Just the palest of oranges was cresting the horizon. Purgatorio's gears began moving, and I turned to him with appreciation. I scratched him under his chin and told him of the evening while I readied myself for the day. I hurried with my morning routine and grabbed my journal before racing down the stairs, Purgatorio followed in my wake.

I entered the kitchen, startling Trish, and settled for a bowl of porridge. I asked if she had seen Nathan, and she shook her head no. I hadn't seen him since yesterday morning, and an unease started to bloom in my stomach. I hoped it was just the pace at which I had eaten my porridge. I left a note for Jaime and headed to the motor park to get my bike. I left the sidecar on it, not knowing why, but felt it would be necessary. I readjusted my bracer and looked at the ankh charm wrapped just below it on my inner wrist. I had found and secured it to a smart looking piece of thick leather that complimented the ankh's shiny surface. I brushed a finger over it as the rising sunlight glistened on its metal. Sighing, I lowered my goggles, signaled Purgatorio to take flight, and drove toward town and what I hoped, were answers.

I didn't want to meet the doctor without Luke, so I found myself outside his apartment once again and knocked on his door. A motherly maid opened the door with wide eyes. She looked behind and around me and then arched an eyebrow.

"What are you doing here, dearie? It ain't much proper for a girl such as yourself to be out and about unchaperoned, you know? And to be visiting a gentleman at this early hour. Appears quite a bit unseemly," she clucked her tongue in disapproval.

"Well, Miss…."

"Mrs. Tobias, Lady Whipley's maid," she said.

"Well, Mrs. Tobias, I am Annabelle Sweeting. I work with Constable Weston in the pursuit of justice and I'm afraid murderers don't care much about the hour. So, if the constable is home, please do fetch him, as I would rather not find another body today," I rebuked.

For some reason, this woman and her judgmental declaration had my hackles raised something fierce. I took pleasure in her startled face at my statement.

"Who is it, Marie?" I hear Luke's voice inquire from within.

Luke opened the door farther and smiled as he looked at me on the front stairs.

"Miss Sweeting, I see we had the same idea to get started early today. Is everything okay?"

He looked between me and Mrs. Tobias and was confused by our conflicting stares.

"Mr. Weston, don't you feel it is ill-advised to have this young lady here, unattended, seeking you out?" Mrs. Tobias persisted.

His face took on a serious expression as he absorbed her words. He took a few moments before responding.

"While I appreciate your concern, Mrs. Tobias, we are at present, in a working relationship. I would not suspect a lady needs to be accompanied when she is attending a male customer at a boutique, nor a patient at a hospital, correct? Therefore, I find this perfectly suitable. If in fact, I were courting Miss Annabelle, which may happen at a later date, then in that instance, yes, a proper escort may be needed," he said, giving me a wink.

"Well, I see your point, but sir, I think you are already far too familiar, if what Lady Whipley says is true," she said.

I whistled with my fingers and placed my arm out.

"If you are really that concerned for my honor, there is always Purgy to keep Mr. Weston at bay," I grinned.

The manticore came in with a screech and nearly caused the maid to faint. I couldn't help but chuckle.

"Miss Sweeting, stop teasing Mrs. Tobias. Mrs Tobias, you now can see she is not as alone as you think. This beastie seems to always be lurking about. Now we must be off. Crimes to fight, mysteries to solve and all of that," Luke said.

Mrs. Tobias gawked at us from the open doorway as we headed toward my motorbike.

"I daresay she will not be returning, and I will need to find a new cleaner," Luke said.

"Well, I could go back and apologize if you wish, but I can't say that I found her very amiable," I replied.

"I wouldn't dream of having you do such a thing. It was quite out of line for her to address you as such, and to bring up gossip as her proof that we are doing anything improper is quite ill-mannered indeed. I think I might have a few words with my aunt as well. To be discussing my personal affairs in front of the help is quite, how did she put it… unseemly?"

We looked at each other and laughed at the whole thing. It was good to have such an easy conversation again. He looked at where my motorbike was parked and frowned.

"Miss Sweeting, I don't believe I will be riding along with you…to… Well, where are we going?" Luke asked.

"I want to meet with Dr. Cannish as soon as possible. I was reading over the notes," I blushed slightly, then continued, "and I feel like his connection to the mysterious Mr. Hillard will help us unravel some of this puzzle," I responded.

"You did a thorough perusal of your notes then?" he said with an arched brow.

"I did," I replied coyly.

"Anything that stands out that you would like to discuss?"

"Hmmm, well I told you about the Mr. Hillard theory, and I guess we need to discover what the markings mean as well," I said.

"Come now, Belle! You torture me!" Luke said, exasperated.

I smiled broadly and tried to stifle a giggle.

"Okay, yes. I read your letter, and I was mortified that it took me this long to find it. I guess I am not a very good sleuth if I can't even discover clues within my own property. I share the sentiments you laid out in the note and if you like we can talk to Chief Inspector Farthing today about remaining a team after this case is laid to rest," I said.

"Thank you for this second chance, I won't squander it." His eyes were intense as he continued, "Belle, I meant what I said back there in front of Mrs. Tobias. I do plan to court you again. I wish to discuss this in more detail after we get through today's conquests. Would that be acceptable?" He said, searching my face.

I watched the hope flicker in his waiting gaze and couldn't help but feel happy.

"Yes, that seems acceptable, Luke. As long as we continue as partners in both aspects, I feel it would be very amiable indeed," I replied.

His smile dazzled as he took my hand in his. He kissed it and then spun me around on the sidewalk in a twirl. I couldn't help but laugh at his playfulness.

"Now that it is partially settled, leave your motorbike here, I will drive you in my auto. Then we can work on this case together and discuss it more on the way to The Yard. Agreed?"

I nodded, and he tucked my arm in the crook of his elbow as we strolled to his motor park. We stole glances at each other and smiled the entire way. Whatever hardships lay ahead, I would remember this feeling and how badly I would fight for it to continue. Purgatorio screeched from the sky above, and I felt his sentiments exactly.

Chapter 36- On The Hunt

It is important in life to follow one's instincts, the majority of the time in love, and definitely in a murder investigation. - Note from Annabelle Sweeting's journal

We arrived at Scotland Yard as the shifts were changing and watched a flurry of bobbies ready themselves for the day ahead. Before we entered the building, I could make out the faint sound of a church bell ringing. It wasn't on the hour, so it caught my attention. I suspected it was the guttersnipes meeting, and I sent Purgatorio in search of Byron. He had been helping with the grounds work in the small garden behind my cousin's house. I tucked a missive onto Purgy's neck, where it wouldn't be missed, directing Byron to send word of what was happening.I hadn't spoken to Nathan since the previous morning, and I needed to know all was well.

Moving past the crowd of men looking for their daily assignments, Luke and I walked purposefully toward the back hall leading to the examination rooms. I felt a tingling sensation up my left arm and looked toward the wall as I passed. The picture of Doctor Cannish's father and the orphanage caught my eye, and I felt pulled in that direction.

A person's history, when not relayed, was often left unshared on purpose, I found. Clearly, the past between the doctor and Mr. Hillard was one of those times. I hated to pry, but it felt almost dire that I did. Whatever their connection it had to be immensely important for this man to be so secretive. I straightened my stance and followed Luke to Doctor Cannish's office.

The doctor was pouring over paperwork and making notes as we walked in. He flourished his signature on a document and looked up as we approached. His eyes were red and tired, and I couldn't help but feel sorry for his recent strain.

"Well, Constable, Miss Sweeting, I would love to say good morning, but it has been anything but. I am sure you heard about the outbreak near Southwark. It was a mite more devastating than the reports had relayed. Thankfully they are on the mend now," he sighed.

"Now onto the more grizzly topics. I am afraid I hadn't had a chance to relay some very vital information to you before I was called away. Let me address them now. I was examining the first girl that you brought me again and I noticed something that quite escaped me initially. While the other children had organs removed, she had one inserted."

"What?! Are you sure, doctor?" I exclaimed.

"Yes, quite sure, Miss Sweeting. And, as it turns out, the organ inserted came from the other girl from Tappers Grove," he grimaced.

"Quite shocking! What could be the meaning of it?" I said, stunned.

I took my journal out and made a few notes. I would have to think about it in more depth later.

"I also believe that the white streak in her hair was the result of bleaching powder. Perhaps she had laid on some wet rags after they had been washed, but I don't believe it had anything to do with her demise," the doctor said.

"Dr. Cannish, I would like to ask you about an old acquaintance of yours. I understand Mr. Hillard is back in town and that you had recently ran into him. For some reason Whitmore believes he is entangled in this investigation," I said.

The doctor's face paled as I said Hillard's name. He fell back into his chair and scrubbed his hand down his face. The stubble along his jaw gave resistance, but he completed the gesture.

"This cannot be. How did I not see it? That despicable man," he said.

"What is the matter, Cannish?" Luke said, rounding the desk and putting his hand on the doctor's shoulder. The man's discomposure was jarring. He was nothing but stoic, or a bit cheeky whenever we met. I felt whatever he was about to reveal would shock us all.

"He's involved," he said.

"How do you know?" I asked.

"To tell you that I will need to go back in time. You might want to sit a spell. I feel like you might need the support," he replied.

Luke and I located two chairs and pulled them in front of the desk. Luke closed the doctor's office door, and we waited for Cannish to begin. He opened the bottom drawer of his desk, pulled out a bottle and a glass, and proceeded to fill the glass halfway with an amber liquid. He took a large gulp and grimaced as the spirit burned its way down his throat. A long sigh escaped his lips before he spoke again.

"I guess not all skeletons can stay buried then?" Cannish started. "It all began thirty years ago, or maybe even before then. Probably when my father decided to take that urchin off the street. Yes, that is when it all began. Let's start there."

My eyes grew large as I tried to refrain from interrupting. His father adopted an orphan?

Chapter 37 - The Doctor's Past

One might wish to forget one's past, but it will always be lurking, waiting for the right moment to pounce.

Luke and I sat on the edge of our seats, waiting for Dr. Cannish to continue with his story. Apparently, there was a more immense association than I had anticipated with this mysterious Mr. Hillard. Cannish looked us in the eyes and sighed. I smiled encouragingly.

"Miss Sweeting…" he began.

"You can call me Annabelle, doctor. I think we have become friends, don't you?" I replied.

"Yes, I suspect we are that. And with what I am about to divulge, I would say I even trust you. My given name is Walter." He smiled to himself. "And Luke, well we've seen some horrible things together, so I guess we are brothers in arms, hey?"

Luke nodded.

"Well, Annabelle…" Walter said, testing the name out. "I recall not long ago you asking me about that old portrait in the hallway of my father, Mr. Tyler Cannish. He was standing in front of the foundling hospital with several children, yes?"

I nodded in affirmation.

"What you didn't know was that one of those children was a Mr. Thomas Hillard. A clever little boy with no fear and tons of potential, as my father would tell me. He saw in Thomas a second son, and I didn't mind the company when he decided to bring him on as a personal errand boy for him. He was about twelve years old then. He grew so much in my father's esteem that the old man decided to send him to school with me. The first year at Eton was perfectly fine, but after that, things became difficult," he said.

A foggy look went through the doctor's eyes, and I could almost visualize the past with him as he continued.

"We were fresh as babes back then. We got into our share of mischief, like all young men should. But then, I started really diving into my studies. The sciences were fascinating to me. I wrote to my father about all the new advances in medicine and chemistry, and he insisted I get Thomas involved as well. Thomas wanted to pursue more romantic subjects, like literature or philosophy. He wanted to be able to spout the great poets to a pretty girl. My father was not impressed. Thomas knew he could lose everything if he didn't follow my father's wishes, so he joined me. He then tried to make it his mission to outdo me.

I didn't mind his antics. If anything, they helped me excel faster than I would have on my own. It wasn't until he started chumming about with Elliott Daven that things really fell apart. Well, that's not exactly true. Elliott was my dormitory mate in the beginning. A real fine gent, always generous and buying drinks at the local pub. Thomas and I were nearing our second year's end, and the chance to apprentice would become available the following semester. We went out to blow off some steam from all the exams, and we ran into Elliott and his new friends, now Father Ned Gaverty, and his little beadle, Zachariah Fieldworth.

Ned and Zachariah were a year ahead of us and chomping at the bit to leave school and start their lives. The two of them were severely arrogant. They still had another year to go, but you wouldn't know it by how they carried on. Thomas and Elliott were enamored by the presumed righteousness of Ned and Zachariah. Thomas and Elliott began to follow them around like pups. I warned them about the faults in their address, but they wouldn't listen to me. It all came to a head when Thomas started failing his classes. My father insisted he buckle down and produce, or he would pull him out. Thomas asked my father that if he was under his thumb, how could he be his own man? That was the last straw. Thomas was given an ultimatum; to finish school and follow me into the medical field, or my father would pull the plug on his funding.

Thomas pretended to fold, took an apprenticeship with an animal specialist, and cut off communications with my father and me. He gave the impression he would diverge into the agricultural medical field. I tried to reach out to him numerous times, but he would mumble something about me being the problem and walk away directly. His work became very dark, from what I was told. Elliott would divulge to me how Thomas was doing such pivotal experiments. He told me of him slicing open live animals and replacing their organs for another species, sometimes dead and sometimes alive. Elliott said some of them lived several weeks before succumbing to complications. Ned Gaverty said it was ungodly, but he could see the potential in it. Zachariah found it all very amusing, and he knew of a few people he would like to try it on. I shuddered at the very thought. We were about to finish Eton when Thomas stopped going completely. Without attending, he failed the remainder of classes and was expelled. My father was furious but couldn't find him anywhere.

Thomas started taking odd jobs at night, very mysterious. It was as if he had become a ghost. I found out later that he was doing unsanctioned medical procedures on the poor. Promising them the world and then taking them for all they had. Sometimes he did help, but most of the time he didn't. I lost track of him for a while. It wasn't until many months later that our paths crossed again.

I was studying under Doctor Randerwelch, a very astute man, for several years as an apprentice. He made things easy to understand. At the beginning of my last year of apprenticing, the doctor invited me to attend the London

Invention Fair. It was quite the spectacle, and I was thrilled to be included by him. The atmosphere was galvanizing, and I could feel myself coming alive there. Everything I had studied for, all the great ideas people were bringing into reality, gave me such inspiration.

I was looking over the most amazing magnifying lenses when I saw her, Miss Eloise Bridgemont. A most attractive creature, and later I found to be intelligent to boot. I hadn't noticed myself still wearing those silly lenses as I walked over to her to beg for an introduction. She laughed at my appearance. What a magical sound that was. I could have listened to it all night. We had just set to walking down a new row of curiosities when my past friends would become my current foes.

Doctor Cannish looked up from his desk confused. It appeared as if he had just realized he was in the present and not in a long-faded memory with a beautiful girl. It made me sigh for the longing I saw in his eyes. I knew how it would end, but I was enraptured with his story. Some of the details were seeping into my brain, and a weird theory was starting to take root.

Chapter 38- The Rivalry

Nothing can outlast the test of time like love and rivalry.

"Well, hmm, now where were we? Oh yes, the invention fair," Doctor Cannish continued.

"I was walking with the most stunning woman I had ever met, conversing about the amazing inventions we were seeing. It was going swimmingly until I heard a collection of unmistakable, raucous laughter. The familiarity of the outburst struck me before the group themselves. Elliott Daven, Ned Gaverty, Zachariah Fieldworth, and Thomas Hillard rounded the corner of the aisle we were in. My one-time friends, now turned barely acquaintances, could hardly conceal their surprise at seeing me there.

Lord Daven requested an introduction, and I remember cringing at the prospect. I was civil and cordial as there was a lady present, but his two lackeys couldn't contain their snickers. Thomas just stared at me with hooded eyes and a grim-set mouth.

Miss Eloise was all charm and took their boyish antics in stride. We moved to continue our exploration, but Elliott wouldn't relent so easily and invited himself along. The other gents continued their own path, but before departing, I caught Thomas' gaze, and he had a queer smirk about him. It sent shivers up my spine. He truly looked overtaken by something. I shook these strange thoughts away and tried to return to the conversation and company as before. Elliott, however, seemed to dominate the conversation and was delighting Miss Bridgemont with terribly embarrassing stories of our days as roommates. I chided him for such antics, but he just continued his assault.

I went along, trying to remain in good humor, but I felt the weight of his ploy as her laughter grew, and she gently brushed Daven's arm. It forced me into action, and I halted her progress to ask if she would allow me to attend her the following day at a museum I planned to visit. She turned a beautiful rose color and nodded her agreement. I was so elated. It only lasted a moment as Elliott tried to make it a party. I informed him that I only had one additional ticket to the exhibit, but he said not to worry he could procure his own. The lady's mother met us then, and we said our goodbyes. I informed her of when I would call and bowed over her lace-enveloped hand. I still remember the sparkle in her eyes.

As soon as she was out of earshot, I turned to Elliott and asked him what he was about. He clearly saw that I was pursuing the lady, and to interject himself was bad form. He laughed in my face. He told me Thomas was right and that I was an immensely selfish being. I couldn't believe my ears. I shared everything with that little urchin, even my father's love, and yet he spoke of me so ill. Elliott continued saying that perhaps a little competition would do me good and take me down a peg. I told him not to pursue the lady as some ill attempt at revenge against me, for what I didn't know. She was far too sweet a creature to be used in such a manner. Elliott Daven scoffed and swiftly turned away in search of his friends. I stood there in thought, wondering how it had happened. How had Elliott Daven taken my brother's goodwill from me, and why now did he try to take the favor of Eloise Bridgemont as well? I was baffled, and I daresay enraged.

The next day I called at the lady's residence promptly at the appointed time. I had brought a beautiful selection of flora to present her with. The doorman met me with a surprised brow raised and told me that the lady had already departed for the museum with Lord Daven. Lord Daven had made it clear that I would meet them there and could not transport her to the exhibit. I was utterly astounded at the sheer audacity of him. I hurried back to my hired carriage. A long, shadowed figure blocked the door as I neared. It was Thomas."

The doctor sighed. He refilled his glass and took another sip. I couldn't help but feel that a betrayal of the worst kind was before him. Thomas seemed to have misdirected his anger for Walter's father onto him. It was terribly unfair and knowing that Eloise was destined to become the future Lady Daven made it heartbreaking. What could Thomas, Walter's adoptive brother, have done to direct the lady so decidedly against the doctor? Why would he go against his own family and help Lord Daven? I leaned forward in my chair waiting for Doctor Cannish to continue.

Chapter 39- A Brother No More

The road to hell is paved with good intentions, just ask Tyler Cannish.

"How could he convince such an intelligent thing that you would rescind on your appointment? As a lord he has the duty of honor to uphold. To issue such blatant deceit and come out smelling like a rose is shocking," Luke said.

"Yes, well, prepare yourselves, it gets worse," Cannish frowned.

The doctor tapped his chin and searched his mind for the right words to convey. Luke and I waited for the next blow to come. Walter continued his narrative.

"Thomas waited in front of the carriage and looked up at me as I approached. I raised a quizzical eye at him, and he smirked. Thomas accused me of destroying his life. He threatened it was for the last time and that it was my turn to suffer. I asked him what he meant. I had done nothing to him. I hadn't even seen him in several months before the invention fair. He laughed at me without humor and shoved a letter into my chest.

The letter was penned in my father's writing. My father had sent a man to discover Thomas in town after he dropped out of classes and went missing. My heart raced as I read the harsh words in such an elegant font. My father was disowning Thomas unless he made amends, went back and finished his failed classes, and joined me in my apprenticeship. He had already conversed with Doctor Randerwelch and cleared the way to make it feasible.

I told Thomas this was ridiculous and that I would write to my father immediately. His path in agricultural medicine was perfectly suitable, and if he had just finished the few necessary assignments, he could move on without incident. Had he confided in me sooner, it wouldn't have gotten this far. A look of surprise crossed his face but then morphed into the angry scowl I had grown accustomed to from him. Thomas told me it was far too late, and he had already quit the other apprenticeship. He was now working for Lord Daven, Elliott's father, as an errand boy.He was continuing his own medicinal studies in private, behooving no one. His eyes grew large and wild as he conveyed the experiments he had been conducting.

I admonished him for taking such liberties with nature and asked him why he wasn't trying to heal rather than dissect. Why did he feel the need to change these poor creatures in so grotesque a manner? He scoffed at me and told me this was exactly what Elliott thought I would say. Thomas told me I didn't understand and that I never could, as I didn't think big enough. That Elliott and the others were right about me. I would always be too straight and narrow, and I didn't deserve what I had.

I argued that I worked hard for everything that we both had. I asked Thomas why he had turned against me and why he decided to confront me in front of Miss Bridgemont's. He wouldn't answer me, he just shook his head, waiting. He looked up as Lady Bridgemont, Eloise's mother, stepped out onto her stoop to leave. Thomas grinned menacingly at me.

"Showtime," he whispered as he took a step toward me and punched me square in the jaw. I fell backward and landed at the lady's feet. She lifted her hand to her mouth in shock and looked to Thomas for an explanation. That is when the ax finally fell."

"You scoundrel! You good for nothing rake! How dare you pursue the upstanding Miss Bridgemont when you have not only ruined my dear sister, Mary, but also left her with child. To think we welcomed you into our home with your respectable airs and gallantry. Your father would be appalled!" I stared in utter disbelief as Thomas shouted his false accusations. "Lady

Bridgemont, I beg you, don't listen to a word this man says. He will claim his innocence, but do not give his claims any purchase. We were once as close as brothers, now, if not for my poor, dear sister's needing me to support her, I would call him out and duel him right here in the streets," Thomas yelled.

"A crowd had gathered, and I looked up at him, mortified. I had no idea he would stoop to such hate-provoked dishonesty. My embarrassment was not complete, however, as Lady Bridgemont looked down at me with disdain. She assured Thomas that Eloise would never associate with such a man as I, and she thanked him for his service for exposing me. I sputtered through my bruised jaw that all his claims were falsehoods, but the damage had been done. Lady Bridgemont scurried off, as did all the onlookers, to spread the lies Thomas spoke that day.

I hurried to try and catch Eloise at the museum, but when I arrived, they were nowhere in sight. I tracked them down enjoying ices together, only to be given the cut direct. It appeared the unsubstantiated news had already reached the lady's ear. By the time my name was cleared, and the truth of the matter related to the Bridgemonts, it was too late. Elliott Daven was weeks into courting Eloise, and I was damaged goods, entangled in gossip.

I happened upon Eloise on the street one day, after she had become engaged to Lord Daven. She spoke sweetly and apologized for ever having believed in the claims. I asked her if she was happy, and she said she was. I told Eloise that was all that I wished for. She kissed me on the cheek in parting, and I almost broke down right there. All my wishes and hopes were dashed by an orphan my father took in, and the lies that those ambitious boys had conjured up about me trying to oust Thomas from my father's regard. Ned, Zachariah and Elliott had thoroughly poisoned him against me. Whether for entertainment or jealousy of my academic achievements, I'll never know. That was the day Thomas stopped being my brother. That was the day my heart was irrevocably broken."

I felt my heart pounding at the conclusion of the doctor's narrative.

The pain of the lost love he endured was truly devastating. I met Luke's eyes and saw a similar emotion mirrored back to me. This would not be our fate. I snapped my head back to Doctor Cannish.

"What kind of experiments was he doing to the animals?"

"Ah, Miss Sweeting, not one to get swept away by the emotions of the past too long, I see. Well, that is good in this case. You need a clear mind in order to pursue such foul cretins as these. I am sure you won't find it shocking in the least. As I may have hinted in my story, he was removing organs from one animal and putting them in another, while still alive. I found out later that he continued this practice in a makeshift laboratory by the docks. He rarely used pain inhibitors and thus the cries of these poor creatures could be heard wailing in the dead of night. I admit, I sought his sanctuary out and reported him time and again until he removed himself from London entirely. At least he had until I saw him recently at the apothecary. Now, I fear our worlds are once again about to collide," he said.

I stood stock-still, taking in all the information. I knew exactly what was happening now, but why? Why would Thomas Hillard be removing organs from animals and orphans and inserting them into other children? The risk was too great. Then again, we knew not the reward, did we?

Chapter 40- The Sins of the Father

Not sugar or spice, but hardships and strife, and coggeries at night, that's what this little girl is made of.

We walked down the corridor with the doctor, all quiet in our thoughts. I felt myself pulled in the direction of the etching of his father with the orphaned children again. A thought popped into my head.

"Which one is Hillard?" I asked.

Doctor Cannish turned back and stood beside me. He looked up and pointed to the boy on Tyler's left. I gasped and leaned in closer. Blinking hard, I tried to convince myself I was not just inventing the eerie likeness I saw before me.

"What is it, Belle?" Luke said, rushing to my other side and peering at the image.

"How is that possible?" he sputtered.

"What are you two yammering about?" Dr. Cannish asked.

"Doctor, I mean, Walter, this child bears a striking resemblance to a girl I know. An orphan who is neck deep in this investigation. Do you know if Thomas had any children?" I asked.

Walter scratched his head in contemplation. "No, I can't say that I do. We haven't spoken in many years. It has not come up within the circle of friends I keep. It is not out of the realm of possibilities though. He could put on quite an act with the ladies, from what I remember," he replied dryly.

A question rattled around in my head, back and forth. Was she a victim, or was she an accomplice? Was she her father's daughter, or was she trying to escape his legacy? I knew what I wanted the answer to be, but my feelings held no weight when it came to the evidence we collected.

We walked toward the exit. The sun shone brightly above, and I shaded my eyes as I looked up. A screech pierced the morning air as Purgatorio dived down with urgency. Rose rushed up to us with a winded Byron racing several paces behind. Her eyes flashed from me to Constable Weston and back.

"You're a bloody bobbie, sir? Well ain't that the cat's kinked tail? Never mind, no time, he's got 'im, miss! The beadle nabbed Nate, he has!"

I grabbed Rose by the shoulders and bent down to meet her eyes.

"Calm down, and tell me exactly what has transpired," I said, trying not to lose my own composure.

She took several big gulps of air and shuttered where she stood. She blinked rapidly, nodded her head, and looked back into my eyes. I tried to be patient, but the thought of Nate's still body kept surfacing to the forefront of my mind.

"I was following him, the beadle that is, just likes you said," Rose started. "He was out and about. I almost lost him by the docks, but I know a few shortcuts, you see? Anyway, I thought I caught 'im spying me out so I moved upward onto the rooftops. I heard the abandoned church bell chime and knew Nancy and Nate were meeting up. I wasn't sure if I should leave or not, but I figures the beadle needed to go home sooner or later, and I could catch ups to him then. I went to meet the others at the old church near the edge of Tapers Grove. Nate and Adam were deep in talks when I got there, and Nancy looked like she had a split lip. Never did find out what that was about. Anyway, we was all there, 'cept little Simon. I think he is still abouts your place," she said.

"Yes, that's correct. He's been helping me with some things. Byron has also been assisting around my cousin's dwelling. So, what happened next, Rose?" I urged.

"So, we were going over how Nancy and Penny found One-eyed Whitmore," she continued. "He said he be reaching out to you but couldn't take the chance of meeting at the smithies like we planned. Then we were talking about those bloody awful packages and how Byron hadn't been able to nab one yet. Marcie was spouting out about how she could if she was given a chance and then Adam set her right down proper. Then Penny started getting fidgety, like she does when something's amiss. I asked her what was wrong, but she couldn't say. We all started peering around but didn't hear or see nothin'. Adam told us about what he and Marcie saw at that ol' lord's house, and boy were we surprised. Then we heard a voice coming from outside. It was that shady Sadie girl. She had spent enough time at Second Chance to know we was meeting when the bell tolls. She came in all frantic-like and told us she was looking for you. We all scattered but Nate stayed behind to hear her out. I ran up to the building across the way to keep an eye out. I saw your flying contraption circling in the air, then I spied Byron running down the lane several blocks away from the church. That's when it happened," Rose blurted.

"What happened?" I asked.

"Damn it girl, get to the point," Dr. Cannish shouted. The anticipation had us all on edge. I couldn't fault Walter for his outburst. This explanation was taking too long.

The girl nodded and continued. "The beadle it was. He came from the side door, I saw him. He must of snuck up behind poor Nate. I saw him hauling Nate out over his shoulder with Sadie following behind watching their back. I could nawt believe it. That wretched little tripe pulled one over on Starling. I had to get to you to let you know. He said to me, if anyone was seen snatched to find you out at once, and so I did," she said proudly.

I grasped the girl in a fierce hug and kissed the top of her head. She looked up at me in surprise and smiled.

"You did great, Rose. Thank you for seeking me out. Where were they headed?" I asked.

"To the beadle's post, I think. In Tapers Grove, it is," she said.

" I wish we knew for sure," I said looking at the doctor and Luke.

As if my prayers were heard, a motor zoomed around the corner and screeched to a halt. Miro came out, struggling with his cane and injured leg.

"Miss Annabelle, I didn't want to leave my post, but I thought I needed to inform you right away. Young Starling, he's been taken," he said.

"Yes, we've heard, do you know where? How did you come by this information?" I asked.

Luke helped him gain back his balance as Lord Thetford reclaimed his composure.

"My invention. Young Starling and I have been keeping tabs on the filthy beadle, and it is a good thing too. I saw him carrying poor Nate. Some other chit was with them, but I didn't know who," Miro said.

"That was Sadie. I fear I may have been completely fooled by her. Oh, poor Nathan. We must get to him at once. What do you think is the best course of action, Luke?" I asked.

I saw Lord Thetford give a start and realized I had displayed familiarity with the use of Luke's name. I didn't have time to care for the improperness of the moment, there was too much at stake to dwell on propriety now.

"If we go in with our motors we might scare the beadle off, we need to be smart about this," Luke replied.

"Zachariah was always a bit skittish. He had a way of being gone before trouble could catch him," Dr. Cannish agreed.

"What about your motorbike, Miss Sweeting? You've driven to the Brass Boroughs before with it, so it wouldn't seem out of place," Byron said.

"Yes, and you are going to come with me," I replied.

"But, miss, I just got out of there, I don't want to go back," Byron sulked.

"A plan is forming in my mind, and I need you with me," I pleaded.

"You've not led me astray yet, miss. Whatever you needs, I'm your man," Byron said.

I turned to Luke, Miro, and Walter with a confidence I hadn't felt in some time.

"Here's what's going to happen…"

Chapter 41 - Gears in Motion

A well-laid plan is wonderfully deceptive. That can also be said about a well-laid trap.

"Here's how we shall proceed," I started.

"Lord Thetford, I need you to continue to monitor your Nassar Navigators. Rose is going to accompany you and if there are any changes she will find one of us at Second Chance to relay the message. I wish you had a separate viewer that was capable of projecting the images wherever you might be," I said.

"That will be my next project, I assure you," Miro said.

"Constable Weston, I need you to take Byron and I to my motorbike. The side car is already attached so we can leave directly. Gather several constables and meet us at Second Chance," I said.

"What can I do, Miss Sweeting?" Doctor Cannish said, looking at me with such an eager desire to help.

"Walter, what I have to ask of you is very difficult, and I don't ask it lightly," I started.

He nodded his head for me to continue.

"I need you to invite Lord Daven out to luncheon," I said.

"What?! Have you lost your senses? That seems quite unnecessary. I can do no such thing. It is quite preposterous," he sputtered.

"Yes, it is, isn't it! And how can he turn it down? His interest will be so overly piqued he will agree. That is when we move. I need you to do this, Walter. Nate's life may depend on it," I replied.

He stared at me for several agonizingly quiet moments and nodded.

"I can see your gears moving. I know when you set your thoughts to it you can be quite fierce. If that is what it takes, then I shall do it. Another child will not be dispatched due to my pride," he conceded.

"Very good, Walter. I daresay you are the lynch pin in this most unorthodox idea of mine. I know you will do your best," I said.

I had hardly taken notice of my metallic manticore as we were so focused on the news that Rose brought us. Looking at him now, I noticed several new dings on his casing. I knelt toward him and stroked the pebbled side of his armor.

"Oh, no, that will not do. Once this is over with, come by the hangar and I will get him buffed out and back to new in no time," Miro said.

I thanked him and moved towards Luke's motor, scooping up Purgy as I went. Byron was hot on my heels, and we all departed for our designated assignments. Luke dropped us off at my motorbike and issued a warning before he left.

He didn't want me to do anything hasty until he arrived at Second Chance. I was more than happy to agree. The stakes were increasing, and I needed a few more pieces in the puzzle before I rushed in. Nate was counting on me, and I wasn't about to let him down.

Byron affixed the helmet to his head, and I asked him if he had any ideas about where the others had run off. He scratched his now fairly clean chin and said he suspected that they would find us as soon as we reached the Boroughs. I worried my bottom lip and then nodded as I started the engine. I tucked a note in Purgatorio's chest compartment and sent him back to Bread Street with a message. My heart began to beat faster as I thought about Nathan's predicament. One step at a time, I reminded myself.

We weaved our way through the busy lanes and watched for the urchins to surface. The wind felt good as it whipped across my face. My goggles were fixed tightly against my skin, but not abrasive. We were several blocks from the foundling hospital when Nancy stepped out of an alley. I slowed the motor and took in her appearance. Just like Rose had said, a nasty cut adorned her lip, and her eyes were wild.

"Nancy, are you okay?" I said.

"Awe, Miss, Rose found you then, she did? That's good, I guess. Well, nawt good for Nate, but then these are nawt good times. We've been keeping an eye on it, no movement yet though. If I get my hands on that scrawny little rodent, I'll strangler her done good, I will!" Nancy said, promising retribution for Sadie's help in Nate's abduction.

"What happened to your lip?" I asked.

"Well, that there is nothin'. I just got the backhand from Mrs. Squires is all. She was deep in the cups you see, and I think she mistook me for someone else. Her eyes were all haunted and weird. Needless to say, she wasn't in a talking mood," Nancy said.

She wiped her hand across her brow and looked around before she continued. "Anyway, what you need me to do? Nate said if he be gone missing, we needed to seek ya out."

"Nancy, I need you to use those remarkable conversing skills of yours," I said.

"What?" she blurted.

"I need you to talk to Father Gaverty for me. I need you to pretend to run into him and tell him about how you just saw Doctor Cannish and Lord Daven heading out to tea together. Can you do that for me?" I asked.

"Well, sure I can. Why am I doing this?" Nancy inquired with slitted eyes.

"Father Gaverty is very protective of Lord Daven, and he wouldn't want the dear doctor to impede their friendship. I need Gaverty out of the way while other things fall into place," I replied.

"Awe, so you's causing a distraction, you are? I get it just fine. You can count on me," she said before dashing off.

"Miss Sweeting, you are quite sneaky for a Glimmer. You are down right Brassy," Byron smirked.

"When lives are on the line, being sly is a necessity, as I am sure you've witnessed before. Nate will not meet the same fate as your sister, nor any other child if I can help it," I vowed.

Byron looked up at me in awe. I replaced my riding goggles and headed on to the Second Chance Orphanage. I prayed the gears I had placed in motion would be enough to delay any harm that may befall my dear Starling. Only time would tell.

Chapter 42- Waste Not, Want Not

The world is rarely just black and white. The trouble is seeing how murky the greys really are.

Byron and I slowed to a stop in front of the building he had recently called home. Purgatorio took to the skies as we took in the scene around us. Dirty children ran through the street playing with foraged toys. I looked up the steep stairs and wondered what Mrs. Squires was up to. My thoughts were halted as Adam and Marcie peeked out from Dark Alley, next to the orphanage. Adam waved us over and slipped back into the darkness. I saw Purgatorio circling overhead, which meant he had delivered my missive to Jaime, and one gear was now moving into motion. I felt a sense of security having Purgy back watching over us as we ventured into the shadows.

"Took you long enough, miss! We've been here for hours, we knew you'd come though. Nate, he said you would, and he ain't no dirty liar," Marcie said.

"Shush, now. We haven't time for your thoughts, Marcie. Miss, what do we do? I think I can take that ol' beadle, but he's got spies all over the place. I don't want to end up in the Thames, like that Viktor Barnes chap," Adam said.

"Viktor Barnes? Do you mean the man who owned the shack we found Janey in? How do you know this, Adam?" I asked, becoming alarmed.

"Words been spreading all along Tapers Grove, miss. They found his body floating by the docks. Looks like someone tried to tie him down, but the rope was weak. Poor bugger. Rumor is that the beadle be the one who done him in," Adam replied.

Byron clapped him on the shoulder and smiled. "None to worry about, Miss Sweeting is a sly Brass, and she already has several games a foot, isn't it so, miss?"

"You have all taken more risks than you should at your age, but I must ask more of you. The beadle and Sadie have our Starling, and we need to get him back. However, we also need to know why he was taken in the first place. He must realize that I would do anything to get him back," I thought out loud.

"I'm none too sure, but it seems that Sadie is a no-good traitor," Byron chimed in.

"I am still unconvinced on that point. Something is needling me about the whole thing. Either she is an amazing actress, or there is something more to this story," I said.

"I told you she didn't have no friends, miss. She's a louse of the worst kind, I'd say," Marcie said.

"Enough, I can't let Nathan spend one more moment in that place than necessary, Miss Sweeting. I owe him something fierce. What's the plan?" Adam said.

I looked at Adam's determined face. I knew they were depending on me. I knew Nathan was too. I heard a shriek from the sky and looked up. Purgatorio glided toward the entrance of the alley, and my gaze followed his path. I could see a constable motor pulling up, and I knew Luke had finally arrived. I turned to the others and knelt before them.

"Adam and Marcie, you are to meet Simon at my cousin's house on Bread Street. Adam you are going to escort Marcie and Simon to Lord

Daven's house, wait until he leaves, and then deliver the flowers and a pack of seeds my cousin will give you. You will need to deliver them directly to Lady Daven, understood?" I instructed.

"Flowers, miss? How is that going to help get Nate back?" Marcie squeaked.

"It's really the note that will be with the flowers that matters, my dear. You see there is a history that I mean to rustle up," I replied before turning to her protector. "Adam, you are to go around back to the building behind the house while they are delivering the flowers. I must know what is inside. Try not to go in if you can, a window will do to see through. I need to know for sure what is in there. There should be a Nassar Navigator still monitoring the place. Flag it down and relay what you can. Rose is watching the other end. She will see you and get whatever information you have back to me. Once you have done this get Marcie and Simon back to Bread Street. My cousin will watch over them. You will need to meet Constable Weston and I in Tapers Grove," I finished.

"Constable? You mean that bloke is a bobbie? He seemed so nice too," Marcie said.

"I am nice, I assure you," Luke replied.

The children jumped as Luke startled them from behind. He flashed me a grin and winked. I felt a sense of calm wash over me now that he was here. Whatever play the beadle was making, we would conquer it together.

"Well, mister, constable, sir….that was quite the trick to be sneaking about!" Byron said, rubbing his shoulder in agitation.

"Oh, is the big bad Byron scared? I thought you were some toughie," Marcie teased.

"You jumped too, you little squeak," he retorted.

The moment of teasing released some of the building tension in the air. I let out a long breath. Staring up into Luke's face, I nodded with determination.

"Off with you two, you know what to do," I said to Adam and Marcie.

They dashed out of the alley and took a right. Luke, Byron, and I followed at a slower pace. When we reached the mouth of the alley, Mrs. Squires was waiting for us. Her hair was in disarray, and she smelled of gin. Bloodshot, accusing eyes stared back at us. Dark circles marred her under eyes. I felt pity for her, but nothing else. Her scowl turned into a sneer as she opened her mouth to speak.

"So you've come to rain down hell on me, Miss Sweeting? Too late you righteous cow, I'm already there," she laughed, before turning her gaze to Luke. "You got some shackles then, Constable? I'm sure we can come to a different understanding, no? I can be nice."

Mrs. Squires approached Luke with a saunter. She brought her hand up to finger the buttons on his uniform. Fluttering her eyelashes up at him, I almost gagged at the spectacle. He tried to gently remove her hand from his person, but she became more forceful and moved in for a kiss. I saw red.

Moving swiftly, I grabbed the back of her loose hair and pulled. She screeched and threw her hands out, trying to gain purchase on Luke as he backed away. Mrs. Squires spun around to face me. Byron stuck his foot out, and she tripped, falling to her knees before me. I released her hair as she fell, and she pushed her hands to her eyes and started to wail. Any pity I felt was washed away by the anger that surged in reaction to her attempts on Luke. I do not know when I became so possessive, but I knew at that moment, the constable was mine.

"Mrs. Squires, pull yourself together. We are not here for you, although after that little display, I doubt you'll be running this establishment for much longer," Luke said.

She stopped her hysterics and looked up, wiping the snot from her face. It was all very uncouth.

"Well, what do you want then? You've done taken all my best snipes.

We were barely scraping by as is. That beadle is a no-good cheat, and I don't want to be tossed away like rubbish in the gutter on the morrow," she yelled.

"What has the beadle cheated you on?" I asked.

She snapped her head toward me and gritted her teeth.

"I'll tell you what he's done. He swore to pay me for the parcel tricks we've been playin' and now he said he didn't have to, since I was knee deep in whatever intrigue he's been playin' at. He said I wouldn't need no money at the gallows, and that's where I would be," she shuddered. "Spat right in my face too, he did."

"What a despicable man," Luke soothed.

Mrs. Squires looked over at him with more warmth now. "He was, he truly was. Then he went on about how he was aiming to take care of the other loose end at the docks. Some Piltner character he roped into this whole affair," she whimpered.

"Mr. Piltner? He supplies fish for Claymores. One of the poor boys we found in the shack was the owner's message boy. He had sent a missive to him. I don't know what he looks like though," Luke replied.

"I can tells you that. He is a horrid creature with pocks all over his face. Madam Jessley down the way at the brothel says she has the worst time getting any of her girls to service him. Pardon such talk, but that's the way around these parts," Mrs. Squires slurred.

I turned to Luke and blinked rapidly. It was the same man that Nathan had met with on the docks all those weeks ago. It couldn't be a coincidence. Whatever the end goal was, it was going to happen soon.

I stared into Luke's eyes and said, "We need to find him now."

Chapter 43- The Beadle's Bargain

With a shake of a hand, a nod, and a wink, the deal is struck before you can think.

Luke sent Constable Williams to the docks to search for the missing Mr. Piltner as we continued on to Tapers Grove. Constable Tallon and Quincy were waiting by Mr. Penzy's residence for us. Shuffling their feet back and forth in agitation, they kept searching the surroundings for unseen threats. The ominous tension was thick as we moved past the desolate dwellings. My nerves were just about to overwhelm me when a familiar face popped out and crooked a finger at me to follow. It was Terrance, the young lad who had lost his best mate, Petey. I remembered him telling me he worked for the beadle sometimes. I wondered for a moment if he was working for him now.

Cautiously, I moved toward the alley he waited in. I directed the other men of my party to keep their distance as I made my way over to the boy. "Awe, miss, I wish you'd nawt have come. You are in great danger, you are. Then again, we all are, aren't we?"

He scrubbed a dirty hand through his shaggy hair.

"Yes, Terrance, I daresay we are all in a bit of a jam. Especially my dear friend, Nate, whom your employer has mistreated so abominably. I need your help to see that his fate is not the same as your dear friend Petey," I replied.

Terrance looked up at that. He looked side to side and licked the corner of his mouth nervously.

"I was thinking the beadle had done poor Petey in too, but I couldn't prove it. He has been terribly distracted lately. Muttering and screaming at anyone nearby, he has. Something about backing the wrong horse, or keeping bad companions. Either way, he has been away for several days, and just returned today with your friend in tow, and that Sadie girl. I peeked in a few times before the beadle yelled at me. I saw that girl watching over Nate. He has a big bloody lump on his head. Doesn't look good, miss," he whispered.

"Did you hear anything about why the beadle took him, Terrance?" I asked.

"He used a big word. I think it was retillabusion," Terrance said, fumbling the word a bit.

It took me a few moments before I could decipher the word he was looking for.

"Do you mean retribution?" I suggested.

"Yes! That's the word, miss," he said.

"That isn't good at all," I said.

"I ain't goin' lie, miss, I am plum scared. This place has plenty of monsters already, I don't know how we are going to make it through if the people sent to help us are fiends as well," he confessed.

"I know exactly how you feel. Come here, take this. Go over to Mr. Penzy's home and stay there tonight. Tell him I sent you and to use this coin as payment," I said.

His eyes grew wide, and he smiled. Terrance snatched up the coin and ran back toward Mr. Penzy's house. At least one child would be safe tonight.

I returned to my travelling party, and we continued to the center of Tapers Grove. We moved past the shack where we first discovered the poor children under the candle sticks. I took my lavender handkerchief out and dabbed at my nose. Both the smells and memories were assaulting my senses. I tried not to let any tears release from my eyes. They wouldn't help anyone right now.

We reached the beadle's apartments and could hear movement from within. The front door swung open, and a man was flung backward down the stairs. His nose was bloodied, and his eyes were wild with fury. On closer inspection, I could see his skin's telltale marks marring his face. It was Mr. Piltner from the docks!

"Zachariah, you're a son of a bitch! You know better than to trifle with me. You must have lost your mind! After I'd helped you with that girl at the docks you treat me like this? I won't take the fall for you!" Mr. Piltner hollered as he looked up from the ground. He pushed himself up and brushed off some dirt before looking back at the beadle to continue the argument. He halted when he saw the beadle's face and, following Zachariah's gaze, turned to find us staring at them both.

A guttural scream broke through the sudden silence as Byron bellowed, "You killed Gwennie!"

Piltner looked back up at the beadle and then took off running. Constable Tallon and Byron dashed after him. I wanted to give chase, but Nate was still in the beadle's apartments and I needed to make sure he was alright. I turned my gaze to Mr. Fieldworth's face and shuddered at the evil grin I saw there.

"Well, Miss Sweeting, so nice to see you. Ah, and Constable Weston, stoic as ever, I see. Do join me inside, I've been waiting for you," Zachariah said.

"Quincy, stay here. Watch for Tallon. Let us know straight away if anything else unsavory is headed in our direction," Luke whispered his instructions.

Quincy nodded and took a post on the street. I raised my arm, and the beadle looked at me in question. Purgatorio moved swiftly through the sky and clutched my outstretched bracer. He nipped at my finger and issued a penetrating glare at the beadle with his red eyes. Zachariah gave a slight shiver in response. We followed his pensive steps into his front room. On the floor was Nathan, bleeding but alive. Sadie was dabbing at his head wound with a wet cloth. They both looked up at our entrance. Nate's body shook with relief, and Sadie frowned.

"Told ya she'd come. She's a Gemmer, and no matter of your disparagement will change that," Nate crowed proudly.

"Yeah, well, all the adults I know would rather spit on ya than coming chasing their own bloody child to this forsaken part of town," Sadie retorted.

"Shut up, you. Not another peep! The adults need to discuss some important things without interruption," Zachariah ordered.

"What precisely are we discussing?" I said, disdain dripping from my words. Luke put a gentle hand on my arm in warning.

"Why a bargain, of course. It's quite simple. You get to keep your lives and take your little snipe with you, and I get a free ticket out of town and no charges brought against me in any part of this mess that the good Father and Daven have cooked up," he said.

The beadle produced a pistol and pointed it at Luke. I gasped. Zachariah's smile widened at his assumed victory at having outsmarted us.

"And to guarantee these are just straight negotiations and no heroics please remove your truncheon, constable," he directed.

"Easy now, I thought you just wanted to talk. You don't need all that fire power for a conversation," Luke said.

"Maybe so, but I'm not taking any more chances. Now remove it slowly and give it to Sadie," Zachariah directed.

Luke did as he said, and Sadie moved to take it from him. She gave me a sheepish glimpse and took her post next to Nathan again. She mouthed "I'm sorry" to me and then looked down at her feet. I wasn't sure what was more disheartening, her being involved in this whole horrible affair, or the fact that we may not make it out of here in one piece. I couldn't let those hopeless thoughts take root. I straightened my spine and stared down the beadle.

"Now that we are comfortable, let's discuss the negotiation, shall we?" Zachariah said, still pointing the gun at Luke's chest.

He moved toward the table on the side of the room and directed us to sit across from him. Once we were seated, he laid the pistol down on the table, still pointed in our direction and easily accessible in case the need arose. Purgy growled, and the beadle tutted at him. I brought the manticore down into my lap as I sat. I realized we weren't as helpless as this beadle thought, but for now I wanted to hear what he had to divulge.

"Mr. Fieldworth, do tell us how you wish to proceed," I said sweetly.

"I knew you were the sensible type. Here's how I see it. I have ample information on the dealings of one Lord Elliott Daven and his trusted followers, Father Gaverty and Mr. Hillard. I have found this scheme to be quite unsavory, and I want rid of it and them. People have died and friendships dissolved, and for what? Nothing to benefit me, I assure you," he said.

"What can you tell us?" Luke pressed.

"Not too hasty, Constable Weston. I need guarantees, I need a way out, and I need your word that no blame will fall at my feet," the beadle demanded.

I took this chance to look the man over. He was shorter than Luke by half a head, with oily reddish-brown hair, and wore a purple hat that clashed horribly. His teeth almost looked rodent-like, with the front two protruding ever so slightly. His cheeks were rounded and gave his eye sockets the appearance of deep holes within his face. He was a stout man, who showed no effect of the poverty and lack of food that his town's people displayed.

Zachariah was a beast. I watched as his greedy eyes calculated how long it would take before we would concede to his wishes. Everything in me wanted to deny his request, but we needed to know what was happening. We needed this little rat to share why these crimes were occurring. Luke turned to me, and I reluctantly nodded. Zachariah smiled broadly at his impending victory. Before we could shake on it, however, a figure darted from the corner of the room and smacked the beadle across the back of the head with Luke's truncheon. I sprung back from my chair in reflex, and Purgatorio stood guard in front of me with his tail spikes ready.

"Animal!" Sadie shouted as she hit the beadle again to make sure he was knocked out. She walked backward until she hit the wall and slid down to the floor, crying into her hands. The truncheon, forgotten, banged on the floor where she dropped it. Luke tried to hold me back as I went to where she wept. Whatever had just happened, she was the key.

Chapter 44- The Truth of the Matter

A world divided by poverty and greed is fertile ground for mistrust and murder.

My heart raced as I neared Sadie in the beadle's apartment. Her body shuddered with sobs that she couldn't contain. The girl had seen hell, of that, I was sure. I stroked her back and looked to Nathan for direction. He shrugged; just as lost as I was.

"Sadie, he was a bad man, but he had information we needed. How can we stop what is happening and prove it if we don't know the root cause or people behind it?" I asked, trying to keep the frustration out of my words.

"Awe, Miss Sweeting, I should have told you everything before. I was just an idiot, believing my pa would help. You are so much braver than he is. You tried protecting me more in a few days than he ever did, and you're nawt even related to me," she cried.

"Are you talking about Thomas Hillard? He is your father, correct?" I offered.

She nodded and hid her face.

"That Lord Daven's to blame. He came to us all chummy with an offer for papa to make some real coin. Papa didn't know the extent of it until he was in too deep. Then he tried to leave and Lord Daven sent me away to the slums. He told my pa that he'd do whatever he needed to in order to get what he wanted," she explained.

"What does Lord Daven want your father to do?" Luke asked from across the room.

"To save his wife, of course!" Sadie said, still sobbing.

I stepped back in shock. Not at her declaration, but at the fact that I wasn't entirely surprised by it. The dots were starting to connect, and I wasn't content with the shape they were forming. Luke crossed the room and picked up his fallen baton, stuffing it back into his holder.

"Where is your papa now? We need to know," Luke urged.

Sadie looked up, her eyes just peering over her folded arms. She stared hard at Constable Weston, looking for some answer written on his expression. Once she was satisfied, she nodded her head in decision.

"He's held up in the back cottage at Lord Daven's house. That's where he does his experiments, you see?" Sadie confessed.

"Thank you for telling us, Sadie. We must venture there at once if we are to discover them in the act before they hear of Fieldworth's treachery," I said.

Luke summoned Constable Quincy from outside and had him help haul the beadle out of his apartments and into a now waiting motor. Still unconscious, the beadle made terrible moaning sounds that brought the neighbors out to see what the commotion was. As they saw him unceremoniously dumped into the back, they let out a cheer. The children spun around, smiling with glee. The weathered faces of the adults showed relief for the first time that I could recall. Whatever the beadle had done must have been worse than we could have imagined.

Purgatorio shot into the sky, spiraling upward. The crowd cheered again, in realization that the real monster had been silenced. A gentle face, and a high position can be the most horrifying of all deceptions when it comes to the cruelty of man. No natural, or in Purgy's case, unnatural beast could ever be so deliberately evil.

I helped Nathan down the stairs, and Sadie supported him from the other side. He was still dizzy but in good spirits. Tallon and Byron appeared from a side road and hurried over to us. They had lost Mr. Piltner and their frustrated looks were evident enough of their dismay.

"No need to fret, Byron my boy. I know where that guy lives on the docks. Just let me get my bearings and we'll go on and give him a real snipe's greeting," Nate said.

"You will do no such thing, Starling! You had me quite scared indeed and you are injured to boot. You, young sir, are going straight to Bread Street and getting some rest. You can relay your knowledge to Constable Weston and I and we will make sure that fiend is apprehended," I said with concern still flooding my emotions.

Nathan looked like he was about to protest, but then another wave of vertigo swept over him, and he released the argument.

"Miss Sweeting, we cannot be at two places at once. We will need to split up if we are to catch them all," Luke said. I could tell from his face that he wasn't happy at his own suggestion.

As we were discussing the best way to proceed, a flash of color caught my eye and I found Rose barreling down the roadway toward us. Her eyes were alert and concerned. I stepped in her direction to gather the news she had to tell.

"Oh, Miss Sweeting! You would nawt believe what we witnessed on them darn contraptions! Lord Daven and Doctor Cannish were at the Daven estate. They was headed toward the front of the house but they caught sight of Adam by the building he was snooping about! Oh, miss, it turned quite violent after that. Lord Daven tried to catch Adam, but he was too fast. When that didn't happen, he socked the doctor right in the jaw, he did. The doctor seemed to be trying to reason with the bloke but was turned out directly. I ran here as fast as I could to tell you," she gasped.

"What about Simon and Marcie, did you see them anywhere?" I asked.

"Ah, yes, Lady Daven invited them in but we stopped watching 'em. I don't know if they got out or not," she said.

Rose's face had a mix of somewhere between about to burst out crying and dead set on saving her friends. I felt the same. We needed to keep moving.

"Has anyone seen Penny? As I understand she had left before Nathan got nabbed, correct? Where has she gone?" I asked.

And as if pulled from the ether, she appeared down the lane with Terrance. I blinked my eyes to make sure I hadn't just hallucinated the whole thing. Luke looked at me in surprise and back at the approaching children.

"Well met, Miss Sweeting. I fear I have some terrible news to relay, however," Penny said.

I gasped at her eloquent statement. I realized I had never heard the young girl speak before.

"Our dear Nancy has run into some trouble at the church. I followed her, you see? She was talking to the father and whatever she said appeared to be quite vexing to him. So much so, that he struck her, gathered her up, and hauled her into the back of the reticulum. Before he shut the door, he murmured something about her being perfect. I didn't like the sound of that, so I thought it best to find you," Penny said.

"Oh goodness, there are so many strings to follow. I fear if we yank the wrong one too soon it will all fall apart," I replied.

"If I can be of help, Miss Sweetin', I will," Terrance spoke up.

I tried to calm my thoughts. So many moving parts all colliding at once. I took a deep breath and looked up into the sky where Purgatorio circled and one of Lord Thetford's contraptions was slowly descending. It dropped a parchment into my hand and zoomed away. I opened the parchment and let out another gasp. It was like an etching, but not. Showing the picture to Luke, his brow furrowed with alarm. Thomas Hillard had arrived at Lord Daven's, and not alone.

Chapter 45- The Tangled Thread

A good mystery is like a tangled ball of yarn. It is unbelievably vexing, sometimes anger inducing, but always satisfying when it is solved.

"We need to move now, Belle," Luke said.

"Yes, we do. What is your plan?" I asked.

"My plan? Well, I thought you would have one," he said.

"I thought you wanted me to take a back seat to your directions as of late. Is that not so?" I said, confused.

"Well, I do have Constable Williams still at the docks, perhaps he can nab Piltner if he goes home. Nate has given me a few other places he likes to hide out there. I'll need someone to relay that info to Williams," he thought out loud.

"Rose, go now," I directed.

Rose shot out like a horse at the tracks. Dust flying behind her down the uncobbled street.

"We need someone to release Nancy from Father Gaverty. I don't like the idea of storming in guns blazing. We need to be quiet about it if we are to catch him. He has been too cunning thus far," he said.

"Penny and Byron, you go with Constable Quincy to the church. Byron take your sling, you are going to have some target practice, I believe. A few well placed breaks to the lower windows should do the trick. That should draw him out. Quincy stay close to Penny, she has a way about her that will let you know when the time is right to interfere. I fear if you walk right in, he will have ample time to hide Nancy, and I need you to not let that happen. We need to catch him red-handed. Hopefully Nancy is still intact," I said.

"Yes, Miss Sweeting, we will not let you down," Penny said.

Quincy nodded to Luke and I, and Byron smirked with the impending damage he would inflict. A small prize for such a large loss. I watched the three dash toward the Second Chance Orphanage and their waiting motor.

"What can I do?" Terrance said.

I looked down at Terrance. His fist was clenched, and he was spoiling for a fight. I loved his courage but didn't want another child in danger. That put me in mind of Simon and Marcie. I needed to know if they were still at the Daven estate or safely back at Bread Street.

"I have a very important task for you," I said.

I reached up toward the sky and whistled. Purgatorio dived down and landed with a screech. Terrance did his best not to flinch. I smiled at his effort.

"Terrance, I need you to take Purgatorio to my cousin's house on Bread Street. I need you to see if Marcie and Simon are there, do you know them?" I asked.

He nodded.

"I want you to have my cousin, Mr. Nethersby, write out a missive to me confirming if they are safe or not. You will place it within Purgartorio, just here, see?" I said, pointing to the compartment in his chest.

His eyes grew large, and he nodded again.

"Make haste now and send him back to find me. The sooner the better," I said.

"I don't know the way, miss," he said shyly.

"I can show him," Sadie said. I looked at her for the first time since we exited the apartments of the beadle. She looked tired and lost. "We can take Nathan home, he needs rest anyway, miss. I know I gave you no reason to trust me, but I hope I can somehow make amends," she said.

"Yes, well I daresay you are working toward redemption with the actions you took in there. Unfortunately, Nate will need transportation. He is in no shape to run. Please show Terrance the way and stay there until you hear from me," I replied.

Sadie smiled and grabbed Terrance's hand. I lifted my arm for Purgatorio to take flight after them. I turned back to Nathan, leaning on a lamp post and smirking at me.

"You know I'm not going to sit this one out, right? I must see it through, miss. I'll crawl to Lord Daven's if I have to," Nate said.

"That's what I was afraid of. Better to keep an eye on you myself than leave you to your own devices," I said.

"What was in the image, Miss Anna?" Nate asked.

"Mister Hillard and Mrs. Squires, dear one," I replied.

"But she swore she never did nothin'! You telling me she swindled us?"

"Nathan, I can't say for sure, but a wise sage once told me not to trust the coggery, and I believe she is what he spoke of. Now, what else, Luke?"

"Constable Tallon is going to take the beadle to The Yard and catch up with us. He is going to apprise Chief Investigator Farthing of our progress. Let us get to it then. We have a meeting with a rather sinister Lord," Luke grimaced.

We all walked back to the Second Chance Orphanage. I took Nathan with me on my motorbike and Luke followed behind. We weaved our way through the streets, a reverse of the journey this morning. The poor dirt roads morphed into cobblestone and wealth the farther we went. I heard a screech and saw Purgatorio across town rushing towards home. I wished I could join him. I wasn't sure I was prepared for what we were to face. I caught Nate looking up at me. He smiled and nodded with determination. I returned the gesture. I hoped Nathan's friends would come out of this okay. A lingering doubt coiled in my belly. I still felt as if something was missing.

Turning the corner, I saw a man standing in the middle of the road. I slammed the brakes and veered to the right, crashing into a cart of flowers. I rolled over the top of the cart and landed hard on the side path. Luke screeched his brakes as he took in the scene. I felt a trickle of blood above my temple and touched the delicate spot.

I looked up just in time to recognize the man from the street, Mr. Piltner, bearing down on Luke as he exited his motor. The pocked-faced man held a knife in his hand. Nate screamed from the side car in warning. I watched as Piltner swung wildly in Luke's direction. A battle cry reverberated from his dry, flaky lips. The knife missed its target, but just barely. Luke took out his baton and hit his assailant between the shoulder blades, causing him to stumble. Piltner recovered quickly. He charged at Luke again, this time leading with his fist. Luke moved to dodge the blow. Piltner feigned the strike of his fist and then plunged the knife with his other hand into Luke's rib.

I ran without thinking. The pain that seared Luke's face was palpable. He pushed the man away from him causing the knife to dislodge from his abdomen. I reached him as he fell to his knees holding his side. Another scream pierced the air, and I looked up to see the knife now rushing down in my direction. The metal gleamed as its arc penetrated the sun's beam. I raised my arm overhead and felt the impact. I waited for the pain to register but it didn't come. The knife had hit the ankh charm connected to my bracer. Piltner stumbled back a few steps. I prepared myself for another blow, blocking Luke from any more damage. *This would not be our fate; this would not be the end of our story.* The chant recited through my mind as I forced myself into action.

"I won't be going back! You should have left well enough alone, lady," he growled.

Piltner advanced toward me again. I hit the button on my ruby encrusted bracer and caught the dagger that sprang out into my left hand. A flash behind Piltner registered in my mind as Nate swept up Luke's discarded baton and swung with all his might at the horrid man. He grunted at the blow, and I took the momentary distraction to surge up and plant my dagger in his gut. His knife clattered to the ground as he groped at the wound I had inflicted. Nathan rushed toward Luke and I. I hauled him to my chest in relief. Luke lay on the ground now, getting paler by the moment. Piltner backed up until his heels hit the curb and fell to his arse, still clutching the dagger inside him. I grabbed the whistle attached to Luke's neck and blew as hard as I could. Nate covered his ears, and I tried to see through the sheen of tears that were threatening to take over my sight.

This would not be our fate; this would not be the end of our story.

Chapter 46- The Better Man

Losing oneself to despair is a common pitfall in life. It is those of us who can crawl from these depths that truly know what it is to be strong.

"What are we goin' do, Miss Anna? He don't look right at all," Nate cried.

I hauled the scarf off my neck and placed it on Luke's wound, soaking up as much blood as I could. I continued to blow the whistle for help. Piltner stayed seated, staring down at his own affliction. I thought to warn him not to remove the dagger, but the vengeful demon on my shoulder kept me silent. I watched his slick hand grasp at the metal. I shook my head and reminded myself of who I was. I would not be responsible for taking a life if I could help it. That is what I fought against. Monsters who have no moral obligation to save a peer if they were capable of it.

"Don't remove it," I said.

Piltner's gaze shot up at me.

"If you remove it, you will bleed out. Keep it there until help arrives," I directed.

"What's it to you? You would rather see me hang from the gallows, I bet. There is no difference, I'm a dead man either way," he moaned.

"It's what you deserve after that stunt, mister. Go around stabbing folks who are trying to save people! Killin' my friends, you have! I should be glad to take that knife out for you," Nate yelled.

"No, Nathan Starling, you listen to me. Whatever evil he has done, we cannot allow ourselves to fall victim to our rage and need for retribution. We must follow the law, and we must hold ourselves higher. This is why we fight monsters, to get them off the street, not to turn into them ourselves," I said.

I blew the whistle again as Nate stared at me with a mix of confusion and tempered anger. I knew how he felt. Looking down as Luke held my scarf to his puncture, I felt it all the more. Hastened footsteps drew me out of my dark thoughts, and two bobbies rounded the bend toward us. Taking in the scene they both blew their whistles fiercely. Finally, a motor with officers rushed toward us. I held Luke's hand and breathed a sigh.

"You mustn't confront them yourself, Belle. You can't risk it," he strained.

"Yes, I know. If Lady Daven has the letter, I don't think I shall have to," I responded.

"What letter?"

"The one I had Marcie and Simon deliver with flowers. The one that told her that a present was waiting for her in the back cottage. The one that is going to set Lord Daven's world on fire if what I suspect is true," I said.

"You clever woman. Why did you not say that before?" Luke asked, clenching his jaw.

"I wanted us to be there, so you could take him into custody when it all fell into place. We must get you to the hospital, Luke," I replied.

"I am going to be okay, Belle. I am not done for yet," Luke smiled weakly.

"Miss, can you please move to the side so we can get Constable Weston loaded up? We already sent word to the staff there to be expecting us. Another motor will be around in a bit for the other man," a tall bobbie with graying hair said.

"Yes, of course. Doctor Cannish should be sought out as well. He will want to oversee the constable's treatment. The man, Mr. Piltner, is the one who stabbed the constable. Please make sure an officer guards over him. Although I don't think he will get far with his wound."

"Yes, miss, we will make sure he doesn't go anywhere. Are you okay? That gash on your head looks painful," he asked.

My hand flung to my head and I felt the lump forming beneath blood encrusted hair. It smarted a bit, but nothing too dire.

"I'll be fine, sir, thank you. If I could get a clean cloth, that would be most helpful."

Constable Weston was already placed in the back of the motor by the time our conversation had concluded. I looked at my motorbike and grimaced.

"Now what do we do, Miss Anna? We need to get to Lord Daven's and your transport is all mangled," Nate said.

I dashed over to the open door of Constable Weston's motor and looked in.

"Yes, but luckily Luke left his motor without taking his keys. How fortunate!"

A screech from above drew my attention to the sky. Purgatorio had found us. He dove down and landed gracefully on the hood of the motor. I reached for the missive I knew that would be hiding in his hollow chest.

"Wonderful! They are both safe and have delivered the package to Lady Daven. I daresay we will be just in time to see the fireworks fly," I said.

"Fireworks? I have never seen those before," Nate replied.

"Come Nathan, let us get to the show before the curtain rises."

"Miss Anna, you lost me now. Are you sure your head is okay?"

I laughed heartily at that, which did nothing to ease Nathan's concern. Moving into the driver's seat of Luke's motor, I adjusted the seating to fit my smaller frame. Starting the engine, a few officers looked my way in question. Mr. Piltner looked up from his spot on the curb, grey and weary. A few obscenities drifted through the open window, but I disregarded them with the rest of the trash slumped in the gutter. Nate had barely closed his door before I slammed my foot upon the accelerator and lurched toward our destination.

I wonder what Lord Daven would do when confronted by the woman he was trying to save. How would he defend his morality when his wife discovered his disregard for the lives of the less fortunate? I shuddered at the horrid truth that revealed itself to me in that moment. The very wealthy would always think their lives more precious and more important than those of the poor. It hurt my heart, but the fact was clearly valid, if history had any say.

Hopefully today there would be justice for those who didn't have the means to claim it.

Chapter 47- The Queen Takes The King

Chess is a game of strategy and foresight. If you can apply the same skills in life then you are indeed a fortunate soul.

Racing down the streets of London was exhilarating. I feared for Luke's health, but I was also in the height of the chase. I would not be able to focus on anything until the last move was executed. Purgatorio chose to fly above us as we made our way to Lord Daven's estate. I tried to go over what we knew about this whole affair. I needed to talk it out. Looking toward Nate, who was a little sturdier now, I felt I needed to share. This, afterall, was his past, his friends, and his heartbreak. He needed to be there just as much as I did.

"Nathan Starling, I must discuss all that I have discovered, and since Constable Weston is not here, I fear the task falls to you. I know you will not like me dredging up the particulars of your friends' demise, but it can't be helped. Are you up to the challenge?"

He nodded.

"Well then, I guess it's best to start at the beginning with these things. We discovered Gwennie at the docks that night when you went to meet Mr. Piltner. If what he said to the beadle was any indication, the horrible man placed her there. Whether he killed her or just moved her for the beadle is still in question," I started.

"I wonder how One-eyed Whitmore came upon her, miss. Seems

strange that he wouldn't just tell us that the pocked-faced wretch was responsible if he knew," Nate said.

"Yes, that is a query indeed. I'm not sure how Whitmore fits into this tale at all really. He just seems to show up and suggest things. It is quite vexing, really," I agreed. "His charm did save me from getting cut today though. So I still believe he is a good sort of nuisance. After Gwennie, we discovered the three children at Tapers Grove."

"Miss Anna, I think you are missing something. The Grave Robber of Greenwich Village. That is when this really all started. You were right, remember? That case wasn't really solved. It was all pinned on a scapegoat so they could continue their nasty dealings," Nate said.

"You're right! That must have been when Lord Daven discovered Mr. Hillard's whereabouts and brought him back to London. He must have had him hidden near the church, but after we came too close, he moved him. Mrs. Squires had told me that Sadie had only been at Second Chance Orphanage for a few months. I think that is when Lord Daven forced Thomas to start using living children as opposed to the dead body parts they were experimenting with before."

"That's disgusting. Why were they messing around with dead parts you think?" Nate asked.

"Well, from what Dr. Cannish told us, Thomas Hillard was no stranger to these kinds of procedures. He did this grotesque work under the guise of an apprenticeship in school. He would swap parts of one animal into another," I continued. A buzzing started in my head as the obvious answer was before me. "Of course! Sadie said at the beadle's house that Lord Daven was trying to save Lady Daven, correct?"

"Yes, miss. Whatcha thinkin'? You have that crazed look upon you," Nate said.

"Something is ailing Lady Daven and rather than seek help from a mortal enemy, like our Dr. Cannish, he went to his old chum. The disowned adopted brother of Cannish. How deliriously cruel."

"What do you mean?" Nate asked, confusion clouding his features.

"Nathan, Lady Daven is the former Miss Eloise Bridgemont and one-time desired sweetheart of Doctor Cannish. Elliott Daven and Thomas Hillard constructed a devious plot to keep Miss Bridgemont and the doctor apart. To think that Lord Daven's animosity would supersede the need to help his poor wife is mind-boggling," I said.

"I can see that. I once heard of a guy holding a grudge so long, he forgot what it was about. But it didn't matter, he was still not talking to the offending fella," Nate said.

"We know that Mr. Hillard had inserted an organ from Gwennie into Janey. So, it stands to reason that whatever is wrong with Lady Daven is an internal organ and they are trying to create a procedure to replace this failing element with that of another unfortunate soul," I said.

"Do you really think it is possible? It would be extraordinary," Nate said.

"It would indeed, but for the part that he's using unwilling children to aid in this endeavor," I retorted.

We were pulling up toward the path leading to Lord Daven's estate when a figure appeared from behind a gaslight. Slowing down we realized it was Adam. He ran to the motor and jumped in the back seat as I parked on the edge of the road.

"Right good timing, Miss Sweeting. You wouldn't believe the happenings up at the Daven place," he said.

"Tell us," I prompted.

"Lord Daven came home early with the doc, looking concerned when he saw me trying to see what was in the back cottage. I dodged him and his servants, but man did the doc take a hit. He was sent away, but not before I spied him picking up Marcie and Simon in his motor. I stayed in the woods by the edge of Daven's property. I figured since the doc was safeguarding the children I should stay put in case you needed me. Then a pretty woman came out of the house and headed for what I thought was the greenhouse at first. She was holding the flowers you sent. She moved very slowly, using a cane, and had to stop a few times as she went. I noticed she was also holding a parchment, and she held it up, smiling. I watched her head to the cottage and walk in. Then the most horrible scream came from her. She stumbled back, and I thought she was going to faint straight away. Lord Daven rushed from the front of the house to aid her. The poor woman started flailing her arms about, trying to get away. Then Mrs. Squires and some gent showed up and hauled the pretty lady into the cottage. There was some yelling and screaming but then it quieted down a bit. That's when I saw your motor. Hey, who's that?" Adam said, pointing behind us.

We turned around to see another motor racing toward us. Squinting, I let out a breath of relief. Constable Tallon and Quincy were joining us. They pulled to a stop next to us and we all got out to plan the next course of action. I wanted to know what happened with Nancy and Father Gaverty, but I would have to ask about that later. We were about to storm a castle, and we needed our wits about us. I couldn't wait to see the king fall.

Chapter 48- Moving Pieces

It is common knowledge that no one's pain is quite as acute as one's own.

"Miss Sweeting, I was told to relay to you that Cannish is taking care of Constable Weston and that it looks promising," Tallon said.

"Thank you, constable. And what of Mr. Piltner?" I asked.

"He is going to live, too," he said dryly.

"Shame, that," Nate sniffed.

"Yes, well I would have hated to be a murderer, Starling," I retorted.

"Not murder, miss. You was a defender of life and not just your own," he said.

"The lad's right, Miss Sweeting. You're a hero indeed," Quincy smiled.

I blushed.

"Enough of that, we have a few more villains to defeat. Constables, what is your take on the situation?" I said, changing the subject.

I repeated what Adam had told us and waited as they thought over the scenario. They wanted to go dashing in like knights, but I wasn't sure it was the best course of action. We were on unfamiliar ground, and I thought it better to draw them out of the cottage. An idea bubbled up to the forefront of my mind.

"Yes, I think this will work. Adam, I want you to go to the same window and peer through with the intention of being seen. Once you snag their attention, dash towards the greenhouse where Quincy will be waiting," I said.

"Why all the pomp and circumstance, Miss Sweeting?" Tallon asked.

"I feel it best to divide and conquer. If they catch wind that the bobbies are here, they will make a run for it. And knowing Lord Daven, he has plans in case such a thing was to occur. By sending the boy in first, they will just think he is a harmless pawn sent to spy, another poor urchin to dispatch of. This will give us more time to get past his servants and catch them in the act. We need to get Mr. Hillard away from Lord Daven," I replied.

"Constable Weston trusts you, so I am trusting you too. Where do you want me?" Tallon said.

"You'll be with me and Nate. We are going to call at the front of the house and see if the Lady is in," I said with a grin.

"But we know she's in the cottage," Adam said.

"Yes, but they don't know we know that. Pulling their attention to the front will give you the cover to sneak to the cottage, and Quincy to the greenhouse," I replied.

Purgatorio screeched from the sky.

"Time to go. Something is happening," I said looking up.

We jumped back into our motors and sped in the direction of the Daven estate. Quincy parked his out of sight of the main gate, and Adam joined him. Constable Tallon, Nate, and I continued up the drive at a slower pace. Once parked, we climbed the stairs to the front entrance and pulled the bell. Several servants from different points of the estate peered out at us, like little mice peering from their holes. *Scurry this way*, I thought to myself.

The door opened to a tall, fit butler. His black eyebrows arched as he took in the sight of us.

"Can I help you?" The butler inquired.

"Yes, is the lady of the house in?" I replied sweetly.

"And who is calling?" His suspicion was evident.

"This is Constable Tallon, Nathan Starling, and I am Annabelle Sweeting," I introduced.

His eyebrows nearly reached his hairline as I said my name. I continued, trying not to raise too much alarm.

"Mrs. Bergenhalt sent us to see if she might be willing to lend us some of her flowers for the party coming up. Everyone knows that Lady Daven has the best around," I complimented.

"Oh, well yes, that is true. The lady is not in just now," he said cautiously.

His eyes darted behind us, and we felt the rats, I mean servants, approaching us from behind. Constable Tallon slowly turned around and shook his head.

"Is the lady accustomed to such intimidating tactics of visitors? I have always seen her as gracious and amiable," Tallon said, still facing backward.

"Yes, well there has been some developments as of late, and the lady is…" The butler looked at me with imploring eyes. I nodded with recognition. He was afraid for her.

"Is Lord Daven at home?" I asked, trying to get anything useful.

"I don't believe…" the butler started.

A shout came from behind the house, and the servants that had been inching toward us started running in that direction. I looked back at the butler and his face was etched with urgent concern.

"Excuse me. I believe I am needed round back," he said dashing past us.

It only took a second before we followed the frazzled man. Turning the corner of the house, we saw Adam surrounded by several of Daven's men. I couldn't believe the smile across the young man's face as he darted this way and that, away from his pursuers. He was having fun. When he saw me, he winked. The men turned, and he took the opportunity to skirt around them and dash toward the greenhouse and the waiting Constable Quincy. Several men followed in pursuit, but he was much younger and faster than them. I felt confident that Quincy and Adam could handle them.

Nathan, Tallon, and I continued to follow the butler towards the back cottage. The door was open and Lord Daven stood outside waiting for news on Adam's capture. I watched as Daven's gaze took in his harried butler heading toward him and then the surprise and rage when he spotted me.

"YOU! How dare you invade my property. Leave at once," he bellowed.

"Elliott, who is it? I need more time in here," a voice said from the interior of the cottage.

"I am afraid you are all out of that," Tallon shouted.

"Who are you? I don't recognize you. Does Chief Inspector Farthing know you are here harassing me? I'll make sure neither of you will have a job in the morning," Lord Daven threatened.

"Lord Daven, I think it is fair to say that you are in no position to voice such threats. I believe that once we see what's in that cottage your words will hold no water with anyone of import," I said.

"Miss Sweeting, you have gone too far! I warned you." Lord Daven seethed with venom. He moved toward us, blocking our path to the cottage. I watched as the butler moved in behind him and peered in the door.

"My Lady!" The butler rushed into the cottage.

"Barnes, get out of there. This has nothing to do with you. She is perfectly fine, just resting," he said.

I tried to run past Lord Daven, but he captured my arm and hauled me toward him. Constable Tallon moved in to defend me, but the lord took out a weird instrument that looked like a spike and placed it near my throat.

"Step back," he warned.

Nate moved slowly while Elliott's eyes were fixed on Tallon. Nathan circled the lord, to position himself behind him. He snuck a peek through the open door and struggled to contain a gasp. I could only imagine what he saw.

"Well now, isn't this nice? We can just wait here until the good Doctor Hillard is done with the procedure. Then you will all see a miracle of modern medical application," he boasted.

"But at what cost? Surely you don't believe trading a child's life is justified. As a devoted Christian you can not say your wife's life is more valuable than others. We are all God's children, aren't we?" I pleaded.

"Of course her life is more important than some filthy urchin! They would just waste away with a perfectly good liver in the Brass Boroughs, but my wife, she makes an impact. She has helped so many people that these guttersnipes should be thanking her for putting their sacrifice to good use," he declared.

Just then, Hillard appeared at the door.

"We got a problem, Daven."

Chapter 49- In Too Deep

Never is a lie worse than when you have entrapped yourself in it.

Lord Daven moved, with me still in his clutches, to face sideways between the cottage door and Constable Tallon. He could now see Nathan and shouted for one of his men to apprehend him. Nate took off like a shot to the back of the cottage before anyone could get close to him. Daven kept an eye on Tallon as he edged his way closer to where Hillard stood.

"What's the issue? Is Eloise alright?" Daven asked.

"It's not her, it's the other one. She's done for. Too much alcohol in the blood, I think," he replied softly.

"Enough of this, release Miss Sweeting at once! Holding her hostage will only make things worse for you," Tallon shouted.

"No, I think she is just fine where she is. Actually, Mr. Hillard, I think we have a new volunteer," Lord Daven said.

"I am certainly not volunteering for anything. You are out of your mind! Release me," I demanded.

He brought the tip of the instrument closer to my throat and I felt his hot breath tickle the wisps of hair around my ear.

"I told you not to persist. You would not listen. Perhaps this is always how it was going to end. I'm sure you have a very healthy liver, Miss Sweeting," he whispered.

Tallon surged forward but stopped short at the sight of blood trickling down my neck. I gave a yelp as Daven shoved me into the arms of Thomas Hillard and pointed the sharp apparatus at Tallon. The constable removed his truncheon and squared off against the lord. I felt helpless as Hillard grasped me around the middle, pinning my arms in the process. I struggled, swinging my limbs wildly to try to break loose. He didn't seem phased at all and picked me up, moving backward through the open cottage door. Nate was nowhere in sight. I hoped that he had not been captured. I did not know where Quincy or Adam were either, and I started to panic.

Crossing the threshold of the cottage, I gained my first look of the gory interior. Mrs. Squires laid sprawled out on a butcher's table. The view around me caused my body to involuntarily shudder. Her eyes, glazed over in death, peered accusingly in my direction. A large, bloody gap marred her left abdomen. I felt the bile in my esophagus threaten to rise. On the other table lay Lady Daven, peacefully sleeping. I presumed that she was sedated by something. The butler sat near her, stroking the lady's hand. The hair on my neck stood on end as we neared another table.

"Stop this, you can stop," I shouted.

"I don't want to be here either, miss. It can't be helped though. He's got my daughter, he has. I just can't live without her," Hillard said.

"Mr. Hillard, he doesn't have her. I do!" I replied.

I turned my head to look him in the eyes, trying to relay that I was telling the truth. He released me and then swung his arm, slapping me hard across the face. I backpedaled into a chair.

"Liar! Zachariah has her, and he and the lord are thick as thieves. I've tried to get her out, but the beadle finds her. He always finds her. He's too well connected in the slums," he said.

"Not this time. She helped us catch him. He was going to tell us all about Lord Daven and this horrible venture. Your Sadie knocked him out," I replied, wincing through my sore jaw.

"Impossible!" he raged.

I tried to get up, but he pushed me down with force. He grabbed a vial and prepared to insert me with something from a syringe. I kicked out, and the vial shattered. The needle, however, still contained a good amount of liquid, and he lurched at me with it. My ruby encrusted bracer no longer held the hidden dagger, as I had plunged it into Mr. Pilner only a couple hours earlier. What bad luck.

I heard shouting outside and wished we had more help. As if in reply to my thoughts, a familiar screech sounded, and Purgatorio broke through the cottage window. He landed on Mrs. Squire's mangled body. His spiked tail swayed with menace as he took in the scene before him. Thomas turned around in reaction to the sound of shattering glass. His eyes filled with fear taking in the aggressive stance of my mechanical beast. Purgatorio flicked his segmented tail and released the sharp barbs from it, sending them into Hillard's arm that held the syringe. Thomas screamed in pain as they punctured his forearm. The force of the projectiles pinned Hillard's arm to the wall and caused him to release the syringe.

I surged from the chair, crossing the room to stand next to Purgy. I took out my amethyst hairpin in case another assault was imminent.

A series of shouts came from the door, and Chief Inspector Farthing surged in carrying a pistol. He looked from Mr. Hillard to Lady Daven and then the butler. His gaze darted over to poor Mrs. Squires with Purgy standing atop and then to me. His eyes bulged wider as they progressed.

"Doctor Cannish, get in here!" The chief shouted with urgency.

"Walter is here?" I asked.

Before Farthing could respond, both Walter and Luke rushed through the door. Luke hurried over to me holding his bandaged side. The fire and fear in his eyes burned brightly as he looked me over for any life-threatening afflictions. I must have appeared a complete fright with my hair down and still a mess from the accident. I moved to wind it up and replace my hair pin. Luke halted my hands and took them in his, bringing them up to his lips.

Chief Inspector Farthing removed the spikes from Thomas's arm and dropped them on the floor, then he hauled him up by the elbow and escorted him out at gunpoint. Thomas yelled on his way out.

"You've doomed her, my dear Sadie! Please save her, brother. Please." Mr. Hillard pleaded.

"Thomas, we are not brothers, we haven't been for a long time. I am, however, not a cruel person, so you can rest assured your daughter is safe. This woman here, that you just tried to slice up, saw to that. Either way you will never see her again, I am sure," Dr. Cannish said.

Hillard's gaze shifted to me at the realization that I had been telling the truth. He swallowed hard and let Farthing lead him away. Walter didn't spare him another look, he dashed over to where Eloise lay still. Moving the butler out of the way, he checked her pulse. He must have found her heartbeat to be pleasing as relief washed over his face.

He turned to me and strode over. Taking my face in his hands, he tilted it to get a better look at the damage done on the top of my head from the motor crash. He gently moved it in the opposite direction to view the small neck wound Hillard had inflicted as well.

"Tsk-Tsk, Miss Sweeting. That's a nasty bump indeed. You always dive headfirst, don't you? I might need to stitch it up a bit, but you should be alright," Dr. Cannish said.

"Thank you, Walter. It looks like you have a nasty shiner as well. I understand Lord Daven is to blame. Also, why is Constable Weston out of bed? I thought putting you in charge of his care would assure his proper recovery," I chided.

"Elliott did not take kindly to the idea of me taking over Lady Daven's care. I thought I had him convinced, but then he saw young

Adam and thought I was making a play to drive her away from him. I guess he didn't need me to do that. He accomplished that all on his own. As for Constable Weston, I did what I could, Annabelle, but he would not stand for it. Once I had him initially patched up he was as bucky as a stallion. It's a wonder that he hasn't split the wound open again," he replied.

Purgatorio dropped down to the ground and trotted over to his discarded spikes. He took them in his mouth and swallowed them. We all watched as they appeared back in his tail where empty cavities had been.

"I didn't know the beastie could do that," Luke wheezed.

"Neither did I," I admitted.

"I think it's best if you both leave now," Chief Inspector Farthing said from the doorway. "We can wrap up this horror scene. You've done enough for your city, I'd say."

"What about Quincy and Adam, are they okay? And what of Lord Daven and Constable Tallon? Did Constable Williams, Byron, and Penny save Nancy from Father Gaverty? Will Lady Daven be alright? I can't go now, there is so much to do," I rambled.

Chapter 50- Trust in Me

Love is really just the expansion of trust. When you share genuine trust with someone the rest falls into place.

"There is no need to put yourself into hysterics, Miss Sweeting. We'll get you the answers you seek, but first we must get all injured parties back to the hospital. We need to clear this cottage of evidence and blood, and it's best if we don't go adding yours and Constable Weston's in the mix," Chief Inspector Farthing said.

"Yes, and the constable doesn't appear to be looking very well at present," Walter said.

I looked over to find Luke buckling. Walter and I rushed together to help support him, and we removed him from the cottage. Tallon joined us outside, and I was relieved he didn't appear to be badly injured. Tallon took Luke's weight from me and helped him back to a waiting motor.

"I'm sorry, Miss Sweeting, I tried to get to you, but the blasted Lord Daven is a crafty one. I was able to subdue him, but only after he slashed my arm."

Tallon displayed a bloody wound on his bicep. I gasped at the jagged line etched there. That odd tool had certainly done some damage.

"Luckily your mechanical creature didn't have anyone blocking his path. He shot down like a comet, never saw anything like it," Tallon said.

I looked behind us, where Purgatorio was trailing us on the ground. His tail still swiveled this way and that, in preparation for any attack. He really was a fierce little thing.

"What happened to Lord Daven?" I asked.

"He's locked up in the wagon over there, along with several of his men, and Mr. Hillard," Tallon pointed. "I daresay the lot should be sent to the sanitarium at once, but we shall see what his powerful friends will do when they hear the news."

"I would hate to be associated with such madness, and a child killer to boot. No, I think that any friends of his would not risk the taint of it all," I replied.

Tallon nodded and helped Luke in the passenger door. Nate came running up from behind. He smiled widely and hugged me.

"Oh, Miss Anna, I am glad you are okay! I couldn't get into the cottage, so I thought we could use more help, and so I got it, I did! I found one of Miro's Nassar Navigators moving about and flagged it down. With the extra parchment you're always needing, I had some in my pocket and was able to write a message out for the ocular viewer. Rose must have run like a thoroughbred mare to get that ol' Farthing out here so fast," he said.

"You clever boy! I am glad you were not caught," I said.

"Ah, me, no way! I've been dodging bobbies my whole life, until you. Do you think a few fat servants are going to take me down? That's just insulting, it is," he smirked.

I hugged him tightly and watched as he and Purgy got into the back seat.

"I have to stay here, Miss Sweeting. Need to help get Quincy to the hospital too. I'll meet you over there," Tallon said, holding the driver door for me.

"Oh no, what happened to Constable Quincy?" I asked.

"He was caught from behind, took a nasty hit to the head. Luckily, your boy came along and fought the man off, and the one who was chasing him too. I'm sure glad he was on our side. Wonder if he's interested in a job when he gets a little older." Tallon suggested.

"Oh, Adam, he is the strong one, you know," Nate said.

"Where is he?" I inquired.

"He stuck around for a bit, but once he heard Miss Sweeting was safe, he said he had promises to keep and you would know where to find him," Tallon gestured to Nate.

Nate nodded from the back of the motor. I guess that was a story for another time. A groan from the passenger side reminded me that Luke wasn't out of the woods yet from his injury. I felt horrible for letting my curious mind chase down these answers when he was in so much pain. I fired up the vehicle and saluted Constable Tallon as I zoomed down the road toward the hospital. I heard Purgatorio power down in the back and sent a prayer up for keeping him energized for when I really was in need. I glanced over at Luke's pale cheeks and saw blood starting to seep through his shirt.

"You take too many risks, Luke. How could you be so careless? You should have stayed in the hospital, not come rushing back into danger when you weren't recovered," I chided.

I wasn't really mad at him, just more fearful that he had done more damage to himself.

He smiled weakly. "I couldn't let you have all the fun now, could I?"

"Is he going to make it, Miss Anna?" Nate asked from the back seat.

"He better, or I'm going to kill him myself," I said.

As if testing my declaration, I glanced to my left and Constable Weston slumped unconscious into his seat.

"No, no, no. You will not do this to me, Luke! Nate, is he breathing?"

Nate leaned forward between the two front seats and checked for the constable's breath. Nate nodded his head fervently, "He is, miss, but it's real shallow."

"Foolish, headstrong man!" I shouted at Luke's hunched figure. "We are almost there, just hold on," I pleaded.

I slammed my foot down on the fuel pedal and raced through the streets, getting curses and stares as I swerved to avoid other drivers. I barely missed a man crossing the street with his dog and shouted an apology through the open window. Fear threatened to choke me, and then a thought like lightning struck. Was this how Luke felt the night he found me bloodied and delirious outside Miro's motor park. Was this fate's cruel sense of karma? Well, just like that night I wasn't going to allow anything to happen to the one I loved. *This would not be our fate; this would not be the end of our story.*

Chapter 51- Misguided Trust

The pain of loving a monster is not knowing what that makes you.

I fell asleep in the chair beside Luke's infirmary bed. He was carted in moments after I squealed to a stop in front of the entrance. Nurse Gilda, the wonderfully feisty nurse that had taken care of One-eyed Whitmore, came barreling through and took charge. I was forced to wait outside while they hooked him up to all sorts of gizmos, trying to stabilize him.

I paced the halls with Nate until a commotion outside drew our attention, and we found Purgatorio roaring inside the motor. I quickly released him, and he chuffed in greeting as if nothing had happened. Several spikes on his tail were still covered in red residue which made me think of Mr. Hillard and his daughter, Sadie. It was a terrible business to have one's father dispatch your friends. Sure, his claim of being blackmailed to save her life might seem quite heroic, but to whom? For Sadie's part, she might feel responsible that they died in her stead. In reality, they died for Lord Daven's blind determination to keep his wife alive. They all had choices, however, and they chose poorly. No matter what one could say about Lord Daven, he did dearly love his wife.

Nurse Gilda finally came out of Luke's room and smiled at me. Relief flooded my limbs, and I would have melted into a puddle on the floor if there wasn't a chair there to catch me. He was going to be fine. He had several serious issues still under observation. I didn't hear much after she said he was going to be alright though. My mind was too full to take in anything else.

After an hour or so, she said I could see him. However, he would most likely still be unconscious. In the meantime, she said I would need to have my head wound addressed. I had forgotten about it until she mentioned it. It was throbbing along with the beat of my heart. I told Nathan to go with Purgy and relay everything to my cousin Jaime. Nathan didn't want to leave me, but I told him I was in good hands and that Doctor Cannish would return shortly. He agreed and dashed away, telling me that he would be back soon. He was just about to exit the door when he ran back and kissed me on the cheek.

"I'm glad you're okay, Miss Anna. Thanks for helping my friends." Nate said with unshed tears in his eyes.

"That's what family does," I said and hauled him in for a tight squeeze.

His eyes shined with wetness, but he brushed it away and raced out the door before anyone could make a fuss. A woman with black hair and kind eyes patched up the cut on my head. She helped me wash the wound and fix my hair out of the way of the stitches. I don't remember her name or talking to her, but I remember the feeling of being taken care of. I drifted along until they let me in to see Luke. I sat by his side and held his hand.

Waves of exhaustion must have finally caught up with me. I woke up to noises outside the open door to Luke's room. Lady Daven was being wheeled in. She was awake and had a yellow tint to her that I hadn't noticed before. I wondered if she had been poisoned. Doctor Cannish followed behind with hurried steps. The rooms became quiet again, and I found myself drifting in and out as other patients were received. I thought I saw Constable Quincy, his head bandaged, walking by. Constable Tallon poked his head in, I believe, but it was hard to tell what was real or a dream.

My neck felt stiff as I opened my eyes to find my cousin, Nathan, Simon, Lily, and Stewart looking down at us.

"Oh, dearest, this is eerily familiar, but reverse," Jaime said. "I fear you two are terrible at keeping out of scrapes."

"It does seem like quite a toll," said Stewart with concern.

"It is a task I will be forever grateful that Miss Sweetin' took on, I will," said a voice behind them all.

They parted, and in walked Nancy. She still sported a busted lip but added to that was now a bandaged wrist and neck. I smiled, and she started to weep.

"You were right to send Penny and Byron, miss. Father Gaverty would have snuck right past that bobbie if it weren't for Penny's know-how. He was fixin' to have me hauled off to that cruddy lord's house and butchered up like the rest of them. He even gave me a right awful burn on my foot, he did. Said it would help me get into Heaven since I was a slum-rat and all, and ain't have no proper baptism and raising up. I was about to tell him that his beadle is the one that gives us churching, but the burn smarted so bad I done passed out. It was when I heard the crash of the glass that I woke up and felt hope," she said.

"Byron's always wanted to take a shot at one of them windows," Nate smirked.

"Yeah, well that ain't all he took a shot at. Turns out Father Gaverty has a secret passage outside his rooms, not sure how Penny knew about that door in the courtyard, but they was waitin' on us just as we came out. You shoulda' seen his face. I thought he might faint from fright, how white he got. Then the ol' bobbie came running when he heard Penny scream bloody murder. Byron popped Father Gaverty right in the eye so he couldn't get away. I can scarce believe it, and I was there," Nancy rambled.

"Fancy this Byron fellow is a good man to have in a pinch then?" A familiar voice floated through the doorway. Everyone turned to find Lord Thetford smiling shyly at the now crowded entrance to Luke's room.

"I know another gentleman that I can say the same thing about," I replied. "Thank you for the use of your wonderful inventions, they surely turned the tide in this investigation. And, yes, I think you would be quite impressed with young Byron. I mean to talk to you about him later."

Miro smiled warmly as he entered the room. Looking down at Luke's battered state, and then to my bandaged head, Miro's brow creased. "I wish I could have done more," he said.

"You've done more than enough, and once again, Purgatorio was my knight and shining manticore. He saved me from a most precarious situation," I replied.

"Oh yes, and Andre is beyond compare, Lord Thetford. I daresay you'll be having new orders in no time," Jaime chimed in.

"Not more beasties," mumbled Luke as he rubbed the sleep from his eyes.

We all chuckled, and each guest took turns wishing Luke a fast recovery and leaving him to rest. When the room emptied it left Nathan, Luke, and I in silence. The fatigue of the day warred with my want of connection.

"Starling, be a good lad and get Miss Sweeting home before she collapses," Luke said.

I blinked my eyes hard and roused myself from my near slumber. "But…"

"No excuses, you are beyond exhausted, and have had a very trying day. I am in safe hands here, so there is no reason for you to stay and fret. There is no point in you having a stiff neck just to watch me sleep," Luke smiled.

"Well, I am quite tired. Are you sure?" I asked.

"Yes, Belle. Get some rest," Luke said.

"Yeah, Miss Anna, you need to rest up, like the constable says. You've got that big party to prepare for too. Your cousin is all a flutter with fabrics strewn about the house. The help needs you back to reign him in," Nate smirked.

A knock on the door interrupted the conversation, and Dr. Cannish entered the room.

"Well now, how are we doing? No more unnecessary heroics, I presume?" Walter joked, raising an eyebrow at Luke.

"I assure you, I will not leave this bed until you have deemed it appropriate. How does Lady Daven fair?" Luke replied.

"Ah, well she has a very bad liver, it appears. I think that with the right combination of vitamins and medicinal herbs we should be able to reduce the inflammation and get her back to a stable state. They were treating her with a highly alcoholic regiment, which in turn made her worse. A dietary change and rest will help alleviate the major symptoms. But I fear it is too early to tell, and we will have to keep a close watch in case the damage has been too sufficient. She has had quite a shock as well. I fear she will need time to come to terms with what her husband has done," he sighed.

"I believe you should stay close at hand. She may need your assistance in the coming weeks," I said.

"I plan to," he winked. Walter examined my head one more time before Nate and I took our leave. He assured us that the constable would be attended to diligently.

We staggered out into the cool night air and hailed a cabbie to take us back to Bread Street. Whatever tornadic disaster that Jaime had made of the house with his linens would need to wait until the morrow, as I could think of nothing other than sinking into my long-neglected bed.

Chapter 52- Feathers Be Damned

The finest frock is neither too simple nor too grandiose. A true artist finds just the right balance.

The following week went by like a whirlwind. The children at Second Chance Orphanage moved to different foundling hospitals that could find space. The orphans didn't feel vastly upset by Mrs. Squires' unfortunate end, but they were disheartened to be separated. I made sure we knew where every one of our little heroes and heroines had gone so they would not be lost in the foundling hospital framework. Also, we needed to call on them to get sized for Lady Bergenhalt's upcoming masquerade. They were nervous yet excited to have a chance to see Glimmer society. Strict instructions to leave their pickpocketing skills at home were issued on numerous occasions. They assured me that they understood the importance of the event and that they would not, as Byron eloquently put it, "rook it up."

Luke was released from the hospital after several days, and his aunt's maid played nurse for him, much to his dismay. I visited him when I could, but she kept shooing me out after an allotted quarter of an hour time limit. She found it very improper that I did not come with a chaperone, since we weren't working on a case right now. I could only chuckle, but I could tell Luke was flustered by her interference.

Jaime made quick work of the children's costumes with the help of

Miss Bethany, Stewart's sister. She was thrilled to be assisting with such a prestigious affair and thanked Jaime continuously. My cousin even surprised me by offering to create my attire. I had not seen it yet, but he promised it would suit me, with scarce a feather to be seen.

I worked in my tinker room creating scarab brooches for all the guttersnipes. I added little symbols to each with an etching tool. For Rose, I etched a shoe with wings; for Byron, a slingshot; for Adam, a strong arm; for Marcie, a fox; for Penny, a crystal ball; for Nancy, a lyre; for Terrance, a candle; for Simon, a cherub; and for Nathan, a starling.

Each of their skills proved to be invaluable in the challenges we faced during the case. I couldn't help but feel a twist of pride and a little shame that the children had to rise to the hardships they faced. Society needed to do better by its youth. I hoped the benefit Lady Bergenhalt had added to her party to help raise funds would shine a light on their plight. Everything needed to be perfect. We couldn't let this opportunity go to waste.

I heard a knock on my workroom door and opened it to find Jaime standing there, disheveled. His shirt was untucked, his hair mused, and his cravat completely missing. Wide, exhausted eyes met mine, and he smiled. "I finished them all! Isn't it wonderful? How do you fair? Are you able to eat with me, cousin?"

"Oh, well isn't this incredible timing. I was just putting the finishing touches on the children's broaches. Come see!" I exclaimed.

Jaime walked in and surveyed the mess I had yet to clean up, but then gasped when he saw the finished pieces lined up and gleaming on the table.

"These are absolutely exquisite, Belle. The craftsmanship is surely beyond compare. You outdid yourself, my dear," he said.

I blushed from the praise and pulled him in for a tired hug.

"Thank you, cousin. Let us go see if the cook can whip us up something quickly, before we faint away from all the hard work we've done. Is Bethany still here?" I asked.

"Yes, she and Stewart are having Trish set up a nice little picnic in the drawing room. A cozy fire, and some hot food will do us a world a good, I'd say," Jaime smiled.

"That sounds beyond delightful," I replied.

Jaime offered his arm, and I slipped my hand into the crook of his elbow. We proceeded down the hall and stairs like the royal couple and couldn't contain our laughter when we entered the drawing room and saw our small party's faces. It seemed that the lack of sleep and overall joy of completing the ensembles and adornments had finally gotten to us both.

We made a happy party as we ate hot ham, freshly baked bread, and cheese with fruit. Trish even brought out several blueberry tarts for dessert. We lounged by the fire and lamented on the horrible circumstances that had led us to discover the wrongdoings of a most respected clergyman. To unearth the evil action of a man of God had everyone in society reeling. With such a post came higher standards. Even Lord Daven wasn't as despised as Father Gaverty and Beadle Fieldworth.

The conversation turned to the children and the challenges they would face in the future without proper support. The Bergenhalt Ball was the natural progression in our discussion, and Jaime became quite animated while describing the costumes he had made for them. I couldn't wait to see them on the children, and what kind of reaction the party would elicit.

Bethany was overjoyed at having been included and promised Jaime if she received any new fabric imports, he would have first rights. She was also elated that he had trusted her with several designs he had been privately working on. The memory of what Lady Bergenhalt had said at tea, regarding him wanting his own shop, returned to me. Perhaps it was time for him to venture out on his own, or rather with the help of some supportive friends. I smiled as they continued to rapture over the newest lace-detailing they had seen coming out of Italy. These were the moments that really elevated my disposition. I could feel the joy vibrating throughout the room, and I knew that whatever travesties came our way, there would be a chance for happiness afterward. We just needed to know when and where to look, and never deny its possibility.

Chapter 53- Righting Wrongs

A future is never guaranteed. A past is never relived. The present is the only thing you have a say in, so do utilize it wisely.

Luke, Quincy, and I stood in Chief Inspector Farthing's tiny office. We waited for him to finish reading the report we had drafted with the help of Tallon and Williams. Farthing worked his curled mustache with his fingers as he flipped to the last page.

"How extraordinary! It looks like we may owe Miss Sweeting an apology, in light of Father Gaverty's connection to this crime, hey?" Farthing conceded.

He looked up at Luke with a raised brow.

I tried to hide the smile threatening to take over my face.

"And I see here that you want to continue as partners then? Leaving young Quincy out in the cold? Tsk-tsk, that won't do," he said.

Before Luke could interrupt, Farthing put his hand up.

"It seems that Quincy has gained some valuable experience from this investigation, and I think it would be wise to have another pair of eyes on your next few cases. He has written a separate report for me highlighting all that he has learned from shadowing you two for the past few weeks, and I find his admiration not misplaced. Therefore, I will honor your request for Miss Sweeting to continue consulting with you, Constable Weston. But, going forward, you will also be taking this young lad along for the ride. Understood?"

"Yes, sir," Luke agreed.

"Now, Miss Sweeting, I believe you had another proposal for me?" Farthing asked with an arched brow.

"Yes, Chief Inspector, I thought it might be beneficial to both parties if we had a league of children in the Brass Boroughs on better terms with The Yard. Not only are they great informants, but they often go unnoticed. We could offer them compensation and a way to make money without having to steal it," I suggested.

"This sounds great in theory, but wouldn't they be in more danger if it was known that they are snitching on their fellow Boroughians?"

"There are so many orphaned children, I think it would be very hard to distinguish whether one is spying or simply hanging about. We could also create a signal or symbol that designates them as part of our secret force. This not only will keep them from getting nabbed wrongfully by the constables and officers, but by not announcing it to the world, they would still go unnoticed to the masses," I replied.

"It is something to think about. I will take it under consideration. Now off with the lot of you. We have a rare lull in cases, so take the opportunity while you can. Oh, and go see Doctor Cannish on the way out, he has a request of sorts," Farthing said.

"All of us, sir?" Quincy asked.

"Just Miss Sweeting I believe, Quincy."

"Thank you, sir," Quincy said.

We all headed for the door at the same time but had to stop and take turns exiting as the space was too small. We laughed at the awkwardness of the situation and said our farewells to Constable Quincy. Luke escorted me toward the back hall, where Doctor Cannish kept his office.

Luke's abdomen still had heavy padding, but his mobility had grown vastly in the past few days. Luke caught me staring at him and smiled.

He reached out and tucked a stray hair behind my ear and waited for me outside the doctor's office as I entered. I took the open chair across his desk and waited for his attention. After a few moments, Doctor Cannish looked up, startled, and grinned.

"Ah, Miss Annabelle, I was woolgathering, it seems. Thank you for dropping by. I have a favor to ask you of a delicate nature, and I wasn't sure how to approach it," he said.

"Well, just be direct. I find that to always work best," I replied.

"Right then. As you say. Lady Daven is in need of a female companion, and I thought of no one better than you. Elliott had kept her quite hidden away with her illness, and she wants to start afresh. She wants her own friends and not the ones that Lord Daven had procured for her through his acquaintances. In short, she needs to detach herself from the vapid sort of females that have surrounded her thus far," he said.

The doctor looked up as he finished with a vulnerability I had not known him capable of. It was quite the compliment, and I didn't take his request lightly. Although the association could taint me, I didn't believe the poor woman should have to bear such undeserved disgrace alone.

"When she is feeling better, I shall call on her. When do you think that might be?" I asked.

The doctor stood up, rounded the desk, and picked me up from my seat into a hug.

"Thank you for this. She shall be returning to the manor in about a fortnight," he replied. He set me down on my feet and beamed with happiness.

"Is it safe to say that your feelings haven't totally diminished over the years, Walter?"

"It is far too early for any of that kind of talk, Miss Annabelle, but I would say you have a nose for truth," he winked.

We shared a laugh, and then I turned to leave. I halted at the door and looked back.

"Shall you both be attending the Bergenhalt masquerade?"

"I doubt she would feel up to going, and with me?" Walter looked unsure.

"Ask her, Walter. Disguises are encouraged, and it might be nice for her to go unrecognized into society for a night."

"I'll think about it. Good evening, Annabelle," Walter replied.

I left his office and joined Luke in the hallway. He gave me a quizzical look, but I just shook my head. We walked in amiable silence. When we reached the outdoors, One-eyed Whitmore was leaning against a lamp post with one leg holding his weight and the other crossed in front, resting on the toe of his shoe. He smiled as we approached.

"Ah, Miss Sweeting, Constable Weston, well met! I must apologize for my absence of late. The world has been ablaze with travesty recently, and I found myself needed elsewhere for a time. I knew you were up for the job though. What a web that was woven, and so very dark. I am glad that you both are here to fight such things," Whitmore said.

"Whitmore, why did you not just go to the constables right away when you knew of the crimes being committed?" Luke said, exasperated.

"Constable Weston, there are two very good reasons for that. Firstly, I wasn't privy to all the players in the game. I had no idea how far and who was involved. With powerful men like Lord Daven you never know who may be on the take. Secondly, you and Miss Sweeting needed to become a team again. You are far greater together, than apart. The Shimmer tells me this to be true, so I must oblige," he replied.

Luke and I looked at each other in confusion. Before we could ask more, Purgatorio made his presence known before diving down to join us. He landed on Luke's shoulder, much to both of our surprise and chuffed in his ear. Whitmore took his leave as we were distracted by the mechanical manticore. We watched Whitmore's retreating form and knew it was not the last time the confounding sage would bring us into his madness. Luke looked up at Purgy.

"What a funny little beastie," Luke said.

"He must understand that we have reconciled. I think he is fond of you again."

"Good, for I am rather fond of you, and I know mine and the little beastie's paths will be crossing quite frequently in the coming days," he grinned.

"Is that so?" I quipped.

"It is," Luke replied.

"And where shall we be going together? We don't have any current cases," I goaded.

"I thought perhaps you would agree to accompany me to the masquerade?" Luke suggested.

"Perhaps I will," I said.

Luke gently nudged his shoulder, and Purgatorio took flight. He reached for my hand and brought it up to his lips.

"I hope to hear your answer soon, dear heart. Until then, I bid you a good evening," Luke replied.

He kissed my hand and then moved closer and kissed my cheek. A blush crept up my neck, and I smiled. He skimmed a gentle knuckle down the tip of my nose and then took his leave, climbing into his motor and driving away. Purgatorio flew down to my waiting arm, and I tucked him into the side car of my new motorbike. Heading back to Bread Street, I felt lighter than I had in months. The future was looking bright, indeed.

Chapter 54- A Masquerade to Remember

How many masks a person wears in their lifetime is far greater than we all presume. Some seem almost invisible.

I stood in front of the mirror in my bed chamber in utter disbelief at the reflection staring back at me. The woman before me was far more elegant than I could have ever hoped to be. The gold embroidered detailing of my attire danced in the lamp light. A midnight blue corset winked through the lacing and made a dreamy background. A white with gold lacing half-jacket closed at the neck, accented with gold cord. The sleeves reached to just above my elbows, with intricate spiral designs cascading down the arms. A midnight blue and gold half-skirt, with a back bustle, flowed dramatically down to my gold half-boots. Snowy white stockings covered my legs and made them look long and graceful. The dress Jaime had made me was truly stunning.

I wore the ankh charm as a choker necklace, and I left my hair down in gentle curls with a clockwork scarab comb, securing the tresses away from my face. A gold mask with black detailing covered half my face, while the other half I had enhanced with dramatic eye makeup; inspired by Cleopatra. I added a few yellow glass accents to my brow arch with adhesive and watched as they glistened along with the rest of my ensemble. I wasn't as daring as to add a blood red lip like the famous queen, but I did add a softer red stain to finish the look. I attached my ruby encrusted bracer, with a very well cleaned hidden dagger back safely within its confines. I wore white half-gloves with gold buttons and were soft to the touch.

I missed the whirling sounds of Purgatorio, and wondered how he was faring at Miro's workshop. As promised, Lord Thetford had taken him back to smooth out the dings and damages Tapers Grove had inflicted on him. He hoped to add a few upgrades as well but would not tell me what they were. He wanted them to be a surprise. I reminded him of the last time he surprised me with hidden enhancements, and he promised he would divulge all when Purgatorio came back.

I twirled around in the mirror once more and grabbed my reticule before turning to leave. Reaching for the door handle, a knock on the other side startled me a moment before I opened it. Nathan let out a low whistle between his teeth.

"Well, I thought to come and brag about my duds, but, I say, Miss Anna, you may have out done the queen herself in that outfit. You are sure to have the tongues wagging tonight," he said.

"Thank you, Mr. Starling, and I daresay that color suits you quite well. Who could have known such a dramatic color could be so dashing," I complimented.

"Mr. Nethersby, of course. And I can't believe it, but not a feather to be seen," Nathan replied.

I took in his dark burgundy jacket with gold and turquoise embroidered detailing, depicting a wonderful hieroglyphic design down the arms. Gold buttons accented the turquoise vest below with blackened swirl impressions engraved into their metal. His pantaloons were charcoal, with a darker black trim along the side seam. The scarab brooch rested proudly upon his chest. Upon his head sat a black derby hat with a satin charcoal hat band. It was positioned at an angle, giving him a debonair look. I started to smile as I saw a burgundy feather and a smaller speckled feather fixed within the side of the band.

"I think he might have snuck one or two past you," I smirked.

He followed my gaze and removed his hat to find the offending additions.

"Well, I'll be. I am sure he just cannot help himself. They do add a nice flair though," he conceded.

"That they do. Shall we tell him how appreciative we are for his excellent designs?" I suggested.

"I think we must, he is in a bit of a tizzy making sure all the other children don't wrinkle their skirts and trousers," he said.

Nathan stuck his elbow out and waited for me to close my door and slip my hand through. It was so sweet to see him working to be genteel and escort me down the stairs. There was still a bit of a height difference, but he had grown at least a head over the winter, so it wasn't as awkward as was expected. It was amazing how we had all changed so much since we had met. It truly made me happy that I decided to come on this journey to the city and take a chance on the unknown. But my father had always said I had an adventurous spirit. I looked forward to where that spirit would take me in the future.

We made our way down the stairs without incident, and then moved to join the rest of the party in the drawing room. All the children were dressed and standing in a line for inspection as Jaime took in any detail or thread that might be out of place. Sadie sat off to the side with Lily, watching as the girls twirled their skirts. I knew she was downcast to not be attending, but there was too much at stake for the orphans of the city and all felt that her presence would derail the perception we were trying to evoke.

Her part in the Lord Daven Scandal, as the persistent royal investigative reporter, Vernadette Chambers, had dubbed it, was widely known. By some she was being called a moral heroine for turning against her father to save other children, but to others, Sadie was part of the reason some children had perished in the first place. If it were not for her, would her father have been persuaded to continue his grizzly work?

Perhaps not, he did say he wanted out, but when they took her captive as a bargaining tool it was out of the question to leave. It is hard to say if his greed would have been worked upon to further continue as well. What can be said is that it was not her fault. She was thrown into an unreasonable circumstance, and she did what all the snipes learned to do; survive. One cannot blame a child for that, but thus was the argument within the "ton" of late. Best to keep her away from such scrutiny.

It would not be long before her father faced his crimes at the gallows. It was hard enough being associated with such villainy, but then to lose one's father in the same scandal could not be easy. That would be a hard day to bear, and we planned to try and support her through that time.

She was quite instrumental in the end, in bringing the horrible business to rights. But family can be strange, and I hoped she would not regret her decision. I prayed her conscience would ease any pain from knowing that she had done right and saved peoples' lives in doing so. Lily was happy to take her back under her wing. While my cousin was still weary of the girl, he knew a bit about bad childhoods, so he didn't hold it against her too much.

Nate explained to his crew what she did for them in the beadle's house. Most of them forgave her, but Byron kept his distance. Gwennie's death was still too close to his heart for reconciliation on his part. I secretly wished that after tonight I could convince Miro to take him on as a butler in training. I had a feeling they would do well together.

"Belle, you look ravishing! I surely have outdone myself. I should die right now as there will never be a better dress to come from this mind, I am sure," Jaime gushed.

"You better not dare stop designing. I am convinced after the "ton" sees your creations tonight, you will be bombarded with requests. You will need to take on your own apprentice just to keep up with the demand," I flattered.

Jaime's hand went to his heart, and he crossed the floor to envelope me in a hug. He took care not to crush the fabric, but his happiness could be felt radiating through the gesture. He took a step back and took my hands in his, holding them at arm's length.

"This really is going to be a dream fulfilled, cousin. To have my clothes donning such a gathering is wonderful, but let us get the children ready to depart. They will need to go over their serving instructions before the party begins!" Jaime exclaimed.

"Motors are standing by, sir," Stewart said from the doorway.

"Excellent, excellent. Let us go then. In a line now, children. Girls in one motor, and boys in the other. There you go," Jaime directed.

I watched as each child passed me, giving their best smile. Their scarabs gleamed in the light. Adam and Byron laughed at something Nate had just said, and Terrance and Simon dashed after them trying to keep up with their smaller legs. Nancy and Penny practiced their walks with Marcie making gagging faces behind them. Rose followed behind and stopped next to me. After a moment of hesitation, she rushed in with a hug.

"Thank you for this. I've never felt so beautiful in my life. I hope your scheme works and some of us find real homes," she whispered.

I took her face in my hands and kissed her forehead. "You are more than welcome, and I wish for the same. If not, at least to raise money to improve your current dwelling, until the right family comes along. Chin up, no more tears now. You have a wonderful and busy night in front of you, Rose. Let us join the others."

We linked arms and walked out of the drawing room toward the front entrance. Jaime followed behind us with a smile he couldn't contain. Everyone piled into the waiting motors, careful not to mess up their clothing as my cousin watched over them. A buzz of excitement followed the happy party moving through the streets of London toward the Egyptian Hall in Piccadilly. We pulled up before the impressive building with its two large columns flanking the doors. There were also two impressive statues above the door arch, standing sentinel and looking down on all who passed. My heart beat with anticipation.

The girls oohed and awed as we got out of the vehicles. The boys snickered at the statues' nudity, but quickly quieted down as Jaime instructed them on the decorum of a gentleman. We ushered the children through the entrance where one of Lady Bergenhalt's servants was waiting to escort them back and prepare them for their nightly duties. The boys tipped their hats to us, and the girls curtsied before following the impressed maid.

Jaime took my hand, and we walked further into the hall. The exhibits were amazing, and the added decor highlighted the regal qualities of the Egyptian empire. We made our way to the back where the dancing would commence. The architecture was incredible, and I found myself lost in its beauty. Tables along the walls had a feast piled high, with delicious exotic fruits, cheese, and bread. The servants brought out more from the back and the appetizing aroma of cooked ham filled the hall. We could hear the chatter at the door as people were starting to arrive. Lady Bergenhalt moved quickly through a door from the back and made her way over to us.

"Well then, this will be quite an affair. Does everything look alright, do you think?" Diana Bergenhalt asked.

"Lady Bergenhalt, you have outdone yourself once again. It is beyond reproach, and we are delighted to be included," Jaime said bowing over her hand.

"Thank you, Mr. Nethersby. I have spied some of the children in the back, and they are looking perfect. Dare I say, your details might outshine the rest of the servants. Now, Miss Annabelle, what do you say to the decor?" Diana probed.

"Diana, you know perfectly well everyone will love it, my dear," Lord Bergenhalt said, coming up behind his wife. He kissed her on the side of the cheek and made her blush.

"Yes, well it is good to have varied opinions, you know. And just look at Miss Sweeting's dress, I daresay she has excellent taste in decor," she replied.

"Lady Bergenhalt, I cannot take credit for this design, it was my dear cousin's. Is it not the height of fashion? I believe he may be destined for great things," I said.

"Truly, Mr. Nethersby? This beauty is your doing?" Diana asked, impressed.

Jaime tried not to blush through the praise and nodded. "I can't take all the accolades, however, as no one could pull it off as our dear Belle here. She definitely makes the dress look better by wearing it."

"I'll say she does," Luke said from behind us.

I felt my neck surge with heat as I turned to greet him. Lord and Lady Bergenhalt excused themselves to go and greet their guests as they entered. I hardly took notice of their exit as I took in Constable Weston's attire. His outfit complimented mine, and the suspicion that my cousin had conspired this result proved correct when Jaime winked at me, from behind Luke, on his way to the front chamber.

Luke wore a gold embroidered vest with similar detailing to my half-jacket. His pantaloons were midnight blue and led down to charcoal grey boots. His mask was the same deep blue with gold threading. A matching top hat perched on his head and was enhanced by a pair of gold filigree goggles. His crisp, white shirt sleeves rolled up to his elbows, and his left forearm was encased in a dark leather cuff with gold detailing and a timepiece embedded in the material.

"You are radiant, Annabelle, a true Egyptian queen! I could gaze at you for days and never get enough. I hope that I do not shame you with my attire. Anything would pale in comparison to it though," Luke complimented.

He lifted my gloved hand to his lips and kissed the top, keeping eye contact throughout the entirety of the gesture. I wished there were no fabric between my hand and his lips. How daring my thoughts seemed tonight. Perhaps it was that adventurous spirit again? A small voice came from our left, breaking the spell.

"Fancy a drink, miss?"

Luke and I turned to find Simon holding a tray of short chalices containing a bubbly liquid.

"Why, Simon, that is a rather daring task for someone so young. And yes, I would be delighted," I replied, taking one. As I picked up the cup I watched for any indication of instability on the tray, but it was solidly level in the boy's arms.

"That's what the maid said too. She's keeping an eye on me for the first few, but I'm more than just a pretty face, miss," he winked.

Luke and I couldn't contain our laughter, and Simon walked away smiling. The crowd around us thickened and the band readied their instruments in anticipation. Flashes of burgundy and turquoise moved around the room offering food and beverages. Murmurs were starting to accumulate, along with appreciation for the children's good manners and lovely attire. We watched as our hosts made their way to the back of the hall where the band was set up. Lord Bergenhalt bellowed for all to quiet down so his wife might address them. It was quite sweet.

"Thank you, my dear. Welcome everyone and thank you for joining us for another spellbinding evening. I want to take this time to make a few announcements before we make merry. First and foremost, congratulations are in order to our new Lord and Lady Bonan. As the newest bride, Mrs. Whitney Bonan will be opening our dance set for us." Lady Bergenhalt waited for the applause to die down before continuing. "Second, I want to take a moment to thank all the merchants and artists that had a hand in this year's event. It truly is an undertaking one could not do alone. You make my dreams come alive for all to partake. Thank you."

Again, she waited. Her eyes found mine in the crowd. "Finally, I wanted to address a subject that came to my attention and has captured my heart. I hope that it might do the same to you."

She made a movement with her hand and a flash of burgundy darted toward her. Lord Bergenhalt reached for the incoming child and picked him up for all to see. It was Simon, beaming out at the guests.

Chapter 55- Mission Accomplished

The sweetest of victories are those won for others. Seeing their joy raises the joy in oneself.

I looked at the sweet boy perched on Lord Bergenhalt's shoulder and waited for Diana to continue.

"You may have taken notice of several children serving you tonight. It was not always planned as such. A thoughtful young woman brought it to my attention that our little ones, like Simon here, are suffering a great injustice. They have lost their families, to either poverty or illness, and with no other relations to take them in, have become one of the many sent to the foundling hospitals. Some are fortunate in their placement, while others suffer greatly. Many never find a forever home and end up barely scraping by with no real education supplied to them." Diana paused for a moment before continuing.

"You might ask why this matters to you. I might ask, why it doesn't?" Her face took on a determined look. "Our town is growing in prosperity and technology, why then can it not grow in charity and generosity as well? We lay the foundation of the future with what we do today. Lavish clothes and parties are a privilege that we have been afforded by birth, marriage, hard work, or luck. There is no crime in sharing a small bit with the future. So, I am asking you today to open your hearts, and purse strings, to help me create something new. A place where these misplaced and forgotten children can go to learn trades that we need. They may not be destined for the lifestyles we enjoy, but they should be given the chance to work for a living, live in a safe dwelling, and contribute to their community."

Lady Bergenhalt took a moment to scan the room and see if her words were getting through. Several faces registered utter boredom, but others showed genuine concern and focus.

"At the far corners of the room you will see two urns. Next to them are stacks of paper and quills. Throughout the night I ask that you take a moment and write down any pledges you feel comfortable making toward this effort. The proceeds will go to the new charity we have formed called Justice for Children. We will offer them training and education. We will offer them a chance," she said. Then she added, "It will also give you a chance to win a variety the wonderful costumes seen tonight, as well as a few amazing custom-made adornments. You can view several next to the urns," she paused.

This new declaration drew everyone's attention. Murmurs of excitement started to waft across the room regarding the potential prizes. Diana looked up at her husband for a moment and then at Simon. Her husband nodded.

"As for Daniel and I, we would like to make another announcement in relation to this effort. We have decided to adopt young Simon here. We hope that this will not only show you how committed we are to helping, but also how we anticipate the addition to our family will enhance our lives. Thank you for listening and have a wonderful night," she finished.

The crowd gasped at her proclamation, and Simon squealed, hugging Lord Bergenhalt tightly around the neck. He reached for his new mother and did the same to her. The crowd cooed and applauded at the new family's evident happiness. Several partygoers made their way over to the urns directly. Luke produced a handkerchief from his pocket and dabbed it gently to my eye. I couldn't help but weep with happiness at the wonderful outcome, and the party hadn't even begun yet.

The Bergenhalts moved away from the band, motioning them to begin. Lady Whitney Bonan and her new husband took their positions. She radiated with pride at being the center of attention. They made several passes of the dance before the rest of the party was permitted to join in. Luke led me to the end of the line, and we met our hands in the middle, waiting for the next turn to bring us in line with the rest of the dancers. Moving in sync, we were soon lost to the music and movement.

Quite a few dances later, we made our way to the refreshment table. The children were still providing wonderful service to the guests. They were told they needed only serve for an hour more than they could have a feast of their own in the back. That had them moving with animation. Congratulations were pouring into young Simon. He was overjoyed but said he needed to help his friends finish the night out. The pride of his resolve and work ethic shown in his new parents' faces.

I popped a grape into my mouth and smiled at all the beautiful gowns swaying on the dance floor. Luke conversed with his aunt, Lady Cornelia Whipley, and congratulated her on the attire she had constructed for all the servants of the party. A presence at my right had drawn my gaze to a tall man with a black suede mask and a woman with a beautiful rosewood cane. It had a rose gold handle that matched her mask. It took me a moment to recognize the swath of white hair on the man's head.

"Doctor Cannish, is that you? You are looking quite remarkable this evening, as is your lady friend," I said.

"What gave me away?" Walter grumbled.

"Your height and your hair, and your perceptive eyes I suppose.

What do you make of this little soiree?" I replied.

"It is quite excellent, is it not, Eloise?" Walter said.

"Ah, Lady Daven, I am glad you could make it. You look much in health. What happy news," I said.

"Thank you, Miss Sweeting. Yes, it has been a whirlwind, I daresay. Walter convinced me that I would not be happy if I didn't attend, and I must say he was right. This has been a wonderful evening thus far, and it is wonderful to see the goodness in the world instead of the evil for a change," she replied.

"I can toast to that," Walter said.

We made plans to have tea the following week, and they left to take in the exhibit in the front hall, where it was less crowded.

"Miss Sweeting, may I have this dance?"

I turned to find Lord Thetford standing behind me with an out-stretched hand. His exotic green eyes sparkled in the lamplight. He wore a charcoal grey suit with subtle black accents. His mask matched and gave him a highwayman esque quality. I saw several ladies looking our way with envy.

"Of course, Mr. Nassar," I replied.

We joined the line and took our positions. Miro started apprehensively but then relaxed into the familiar set with ease.

"I wasn't sure if I should attend, to own the truth," he said. "I was still concerned by my brother's legacy, but it seems my plight is old news at this point," he quipped.

"I told you it would not be forever. And I daresay you have caught the eye of several young ladies tonight," I smirked.

He followed my gaze as a couple of this season's finest debutantes watched him and whispered from the side of the room. They blushed and giggled when they were caught staring. Miro looked back at me with a quizzical brow.

"So, all my faults and tainted associations have been eliminated by the newest scandal?" Miro said, surprised.

"Isn't society fickle? I daresay you'll be on the top of all the mama's lists by the end of the season. You are a lord now," I said.

I laughed at the sudden look of horror on his face. We did several more turns before the closing sequence ended with a mutual bow. We continued our conversation as he led me from the dance floor.

"So, how does Purgatorio fare?" I asked, concerned.

"He is almost ready, I am just working on one slight adjustment, and he will be back in your company directly," he smiled.

"It is quite remarkable how attached I have grown to him. He really is a marvelous invention. I look forward to seeing your new Nassar Navigators taking flight soon. Is it true that several businesses have agreed to test out the parcel deliveries with them?" I asked.

"It is. Although, they will need to have someone man the controls to get them to the correct locations, but I think it will save time and increase profits if they succeed. There will be a few bugs to work out, making sure they don't drive them into the airships and such, but I think it is going to revolutionize how we transport items."

His eyes were alight with the excitement he felt for his new conquest. Such passion made one want to be creative as well. We all want to experience the flutters of purpose course through us. Luke quietly joined our party and listened to the newest details of the parcel delivery system Miro was implementing. All animosity had been resolved between them, and they seemed to get along quite nicely. Jaime joined us and gushed over Lord Thetford's attire before once again thanking him for Andre, his mechanical peacock. A rather tall, dark-haired man stood behind him, waiting patiently.

"Ah yes, where are my manners, apologies all," Jaime started.

"This oak of a man behind me is Mr. Chadwick Telvencott, and he is the editor for the royal newspaper. This is my dear cousin, Miss Annabelle Sweeting, her crime solving partner, Constable Luke

Weston, and the wonderfully inventive Lord Miro Nassar, Earl of Thetford. Belle, I believe you might be familiar with his crime investigative reporter, a Miss Vernadette Chambers?" Jamie asked.

"Yes, she has been quite thorough in reporting our latest case. A bit demanding, but I daresay she gets down to the bones of it all. I like that she verifies the facts, unlike the gossip rags that seem to throw the "ton" into such hysterics. The queen must be quite pleased to have such a dependable news source at her command," I replied.

"That she is, Miss Sweeting. Miss Chambers has been an excellent addition to the Royal Gazette.

"It is nice to make your acquaintance Mr. Telvencott, are you here for the paper, or to enjoy yourself?" Lord Thetford said.

"A little of both, it would seem. I was not expecting the announcement of a new charity nor the adoption, were you?" Mr. Telvencott inquired.

"Not at all, quite brilliant. I will look forward to reading the article about it," Miro replied.

"I must excuse myself, my leg still tends to ache after a time without a cane. It was a pleasure seeing you all, and making your acquaintance. I will pop over two days hence with Purgatorio, Miss Annabelle. Will that be convenient?" Miro asked.

"Sounds splendid," I replied.

"Well met," said Mr. Telvencott.

"I'd like to pick your brain about something, do you have availability sometime next week, Lord Thetford?" Luke asked. His request surprised both Miro and me, and Miro nodded his head.

"Wonderful, I will coordinate with you early next week then," Luke shook his hand.

Miro bowed and took his leave, his limp becoming evident as he departed. Jaime and Mr. Telvencott moved on for more introductions, leaving Luke and I to ourselves.

"What was that about?" I said.

"Just an idea that I wanted to expand upon. If anything comes of it, I will let you know. For now, I would like to chat it over with Lord Thetford to see if it is plausible first," Luke replied.

He gently pinched my ear lobe and smiled at me. I looked around to make sure no one had seen the intimate gesture. A blush creeping into my cheeks made his smile grow bigger. I tried to give him an affronted demeanor, but I couldn't hold the look for very long. We both laughed as we glided past the other guests toward the front exhibit hall. We wove in and around the beautiful artifacts they had on display, enjoying each other's company. Gazes of longing, secret hand brushes, and whispers of future dreams mingled with the objects of the past in that hall. It felt like the stars had finally aligned. A new mantra resounded in my mind.

This would be our fate. This would be the beginning of our story.

Chapter 56- Resolution

Perceptions are like stained glass, different from every angle. Let mine continue to hold this rosy hue.

Two weeks later

***

Purgatorio roared as Andre continued to follow him around the drawing room. His new shiny rose gold casing was beautifully affixed to his new and improved core with top-of-the-line titanium rivets. Miro had made good on his word and removed every dent from his metallic hide, adding a longer active energy source. He also added new dials that would allow for collecting images as well as a beacon that could be activated if an urgent need arose. Luke really liked that feature. Purgy's mane, now made up of supple dark leather sections, adhered to his head with the same titanium rivets of his body and rose gold metal-edged tips. Purgatorio's new mane rippled with his agitation at the peacock's antics. To see a mechanical beast displaying such emotion was comical.

"Come now, enough of that bickering. We are celebrating after all. I had joked last year about Constable Weston being promoted, but now it seems I have in fact had a premonition! Congratulations, Inspector Weston! You have earned it and then some," Jaime said, clapping his hands together.

"Yes, yes, what a right good bobbie you make, sir," Nathan agreed.

"There truly is no one more deserving of the title. I look forward to continuing our investigative adventures together," I added.

"I look forward to working for you as well, sir. Congratulations," Constable Caleb Quincy said.

"Let us toast then, to the new Inspector. Let his bravery never overpower his intelligence, and let no criminal outrun his determination. Cheers to you," Miro said.

"Thank you all for your well wishes and putting together this gathering," he started. "I think we all know that while I have earned the title, this has been anything but a singular endeavor. Miss Sweeting has poked and prodded me in the most vexing way to find viable clues and in turn made me a better detective. I am very lucky for that chance moment all those months ago when I witnessed a guttersnipe pickpocket a charming lady at a train station. That instant has irrevocably changed my life for the better. This success is yours too, Belle."

I looked around the room at our friends gathered together. His aunt, Lady Whipley, dabbed her eyes with a handkerchief, and Doctor Cannish raised a glass while keeping a hand on Lady Daven's shoulder. Stewart and Bethany spoke animatedly in the corner, while Lily and Sadie moved in and out of the room, bringing delicious tarts and refreshments that Trish had been instructing Sadie how to make.

Lord and Lady Bergenhalt grinned as Simon sat next to Purgatorio and played with his whiskers. They had done very well at the benefit, and plans were already in motion to build an academy and new lodgings for abandoned children. All poverty wouldn't be erased, but it was a start and a good one at that. The other children were all looking forward to when they could attend. Byron and Miro had got on quite well, as I had anticipated, so he was currently employed as an errand boy and apprentice butler. It would be a waiting game to find more permanent places for the others, but we were hopeful.

The trial of Lord Daven, Father Gaverty, and Beadle Fieldworth was to be held in a fortnight. The Royal Gazette was doing its best to keep the story at the front of everyone's mind. Mr. Hillard and Mr. Plitner, being of no real consequence to society and quite friendless, were already headed toward the gallows. The struggles that Sadie would deal with in the coming months would be tremendous. She was keeping busy and making great strides, by all accounts, but I knew the internal guilt must be grating on her. The right choice was made, however connected one was to the villain. There was no way to justify his wrongdoing, no matter how one tried. The children's deaths might be argued to be the result of his need to protect his own child, but to desecrate the bodies in the Greenwich Graverobber case was done under no duress. Mr. Hillard had been brought in for greed, and in doing so, put his daughter in danger in the first place. The more I learned the more I felt that a vicious man deserved a vicious end.

I watched the people in the room around me and felt my heart calm. With each season, I found myself surrounded by more wonderful acquaintances. Of course, I had met several deplorable humans as well, but this made it worth it. There cannot be this lightness without the dark. There cannot be triumph without a foe to thwart. There cannot be an inspector without a crime to solve, and his assistant, of course.

Luke made his way over to me and took my hand. He lifted it to his lips and smiled before he kissed my knuckles. Crime had brought us together and almost tore us apart. It was an interesting perspective I had stumbled on. Could one both love and hate a crime most foul? Although I may hate the horrible deeds of the wicked, I cannot help but love the puzzle they present. What does that make me?

Righteous? Vengeful?

Luke looked at me with a quizzical brow. Probably picking up on the warring emotions my thoughts were emitting across my face.

"It's nothing. I was just thinking what someone would do who seeks justice if no crimes were ever committed?" I offered.

"Unfortunately, we will never find out that answer. But, if I had to guess, I would say they would put their powers to invention. For what is a crime but little elements that lead to a whole picture, right? To create something to better the world would seem similar. Putting together pieces to bring something beneficial to society," Luke replied.

"Quite well put, Inspector Weston. It seems you have grown wiser with the promotion," I said.

Luke pulled on a loose curl that framed my face. His expression was clear of any pretense and flush with emotion.

"It was not the promotion that has opened my eyes, it was you. You have a goodness and a fierceness that will not be contained, and I regret ever trying to. We are two halves of a whole, you and I. Those wonderfully determined elements in you bring out the best in me. I see that now," Luke sighed.

I grabbed Luke's hand and led him from the drawing room to the hall. My heart raced with nervous anticipation. The spark between us that had almost died was flickering, waiting for a jolt of fuel. Stretching up on the balls of my feet, I took his face in my hands and brought it down to mine. A whisper of a kiss soon melted into more. His left hand cupped the back of my head while his right held my lower back, pulling me closer. His smile broke our kiss.

"I believe you've been promoted as well." Luke smirked.

"Oh really? To what?" I asked.

"Master thief," Luke said.

"And why is that?" I pouted.

"I think it's quite evident, my Belle."

I shook my head smiling, not quite in on his meaning, but liking the way my name sounded coming from his lips.

"Well, it's my heart, dearest. You've stolen it without me even noticing," Luke admitted.

I looked up into his warm brown eyes and gasped.

"That just cannot be, Luke. I would never steal something so important," I smirked.

"How then, did you get it?" Luke played along.

He tipped my chin up to his face gently between his thumb and pointer finger.

"I believe it was a fair exchange, sir. One fiery, strong-willed heart with a nose for trouble, for one strong, dependable, courageous heart with a talent for patience," I responded. My breath hitched as I faced the intensity in his gaze.

His eyes sparkled like cinders in the hallway gaslights. I felt his joy mingle with my own as we held each other for a few moments more. Luke kissed the tip of my nose and tucked a curl behind my ear.

"Yes, I think that may be the most important bargain of my life. I will do my best to keep it safe," he promised.

My heart fluttered at his words. Touched by his declaration, I basked in the feeling and the potential promise of our future.

"As will I, now back to your adoring guests. We mustn't keep them waiting," I said.

"They could wait for an eternity if it meant I would be with you," he replied.

I pulled him in for another quick kiss and then smoothed out my half-skirt and hair.

"You know I might have to apprehend you for stealing kisses, Miss Sweeting," Luke's eyes twinkled with mischief.

"Didn't anyone tell you to never trust a cogger, Inspector Weston?" I winked.

Luke looked around to make sure we were still undiscovered. He emitted a low growl before pulling me close and kissing me deeply. I felt my neck heat and my belly flutter. He tore away with evident effort and grinned.

"There is no deception in how I feel for you, sweet Belle. And by the blush on your cheeks, I am most certain our feelings are in unison. If I am mistaken, I am happy to investigate this further," Luke said, raising his brow in challenge.

I laughed at his cheeky expression.

"I am sure you would be. However, you are needed in the drawing room," I smiled.

"Perhaps tomorrow then?" Luke asked, reaching for my hand.

"Perhaps," I replied. We interlaced our fingers, losing ourselves to the revelation of our mutual desires. Neither one of us wanted to let go of this moment we had found. We begrudgingly released each other though, when footsteps sounded down the hall.

Smiling, we walked back into the crowded room filled with laughter and friends. My cousin elevated a knowing eyebrow in my direction, and I fought to keep the chuckle from escaping my lips. The merriment continued throughout the night. Luke and I stole glances and smiled at each other whenever a lull in conversation afforded us time.

The joy of this night would need to sustain us. I felt a strange tingle of something dark and sinister on the horizon. Weirdly, I looked forward to it. To the challenge and danger of another puzzle, to working with Luke to unravel the tangles, and to know I was doing something important. Because isn't it our life's goal to leave a lasting impact on this world?

Yes, I felt the truth of it down to my bones. I would not go looking for trouble, it usually found me anyway. But I just knew that when the time came, I would have a hand in putting the world back to rights. It was my undeniable calling, and I would answer every time.

The End

About the Author

LK Billips lives in Wisconsin with her wonderful husband and daughter. She has a BA in Comprehensive Art and Certificate in Museum Studies. While art has been a staple in her life, the passion for writing could no longer be ignored. She enjoys crafting, reading, going for walks by Lake Michigan, and playing with her fur babies, Gizmo and Mr. Darcy.

You can connect with me on:

- https://lkbillips.com
- https://www.facebook.com/LKBillips
- https://www.instagram.com/lkbillips

Subscribe to my newsletter:

- https://lkbillips.com/contact-bonus-material

Also by LK Billips

The Catalyst

This is the first story in the Annabelle Sweeting Mystery series. It follows her on her first adventure arriving to London, and the whirlwind of puzzles that soon follow.

Annabelle Sweeting has come to London. Set in a steampunk world, a country girl with a quirk for gears and fashion makes her way through the busy streets in the hopes of discovering herself. What she does discover, however, are two dashing men vying for her attention, an unexpected series of murders, and an underestimated talent for being in the middle of it all. Can she navigate her way through the haughty "ton", help the handsome constable solve the murders, and not get killed herself?

This story follows Annabelle through the cogs and gears of an altered London in the 1800s. She learns how to navigate society and her own ambitions.

The Compass

https://storyoriginapp.com/giveaways/ ae34fe86-9e7e-11ec-b0f6-038473eefef9

This prequel tells the back story of Jaime Nethersby. The carefree, fun-loving cousin of Annabelle Sweeting hasn't always had it easy. His childhood has been wrought with dark memories, and some questionable family gatherings. This short story gives you a glimpse on how their friendship began, how Jaime came to his current vocation, and how their family bond was made stronger than ever. This can be read before or after The Catalyst.